ELAINE

Stephen Ferris

Nexus

First published in 1994 by
Nexus
332 Ladbroke Grove
London W10 5AH

Copyright © Stephen Ferris 1994

Typeset by TW Typesetting, Plymouth, Devon

Printed and bound by
Cox & Wyman Ltd, Reading, Berks

ISBN 0 352 32905 X

This book is sold subject to the condition that it shall not,
by way of trade or otherwise, be lent, resold, hired out or
otherwise circulated without the publisher's prior written
consent in any form of binding or cover other than that in
which it is published and without a similar condition
including this condition being imposed on the subsequent
purchaser.

This book is a work of fiction.
In real life, make sure you practise safe sex.

1
Conceit and Deceit

The man was completely naked, apart from a heavy leather collar about his neck from which a loose chain led to a beam above. Both arms were strapped behind him, wrists to elbows, and he wore a blindfold. He was standing on his toes, his heels clear of the floor and the quivering of his strained leg muscles indicated that he had been in that position for some time.

The woman behind him was speaking to him in low but menacing tones. She was in her forties, with a voluptuous ripeness about her figure, and plenty of that could be seen. She wore black, thigh-length, wet-look boots with six-inch heels and elbow-length gloves to match. A cat mask covered the upper part of her face. Apart from that, she too was naked, except for a brief basque or corset, which started below the navel and extended up to just below her breasts, where cups supported but in no way concealed the ample bosom, pushing it out in an exaggerated fashion. As she strutted to and fro her buttocks and a mat of pubic hair were clearly visible.

She drew a slender, whippy cane through her fingers and her voice purred with lust. 'Getting tired, are we? Like to rest those sore muscles? No reason why you shouldn't. Except that when your heels come down, they rest on a pad which completes a circuit. The red light comes on and your caning begins again, and goes on until you get up on your toes and the light goes out.' There was no humour at all in her sudden laugh. 'Too bad you can't just step forward, isn't it? But I thought of that, didn't I? That's why your toes are tied to those staples in the floor.'

The man moaned softly in despair.

'Louder! I want to hear you beg!' At that moment, tortured muscles could take no more. The man's heels sank under the strain and the light came on. Like a pouncing cat the woman leapt forward, teeth drawn back in a vicious grin of delight, her cane lashing frenziedly at his unprotected, bare buttocks, already marked from previous beatings. He shrieked and attempted to rise onto his toes again, but the effort was too much and the extinguishing of the light was too brief to interrupt the fierce punishment.

'I own you!' the woman spat. 'You are mine to do with as I want. Your will is of no consequence.'

Standing before the monitor attached to the hidden TV camera, a tall, dark-haired woman with glittering eyes drew in her breath with a sharp hiss of satisfaction as she reached out to stop the recording. 'Just as I now own YOU, my dear Mrs Christina Lucio, MBE, wife of one of our most prominent industrialists; patroness of numerous charities; glittering star in the social firmament. What prophetic words. "Your will is now subject to mine!" I like it.'

She numbered the tape with great care and placed it with a pile of others.

As the telephone bell shrilled, the pretty blonde in the crisp, white blouse leaned across the large oak desk and picked up the receiver. 'Sir James Hamsett's residence. Oh, Mr Carmani. I'm sorry. Sir James can't speak to you now. He is just leaving for South America. He'll be back next week. Shall I make an appointment for you? I see. I'll tell him to expect your call when he gets back. Yes, this is Elaine, his private secretary . . . Mr Carmani! I'm shocked! I'll bet you say that to all the girls.' As she hung up, she mouthed the words, 'Dream on!', then sat back and smiled a little as she stared out of the window into the sunlit garden beyond. This was certainly a great place to have an office and she was very lucky to have such a good job – and such a great employer. There he was now, giving last-minute instructions to John, the chauffeur.

She savoured this opportunity of inspecting him while he was unaware of it. Handsome, no doubt he was. Tall and with hardly any middle-age thickening of the waistline. Forty-five, but still able to compete with younger men at squash. Still virile and active, too. With a sudden sensation of dampness between her legs, she recalled just *how* virile and active he had been just a couple of nights ago. She had been a virgin until she had succumbed to his blandishments, therefore she had no yardstick by which to judge his love-making, which seemed to her to be entirely satisfactory. The occasions on which they had made love together had been too few and far between, she decided. A conference here. A seminar there. So few excuses to spend the night alone, together, in some anonymous hotel room.

As she watched, Lady Isabel Hamsett came across the lawn with a basket of flowers to make her own farewells. About the same age as her husband, she was still beautiful in a faded, English rose, sort of way. James seldom discussed his relationship with his

3

wife, but Elaine gathered that his had been something very close to a marriage of convenience – the union of two great financial dynasties. There were no children of the marriage. Perhaps her Ladyship's greatest asset was her social grace, which was of enormous value on the many occasions when entertaining, and being entertained, was a business necessity.

Elaine decided that she was definitely jealous of her Ladyship, who had this wonderful man all to herself every night, yet made so little of her opportunities, even to the extent of having separate bedrooms, that the poor guy felt obliged to look elsewhere for sexual relief.

Now Sir James had turned away and was coming up the front steps. He would be coming to his office for a last-minute briefing from his faithful PA. Why did her heart always seem to speed up when she knew he was coming into the same room? Then he was there and she was in his arms, smothering his face and neck with kisses. 'Oh, James. James! What am I going to do without you for a whole week? I want you *now*. This minute!' She detached one arm from around his neck and pressed urgently at the front of his trousers, feeling the immediate response she had come to know well.

He pulled away at once. 'Not here, Elaine. Not now! Never in this house. You know the rules.' Seeing her pout, he relented and opened his brief-case. 'Look, I've bought you a going away present. Something for you to wear for me when I come back.'

The package was quite heavy and, she guessed, bracelet or necklace-sized.

'You're so good to me. I *do* love you and of course I'll stick to the rules. I don't have to like it though, do I?'

Sir James grinned at her enthusiasm and patted her shoulder. 'I'll be back before you know I've gone. How could I stay away from that body for long? No ... no ... Don't start again, there's a good little thing. Look. There's this Cartwright thing still brewing. I hoped it would be ready for signature before now, but they've been dragging their feet. If they send the papers through before I get back, give them to Isabel to sign. She has power of attorney for everything.'

He kissed her briefly and turned to go. 'Don't forget to put that present in a file or a brief-case when you take it upstairs. We don't want anyone seeing it!'

She watched from the window as he ran down the steps to the car. At least, she thought, the farewell kiss for his wife was no more passionate than her own. Then the Rolls was gone and she turned away from the window feeling empty and lonely.

She tucked the gift away in a drawer until that evening and then, business of the day completed, she slipped it into a brown envelope and took it upstairs to the little room she occupied. Unable to restrain her curiosity any longer, she sat straight on the bed and unwrapped it. Inside the pretty paper was a jeweller's box but, when she opened it, the contents were not exactly what she had expected. True, there was a beautiful Cartier watch, but there was also a little parcel of material and a note. She unwrapped the parcel and grinned as she saw that it was composed of the most outrageously flimsy set of bra and panties. The note said: *Darling Elaine. Be wearing these when I come home. Then I shall want to see you in just the watch! Love James.*

As she undressed and showered she smiled constantly at the recollection of the gifts and the note.

Emerging fresh and pink from the bathroom, she stood in front of the full-length mirror and inspected herself. Her robe bothered her and she slipped out of it and let it fall to the floor, appraising her reflection critically.

Long, blonde hair, now hidden by a towelling turban. High cheek bones; steady blue eyes and the creamy pink complexion of a natural blonde. Her gaze travelled down, past her shoulders to her breasts. Just about perfect, for a 23-year-old, she decided. Not too heavy, but very firm, with the rosebud nipples and large area of pink aureole which went with her natural colouring. She drew in her stomach and allowed her eyes to wander down over the distinct demarcation of her rib-cage to her perfectly flat belly, leading to long, tapering legs. At the junction of body and legs, an exquisite triangle of fair, curly, pubic hair gave the third confirmation of the fact that her hair colour owed nothing to artificial aids.

Looking at herself, naked, excited her and she went to find the skimpy underwear she had been given. Slipping into the bra, she examined herself again. Fragile as gossamer, it lifted her breasts to an even more pert angle, if that were possible, yet concealed absolutely nothing. She had not noticed, until then, that there were peep-holes for her nipples. When she put on the panties they were just as transparent, and the crotch was split, so that the golden hairs on her pubes were clearly revealed.

The clothing excited her even more and she felt the old, familiar, moist heat growing between her legs. She reached down and began to massage the open crotch area, her other hand passing lightly across her breasts, brushing the exposed nipples into erection. 'Damn you, James, for going away and leaving me so

6

randy. I want you – *Now!*' She gazed once more into the mirror, imagining his hands where her own were; his hot breath on her neck; his strong, white teeth on her nipples. Unable to bear it any longer, she sank onto the bed on her back, opened her legs wide and began to masturbate. From long experience she began teasingly, by running her fingers up and down the wet, warm, pink area just inside her labia and, when that was thoroughly excited, slipped two fingers into her vagina to find and massage that *special* place behind her pubes, pressing quite hard against the bone. Finally, she allowed the end of her thumb to occasionally brush against the tip of her stiff clitoris, gasping with pleasure every time it did so.

In this way she knew she could extend her pleasure for the maximum period of time, bringing herself to orgasm only when she could not bear the exquisite sensations any longer.

Her breathing became heavier and the finger and thumb of her left hand, working first on one nipple and then on the other, began to pinch and roll and pull almost viciously. One erotic fantasy after another drifted through her mind. A man's body, hard and lean, pressing down on her. The warm gush of his completion as he thrust and thrust again. Now the moment was upon her and was not to be denied. Her breath whooshed out in one, long, continuous, gasping moan, her hips rotating convulsively, leaping off the bed to meet the now frantically-moving hand as she pulled and pinched her nipple as hard as she could. With head rolling uncontrollably from side to side, she spent copiously, covering her hand in love fluid as she cried his name again and again. 'Oh James. James. James!'

Drained and slaked, she rolled onto her side. Without bothering to remove the underclothes she pulled the sheet over herself and with hand still clasped between her thighs she drifted off to sleep.

It was a few days later that the Cartwright papers came through for signing. Elaine had had a heavy day at the typewriter, catching up on correspondence dictated by Sir James before he left, and rose stiffly from her machine to greet the courier. She checked the various parts of the house by telephone, to track down Lady Isabel, eventually getting an answer from her bedroom. 'Just bring them up, Elaine. I'll sign them here.'

Elaine was aware of a certain curiosity as she mounted the stairs. She had never seen the bedrooms and wondered what they were like. She knocked and was told to come in. Entering, she saw that this room was the same style as the rest of the house, with a low, beamed ceiling. The bed was vast and expensive, the carpet thick and soft, and the whole of one wall was occupied by what she guessed was a wardrobe which had full-length sliding mirrors as doors. She was a little embarrassed to see Lady Isabel lying naked on her stomach, on a padded bench, attended by a sturdy, brown-haired girl dressed in halter and shorts, who was rubbing oil into her back. Even in her confusion she had time to notice that her Ladyship still preserved a voluptuous, if slightly plump figure.

'Oh! I'm sorry. I didn't know . . .'

'That's quite all right, Gretchen is just finishing. Bring them over here and fetch my spectacles from the dressing table.'

Elaine put the papers on the padded bench in front of Lady Isabel who raised herself on her elbows and squinted through her glasses as she signed them. Her breasts, thus almost completely revealed, were heavy and pendulous.

All the right equipment, thought Elaine, and all going to waste.

As she handed back the papers, Lady Isabel delayed letting go of them for a moment, so detaining Elaine while she inspected her over the tops of her glasses. 'You look tired, dear. Had a heavy day?'

'I'm afraid so, your Ladyship, but I don't mind.'

'Nonsense, child! Your shoulders must be aching like mad. Look, I'll tell you what. When you have given the papers to the courier come back up. Gretchen will have finished by then and she shall give you a massage.'

No really. I couldn't! I've never . . .'

'Don't be silly. Gretchen has such marvellous hands. You'll feel wonderful afterwards.'

Elaine smiled, a little awkwardly. 'All right then, if you're sure that's all right. I am a bit stiff and sore.'

She went downstairs and saw the courier on his way. By the time she got back to the bedroom, Lady Isabel was sitting at her dressing-table, wearing a silk robe and applying her make-up. Gretchen smiled and patted the bench top. Lady Isabel turned from her mirror. 'Just slip your blouse and skirt off, dear. Are you wearing panty-hose? I should take those off, too. No need for more than that.'

Thankful at least for that, and for the fact that she was wearing 'sensible' brassiere and knickers, Elaine did so and with a certain unease, climbed onto the bench and lay face down.

Gretchen stepped up beside her and began to rub her shoulders and neck. Elaine immediately realised that Lady Isabel had not been exaggerating. Gretchen did indeed have marvellous hands; warm and strong, yet soft. She seemed to know exactly where to massage and manipulate to relieve the aches and tensions. Elaine found herself murmuring, 'Mmmmm! Wow! That feels so *good!*'

Gretchen transferred her attention from the shoulders and neck to the spine, pressing with her thumbs on either side of it all the way down to the small of her back, then rubbing the same area with the sides of her hands on the way back. Elaine's bra strap kept getting caught up in this operation and it seemed perfectly natural when Gretchen, with a murmured, 'Excuse!', unclipped it and slipped the garment down over her elbows then drew it away from beneath her in one practised movement.

The massage went on and Elaine found herself wanting to purr like a cat because it was so soothing and relaxing. Lady Isabel spoke over her shoulder. 'Use the aromatic oil, Gretchen. That makes such a difference.' Gretchen paused in her work for a moment, then poured a few drops of cool, sweet-smelling liquid onto Elaine's back and gently but firmly began to massage it in.

Elaine thought that she had seldom experienced such pleasure. She felt pampered, relaxed and almost sleepy. The oil spread over her lower back and then, with another murmured, 'Excuse!', Gretchen pulled her knickers down and off, leaving her naked.

For a moment she stiffened, but Lady Isabel who had been watching said, 'Don't worry about that, my child. The oil would spoil them and we're all girls together.'

Elaine relaxed again and enjoyed the sensation of the oil being worked in all the way down to her feet. Gretchen then returned to the gluteal area, thoroughly massaging the soft cheeks of her bottom. Elaine decided that it felt very good indeed. Quite a turn-on, in fact. She even managed not to tense up when Gretchen gently parted her buttocks and allowed a little of the oil to dribble right into the cleft. Elaine felt it trickling through to the bench below and thought, 'If she's going to massage *that* in this could get quite interesting!' She hardly expected that to happen and wondered if it might be wishful thinking.

When Gretchen's hand inserted itself between her thighs and massaged the sensitive inner skin, Elaine knew that she should have clamped them together chastely, but instead she parted them slightly, her bottom beginning to stir to the rhythm of the massage.

The rubbing hands moved further and further up her inner thighs until Elaine could just feel them brushing against her pubic hair. Teasingly, they did not go further than that and she was embarrassed to find herself half hoping that they would. She was getting quite randy and, when Gretchen invited her to turn over, she did so, conscious of the fact that at least a part of her willingness to do so was to show Lady Isabel what a really desirable body could look like. She glanced across at her. Maybe she could see Elaine reflected in the mirror. If so, she appeared to take no notice.

'Hands behind head, please.' Gretchen positioned them for her and she was not displeased at that. In this position her breasts were lifted to their best advantage and she was proud of them. Glancing down, she was amused to see that her nipples had already responded to the massage by erecting themselves. She relaxed and allowed the girl to rub oil into her armpits and upper arms. This really was most relaxing! She closed her eyes and extracted the greatest possible pleasure from the continued application of oil. Dripped onto her flat stomach and rubbed in. Spread down her thighs and legs. Surprisingly, the foot massage was very sexy.

When the cool, sweet oil dribbled over her breasts, she was ready for it and arched her back, thrusting herself up eagerly, towards the hands which she knew would follow. Languorously opening her eyes, she saw, with a slight shock, that at some stage Gretchen had removed her halter. As she bent over her work, her full, milky-white breasts dangled, jiggling slightly with her movements. Elaine was fascinated by the fact that her nipples were pierced and ornamented with small gold rings. She had never experienced sexual contact with a woman and the desire which she found rising within her to touch and fondle was somehow alien and a little frightening. Tentatively she removed her right hand from beneath her head and reached out to touch Gretchen's waist; thrilling, in a way she had not expected, at the feel of bare, female skin.

Gretchen smiled down at her and, disappointingly, removed the wandering hand, but only to turn it palm upwards, pour a little oil into it and plant it firmly under one hanging breast. Wonderingly, Elaine smeared the oil across the naked flesh, noticing the contrast of the gold ring with the soft, yielding quality of Gretchen's breasts. She lifted each in turn, thrilling at their sheer weight and size, then gasping as Gretchen's right hand moved down to probe between her legs, separating the pink lips of her labia with slippery fingers.

Elaine let her hand trail down over Gretchen's bare belly until it was arrested by the material of her shorts. She looked a question and Gretchen nodded, smiling. With trembling fingers, Elaine unbuckled the cloth belt, unfastened the securing hook and tugged down the zip. The shorts fell to the floor and Gretchen kicked them off to stand, naked, with legs planted invitingly apart. Elaine slipped her hand between the parted thighs and felt the moist heat above the brown pubic curls. Then, with a little sigh, she allowed her fingers to explore the secret, pink slit. Gretchen responded with a sharp intake of breath then lowered herself slightly, as though to encourage further intrusion.

Then, unexpectedly, Elaine felt another pair of hands on her body, one massaging her left breast and the other joining Gretchen's in its masturbatory work between her legs. Lady Isabel, naked again, had come over and now stood on her left side. Elaine saw what the padded bench had previously concealed, that her nipples too were pierced and ringed. With only a moment's hesitation Elaine held up her left hand, palm upwards, and Gretchen paused in her labours to pour a little oil into it.

Elaine found that she loved the novelty of having a completely nude and sexually compliant woman on either side of her equally naked body. She let her oily hands wander freely over bare breasts, bellies and buttocks, finally settling on employing her expertise in masturbation to excite both women at the same time. From the way they moved she could tell she was getting to them. And there was no doubt that they were getting to her! The feeling of a hand on each breast and two between her legs made it hard for her to keep down the rising tide of lust. She wanted an orgasm and she wanted it *now*. But first that bitch Gretchen was going to find out that she was not the only one with stimulating fingers. She concentrated on her work, fighting down her own desires, and was rewarded quite soon by the sight of Gretchen in the throes of orgasm, her head thrown back, body arched, hips thrusting and knees turned to jelly. Then Elaine could wait no longer as her own crescendo mounted and she came too, her gasping cries blending with Gretchen's.

She lay for a while absorbing her feelings. Her orgasm had not been the violent affair she sometimes achieved and yet . . . And yet . . . She puzzled over the difference between her present state and what she felt after being with James. There was no doubt that this was different. A warm, comfortable, fuzzy feeling. She felt no urgency to cover herself or to get up. Maybe, she thought, when a woman is with a woman there is nothing to prove. No need to exaggerate for the sake of male ego. These women would know, without having to be told, exactly what they had done. They had given of themselves, not entirely for their own gratification, but for hers and they knew how and where to touch to provide pleasure. Elaine was not used to that and found herself feeling grateful and loving. She wanted to kiss them and stroke them and to give in return. And with that thought came renewed passion as she realised that, for the first time in her life, she could easily achieve a second orgasm.

She noticed only then that the hands had never stopped fondling and probing. That her lovers – and what an accurate word that was, she thought – had used their experience, as she had used her own on them, and had anticipated what she would be thinking and feeling. They were going to bring her to climax again! She gazed at them with soft eyes and opened herself to their ministrations. After a while she reached up and drew them down to her, one after the other, kissing each passionately, with open mouth and tongue flickering, then indicated that they should do the same to each other.

As they leaned across her, their breasts hung before her face. Tempted by their opulence she reached up to take one in each hand and drew them towards her mouth. While she licked, sucked and nibbled softly at one nipple she toyed with the gold ring on the other, twisting and tugging very gently; something which seemed to give obvious pleasure, taking it in turns to treat each lover the same. Then unable to resist the temptation any longer, her hands reached out between their thighs again and her own legs parted wide. With knees slightly raised, her whole body was crucified on the altar of lust and love, an expression of her total vulnerability and surrender.

Presently she felt Lady Isabel coming to the boil, and observed with considerable pleasure, the unmistakable signs of orgasm; the rippling of the naked stomach, the heavy, moaning breathing and the pulsing grip of the vaginal walls on her fingers. The excitement of watching this precipitated her own climax – the same warm, cosy, totally delightful sensation as before and, quite soon after that, Gretchen came again.

This time none of them stopped what they were doing but went on kissing, licking, fondling and stroking. To Elaine this was a completely unique sensation. A feeling of total relaxation and freedom. She could feel years of stress soaking out of her with the release of her own juices. Time seemed endless as uncounted mini-orgasms washed over them. There was nothing in the world except the giving and taking of sexual pleasure.

Finally, like the tiny waves on a shallow beach, the

ripples of orgasm grew smaller and smaller and, by mutual consent, they stopped masturbating each other and just clung together, kissing and stroking, savouring the afterglow. Then it was time to return to reality. To get up and dress. Elaine realised, with a start, that two hours had elapsed since she entered the room. It hardly seemed possible, yet it was true. There was almost no conversation between the three women. None seemed necessary. Unlike a sex session with James there was no need for prolonged discussion about, 'How was it for you?' Each knew how it was for the other without asking.

As Elaine made her way back to her room, to shower, she tried to sort out her emotions. She had often wondered about the motivation and feelings of girls she flippantly described as AC/DC. Now she found she was 'that way', herself, and had a much clearer understanding of exactly what the attraction was. She also had a much better insight into her sexual relationship with James now that she had some other experience to compare it with. It also clarified the reason James sought her sexual favours in preference to his wife's. She wondered, idly, if he knew about Gretchen, then decided that he must do.

2
Return Engagement

Elaine had just finished dressing when she heard the sound of the Rolls on the gravel drive and saw from her bedroom window that Sir James was home. She hastily stripped again before putting on the presents he had bought for her – the flimsy undies and the watch. She ran downstairs, not quite sure whether her excitement was at his homecoming or the thought of what she was wearing under her blouse and skirt – a secret only they would share.

Sir James was in the study talking to Lady Isabel, who looked up as she entered. 'Goodness, girl. You look quite flushed. Have you been running?'

'I'm sorry, your Ladyship. I wasn't expecting Sir James so early and I was a little behind with my dressing.' She went over to the desk. 'Good morning, Sir James. I trust you had a pleasant trip. Here are the letters you dictated before you went.' She held out the basket of correspondence deliberately using the hand with the watch on it, looking for the faintest sign of a reaction. When it came, it was almost imperceptible, but definite, and she knew that he was picturing what she had on underneath her outer clothes. Knowing how easy it was for her to arouse him she moved around the desk so that she could see into his lap. She experienced a thrill of triumphant glee when she saw his penis stir and grow; pushing against the material of his trousers. She would make him pay for being away for a week! She shifted closer and leaned down behind him knowing that her perfume would waft across his nostrils. On the pretext of pointing out some detail in the letters she allowed her breast to nuzzle gently against his shoulder, saying, 'I got everything ready for you, as you asked, Sir James. I think it will all be clear to you, but if it's not, I can take down anything you've thought about while you've been away so that you can deal with things properly.'

The bulge in his trousers reached positively tent-like proportions and she knew that as long as Lady Isabel was in the room she could keep him in his chair as firmly as if she had lashed him to it. It was a delightful feeling of power and ownership.

Sir James cleared his throat and pretended to search in his trouser pockets for his keys in order to ease his discomfort. 'Isabel, my dear. I shall have to go out almost immediately to a business meeting and I'll take Elaine with me. I may need some notes taken.'

Lady Isabel smiled. 'Elaine and I have been seeing quite a lot of each other while you've been away. She has been taking walks in the garden. One afternoon she made Gretchen and I both come. It was most pleasant.'

Elaine stared at Lady Isabel, who looked back with total innocence. She suddenly realised that the prank she was playing on Sir James was being played on her by Lady Isabel, and she flushed with embarrassment at the memory of the occasion on which she had made her Ladyship and Gretchen both come. She hastily found an excuse and scuttled off.

She had regained her composure by the time Sir James was ready to leave. He had elected to drive the Rolls himself and she climbed into the front seat beside him. As soon as they had cleared the grounds of the house he turned to her. 'Little bitch! You need your bare bottom spanked!'

She wriggled, contentedly. 'Oooh, lovely, James! Is that what you're going to do with me?' She reached across and, before he could stop her, unzipped his fly, diving her hand inside to grasp his penis.

He exclaimed aloud and the car swerved across the road. 'For God's sake, Elaine! Not here! Not now!'

She released him, pretending to sulk. 'Always the same thing. "Not here, Elaine. Not now, Elaine." You've been away for a week and I thought you would want me. Of course, if you don't, I shall quite understand,' she sniffed, her nose in the air.

In response, Sir James swung the Rolls off the road and down a cart track leading into the depths of a wood. When they were well out of sight of the road he pulled the car to one side and stopped. 'Right!' he said. 'Out!'

Elaine chortled at her power to make this man do as she wanted. 'Oh, Goody! An open air one. We've never done that before.' With his arm around her waist, propelling her forward, they went deeper into the forest. When they arrived at a grassy place Elaine swung round and planted a firm, wet kiss on his lips, then slipped out of his arms and ran to the middle of the clearing. Her eyes shining with excitement and mischief, she said, 'You stay there, my darling. I'm going to strip for you now, and show you your presents.'

As he leaned his back against a tree and watched, she commenced a slow, rhythmic movement of her body; not so much a dance as a sheer animal mating display. Her hips and belly gyrated and her breasts jiggled. Slowly, very slowly, she unfastened her blouse, button by button, her eyes never leaving his face. She held it closed chastely, across her breasts, while she slipped it off her shoulders, rolling them provocatively. Then she flung it wide open and stood stock still for a moment, displaying to best advantage her firm, upthrust breasts behind the gossamer bra, her nipples exposed and erect.

She took off the blouse completely and threw it away, not caring where it went. Her hands went to the waistband of her skirt and she unclipped it with tantalising slowness, undulating her bare belly all the time. Inch by inch she eased the skirt down over her hips, exposing more and more naked flesh, until the tops of the flimsy panties were visible. Then she dropped the skirt and kicked it away. For just a moment she allowed him to see the effect of undies, grip-top stockings and high-heeled shoes, then she turned away in mock modesty. With her back to him she slowly bent further and further forward, knowing that the single cord between the cheeks of her bottom, which formed the back of the panties, hid nothing from him. When she was down as far as she could go, she looked at him between her legs, her blonde hair hanging down to the ground.

She sat down on the grass facing him and, with exaggerated high kicks, disposed of her shoes. She rolled her stockings down until the tops came past her toes, then fell onto her back. Keeping her legs straight, she raised them to a vertical position, then slowly parted them until they were as wide as they would go. Grasping the tops of the stockings, she slowly peeled them off and threw them after the rest of her clothes.

Rejoicing at the physical reaction in him which, even at this distance, she could see her performance had had, she rose to her feet and stood with legs and arms apart, head back and breasts thrusting forward. Then, staring into his eyes, her voice hoarse with wanting, she said, 'And now – just the watch, my darling. Just as you asked.' Still fixing him with her steady stare she reached behind her, unfastened the bra clip and cast the garment away. The flimsy panties followed and she stood gloriously naked, then collapsed onto her back, her knees raised and parted, her arms stretched out towards him. 'Now, darling! Now!'

She heard the swish of grass as he crossed the space between them and then he was on top of her, his weight crushing her into the sweet-smelling clover. With urgency she reached underneath him and tugged down his zip and then he was in her, the full length of his rock-hard penis slamming up inside her time and again, so that her whole body shook with the impacts. She cried out with the joy of feeling him inside her, then he shuddered, gasped, and she felt the warm flood of his sperm spurt up to bathe her inflamed passage.

His penis softened and he rolled away from her. Panicking, she tried to pull him back. 'James! James! I haven't finished! Don't leave me in this state, for God's sake! Help me!'

He kissed her forehead. 'Don't worry about it. We can't always both finish at the same time. You were great Elaine. Thanks!'

She could not believe that he was getting up and adjusting his clothes. In a frenzy of frustration she moaned and masturbated frantically, but the moment was passing fast. She clasped both hands over the centre of her frustration and rolled onto her side feeling cheap and used.

James was already on his way back to the car as she got up wearily and started to find her scattered clothes. It occurred to her that perhaps her experience with Lady Isabel and Gretchen had spoiled her for men. Did that happen? She did not know. It was all outside her experience and she felt suddenly vulnerable and weak.

When she got back to the Rolls, James was studying a map and smoking a cigarette. He offered her one but she declined. 'Well, we must get on or we'll be late. Thanks again darling. That was tremendous.' He leaned over to brush her cheek lightly with his lips, then started the Rolls, turned it and drove back to the road.

Elaine was a silent companion for the next few miles, but then recovered her buoyancy, as is the way of the young. After all he was right. They had been very lucky, so far, in the number of times their orgasms had coincided. And after all, he *had* been without for a week and so would be naturally eager. It was her own fault really if she had not been able to keep pace with him. It would all be all right next time.

Presently, they came to a very high wall, with wire on top, all along the side of the road. It seemed to go on for miles, until they arrived at a huge and ornate pair of gates. James stopped the car by the gates and a gatekeeper dressed entirely in some sort of black uniform came up to it. Peering into the car, he said, 'I'm sorry, Sir James, but I don't know the young lady. You can go in, but she can't.'

'That's all right. She is my private secretary. I need her for note-taking.'

'I'm really sorry sir, but you know that I can't let her in.'

Sir James sighed. 'Oh, very well. Let me use your telephone.' He climbed out of the car and went to the gate-house. Elaine could see him talking on the telephone, occasionally gesturing in her direction, then the gatekeeper took up the phone, obviously receiving instructions. James came back to the car and Elaine expected the gates to be opened, but instead she was invited to get out and wait with him, while the gatekeeper climbed into the driving seat of the Rolls and took it away.

A moment later, a long, black limousine with tinted windows purred down the drive and stopped just inside the gates, which opened electrically. They went in, climbed into the limousine and the chauffeur turned it to head back up the drive. The grounds had obviously been laid out by a skilful hand because, as the drive twisted and turned, occasional, teasing glimpses could be caught of a great house; then, like a curtain being drawn on a stage, the whole was revealed in all its splendour. Huge, rambling and magnificent, surrounded by bowling green lawns and sparkling fountains. There was money here, Elaine thought.

The limousine swept to a halt outside a large and imposing door. James and Elaine got out and passed into the dim depths of a cool entrance hall. A woman in an ornately embroidered, and ostentatiously expensive, silk kimono came to meet them, holding out both hands to Sir James and kissing the air beside both his cheeks. 'Sir James. It is wonderful to have you with us again.' She turned her smile to Elaine. 'And this is Elaine, of whom you have given such a flattering description. He did not do you justice, my dear.'

'Elaine,' said James. 'I would like you to meet

23

Madam Cecilia Maximilian, a very old friend. Madam Max, I find that I shall not need Elaine to take notes after all. Would you be kind enough to entertain her while I do my business?'

'That would be my greatest pleasure, Sir James. Off you go and leave her with me. Come into the drawing room, my dear. Perhaps you would like some tea?' She led the way into a vast, panelled room with comfortable chairs and sofas and operated a bell-pull on the wall. 'Come and sit here beside me and tell me all about yourself. You are Sir James' private secretary are you not?'

Madam Maximilian had the sort of social grace which made conversation with her extremely easy, so that Elaine was relaxed enough to be able to spare part of her mind for an appraisal of this woman. She was slim, dark-haired and beautiful. Elaine could not make up her mind whether she was in her thirties or forties. Her skin condition made the former seem likely, but her hair style, severely drawn back in a bun, aged her a little, although there was no trace of grey in it. Her eyes were her most striking feature. They were very dark and had a piercing quality which made it difficult to look straight into them. When Elaine did, the sensation was that of a laser beam scraping the back of her skull. 'Elegant,' thought Elaine. 'Elegant – in a continental sort of way,' she qualified.

Presently there was a soft knock at the door and, on being told to enter, a maid in black dress with white apron and cap, pushed in a laden tea trolley. There was something odd about the maid, although Elaine could not quite put her finger on it. She was very heavily made up for a domestic servant. Her hair was very blonde indeed, almost like a wig, and her black, patent leather shoes had the highest heels Elaine had ever seen. She did not speak at all and seemed to be extremely timid, glancing around her nervously, as if expecting to be leapt upon by a tiger. All these things were odd, yet Elaine sensed that there was more to the oddness than that.

Madam Maximilian dismissed the girl with a curt wave and she left quickly as though relieved to go. Elaine put the puzzle out of her mind. It was none of her business if people chose to employ potty servants and anyway, she found that she was hungry. The tiny sandwiches were excellent and she ate with a keen appetite. Madame Maximilian watched her but ate little herself, apparently enjoying Elaine's pleasure in satisfying her hunger.

She finished her tea and wiped her mouth, a little embarrassed at how much she had eaten. Madame Maximilian, good hostess that she was, sensed a void and filled it. 'So, my dear. Have you been with Sir James a long time?' The topic of Elaine's work engaged them for a while and then Madam Maximilian changed the subject. 'I must tell you, child, that your hair is quite the most beautiful I have ever seen. May I touch it?' She reached out and took a few strands between finger and thumb. Elaine allowed her to do so, not knowing how to react. 'So beautiful and so soft. You know, Elaine, from what you and Sir James have told me, I can tell that you are good at your job. I am in need of a personal secretary myself. If you ever decide to leave Sir James I hope you will let me know at once. You will find that I can match, or more than match, what you are getting at present.'

Again Elaine was caught flat-footed, not quite knowing how to respond, but she was saved by the return of Sir James. Madam Maximilian saw them to the door. 'Goodbye, James. I hope we shall see you again soon. And you too, Elaine. Don't forget what I told you.'

The limousine whisked them to the gate where the Rolls had been returned and was waiting. On the drive back, Sir James was deeply preoccupied, answering any attempt at conversation with surly grunts. Only when they were almost home did he speak. 'I have to go to South America again. I don't know how long I'll be away. Get me a ticket for tomorrow night.' It was not unusual for him to jet about all over the world and his grumpiness made her afraid to ask questions. One way and another, it had not been a very satisfying day.

The time until his departure seemed to speed by in a blur of business duties and they had no opportunity to be alone to make love to one another. So it was with a sense of failure at her inability to close the gap which had opened between them that Elaine watched the Rolls carry him away to the airport. It came as something of a relief to be able to ease off a little – if taking on the mountain of dictation he had left could be called easing off.

Elaine was working at this the next day, when Lady Isabel came into the office. She seldom came there and Elaine was a little surprised. The older woman came over to where she was typing and rested her hands on her shoulders. 'Elaine. I worry about you. You work too hard.'

'It's all right, your Ladyship. I like my work.'

'After what we have done to each other, I think it would be all right if you called me Isabel when no-one else is around to hear.' She smiled faintly, and rubbed her thumbs into the sore muscles on either side of Elaine's neck, reminding her of that delightful massage session.

'Thank you, your La . . . I mean Isabel. You know,

it was awful of you to embarrass me like that, the other day. I didn't know where to put myself.'

Isabel chuckled and there was a mischief in her voice which belied her age. 'You are so young and so fresh; so innocent. You practically demand to be teased. And you do blush most becomingly. One day perhaps, Gretchen and I will be privileged to see if that blush goes all over, or stops at the neck. But there, I see I am doing it again. I'm sorry, my dear. I'll stop.'

Elaine felt that this woman was the closest thing to a mother-figure available at present and in her confusion, she needed to talk to someone. 'Isabel. I want to ask you something, but it is personal, and I am a little scared.'

'Don't be afraid of me, Elaine. Ask anything you want. If I don't know the answer, I will tell you so. If I know, but don't want to tell you, I will be truthful about that, too.'

'Well. You and Gretchen. You're . . . You're . . . I mean, both of you are . . .'

'Lesbians, is the word you are groping for. Queer. Homosexual. Those are other names. We prefer to think of ourselves as human beings and lovers.'

'Does that mean that you really don't like sex with men?'

Isabel smiled again at the naivete of the question. She came around the desk and sat down, facing Elaine. 'I have had, and still do have, sex with men. After all, I am married to James and one has obligations. Some men are very good lovers and it is a joy to be with them but they are rare and occasional. It is much commoner to find that a woman, making sexual love with another woman, is more concerned about her partner's pleasure than a man would be. For myself, I prefer to get my excitement with

Gretchen. She, on the other hand, also enjoys the attentions of the occasional man.'

'And you don't mind that?' said Elaine, in wonder.

Isabel shook her head. 'How young you are. Just because you love someone doesn't mean that you own him or her. When Gretchen gives herself to another – man or woman – she takes nothing from me. I still have all her attention and love when we are together.'

'So, if I liked . . . I mean, if I *really* enjoyed what we did the other day, it doesn't mean that is the only way I shall be able to love in the future?'

'I could see that you enjoyed it. What we did was loving and giving. If you don't get the same pleasure from a man, it is just because you have not found one who has the same capacity to love and to give. You will, one day. And when you do, I advise you to cling to him and not let him escape. As I said, they are rare.'

Elaine sat for a while in thought, and was somehow reassured. Maybe she was more 'normal' than she had been thinking lately.

'Another thing, Isabel. More personal. Do you mind?'

'No. Go ahead.'

'Your . . . Your . . . Yours and Gretchen's . . .' Unaroused, she could not bring herself to say 'nipples' to this woman. She fumbled and found an alternative. 'Your gold rings. I mean, why? I don't understand.'

'Ah! That's a little deeper. I'm not sure you are ready for that yet.' Seeing Elaine's obvious disappointment, she relented. 'Gretchen and I try to do everything we can to please each other. We both enjoy bondage and the nipple rings have a place in that activity.'

Elaine was incredulous. 'Bondage! You mean tying each other up and hurting each other?'

Isabel was visibly shocked. 'Tying up, yes. Although we call it restraint. Pain? What is pain? When you masturbate do you not sometimes pinch your nipples until they hurt? At exactly the right time, in the right place, applied to the right extent, pain is a pleasurable stimulation. If all those things are not right, there is only pain without pleasure and to inflict it is not a loving thing to do. Hurt each other? Certainly not! You're confusing bondage with sadism. Sometimes the two go together but by no means always. We have nipple rings because we are both very sensitive in that area and we found that nipple clamps, the alternative, hurt.'

'But, what do you get out of it. I mean, what does it do for you both?'

'Ah! Well! This is that area I was talking about when I said there might be a question I couldn't answer. It is something you have to experience to understand and I'm not sure you are ready yet. What Gretchen and I do is no secret from you and anytime you want to watch you are welcome. An audience increases the intensity of what we feel, so we wouldn't mind. You have only to ask. Let me know when you have thought about it.'

Over the next 24 hours Elaine *did* think about it. The astounding conversation filled her waking thoughts and her masturbation fantasies began to centre around what she imagined the couple might do. The novelty of discovering yet another, unfamiliar, sexual stimulation was a powerful motivator for her curiosity and so, when she saw Isabel in the garden, she joined her for a stroll. 'You remember what you were saying about watching,' she began. 'Well. I've thought about it and I think ... That is to say, I've decided ... Or rather ...'

'For goodness' sake, girl. You'll never get it out. You want to watch. No problem. Come to my room at three o'clock this afternoon. I'll tell Gretchen we're expecting you.'

Elaine spent the time until three o'clock convinced that she had made a mistake. But, impelled by her insatiable curiosity, she found herself tapping on the door of Isabel's room with a thudding heart.

Gretchen opened it and as she went in, Elaine jumped with surprise. On the broad double bed, Isabel was spreadeagled, completely nude, face up, her wrists and ankles secured to the bed posts with white silk scarves. Her eyes were covered by the sort of blindfold which completely shuts out all vision. Cords were attached to each nipple and led up to a beam above the bed, so that her nipples were subjected to a very slight tension as a small part of the weight of her breasts hung on them.

Gretchen led Elaine to the bedside and they looked down on the naked woman. 'We do not speak when we are in restraint, except in an emergency, so Isabel has asked me to explain,' said Gretchen. 'She has been like this now, for one hour, unable to move or see. The tension on the nipples is adjusted so as not to be painful. Any time she wishes to feel her nipples being pulled, she just has to move her chest.' At those words, Isabel jiggled slightly from side to side so that her semi-suspended breasts pulled at first one nipple then the other.

'She knows that when her hour of restraint is up something will be done to her. She does not know what. All she knows is that, whatever I choose to do to her, she has to submit to it. She has had an hour of anticipation and it is that hour of waiting for the unknown that she enjoys. What comes at the end of that hour may be pleasant for her, or it may not. That is not her choice, it is mine and depends on my mood on the day.'

She stooped over the helpless form on the bed. 'So, Isabel. Your hour is up and Elaine is here to watch. What shall I do to you today?' She took hold of the cords and tugged gently upwards. 'Shall I tighten your nipple cords until your full weight hangs on them?' The sightless head shook. 'Shall I hang you up by the feet with your legs apart and cane you between your legs?' Again, the head shook. 'Aha! I have it! You shall be shaved. It is a long time since I did that to you and it has all grown back again. I shall make you as smooth as silk down here.' She ran her hand through Isabel's pubic hair. The head shook even more violently and the area under Gretchen's hand twitched in anticipation.

Elaine watched, fascinated, as Gretchen fetched a shaving mug, brush and soap. Working up a lather, she spread it all over Isabel's pubic hair, working well down between the stretched legs. When the hair was all covered she took a safety razor and began to shave. The lather was being scraped off when Elaine realised that the hair was not coming with it. There was no blade in the razor. She opened her mouth to say something to Gretchen but Gretchen raised a finger to her lips and cautioned her to silence. When Gretchen had laid razor strokes across the whole pubic mound and between Isabel's legs, she wiped away the residue of lather with a damp cloth, then blew on the wet area. 'See how cool it feels without all that nasty hair. Elaine can see every part of you now. But before I let you go, she also wants to see four good orgasms.'

She took a tiny vibrator from a bedside drawer and

31

switched it on. At the sound, Elaine noticed that Isabel's vulva actually twitched and contracted expectantly. Stretched out as she was, with legs widely separated by the pull of the scarves on her ankles, her labia gaped open to reveal the entrance to her vagina. That too, contracted rhythmically, in anticipation of what she knew was coming. She squirmed as Gretchen inserted her finger and thumb to pull the labia even further apart to expose her clitoris. Very gently and delicately, Gretchen touched the tiny button of flesh with the tip of the buzzing vibrator. Again and again, she dabbed, eliciting a strong wriggle and a stifled moan each time. Isabel rolled her torso from side to side as far as her bonds would allow so that her breasts, held by the nipples, were pulled first one way then the other. Gretchen looked at Elaine. 'Will you carry on with this?' Elaine sat on the edge of the bed, took the vibrating instrument from Gretchen and began to imitate her actions. She found that she was being turned on by what she and Gretchen were doing. She tried to guess what it would feel like to be brought forcibly to orgasm but it was outside her experience. She could tell however, from Isabel's reactions, that for her it was a pleasurable sensation.

After watching for a while to see that the job was being done correctly, Gretchen began to rub her hands all over Isabel's upper body, first stroking lightly, then pressing and grinding, with the heel of her hand, at the place where the pubes projected above the clitoris. Elaine guessed that she was duplicating the stimulation caused when, with penis fully inserted, a man's skeleton impinged upon a woman's. Then she reached out and took one of Isabel's breasts in each hand, gripping tightly and lifting them, then pulling down against the nipple cords. Isabel's moans and wiggles became frantic and she came to orgasm.

'One!' said Gretchen. And the treatment continued. It was interesting to Elaine that Isabel's orgasms, unlike the ones when they had kissed and fondled, seemed to become more intense each time and she guessed that on the previous occasion Isabel had already come to orgasm several times when alone with Gretchen, before Elaine joined them.

When Gretchen counted, 'Four!', the whole of Isabel's body was leaping and jumping and her moaning was intense, her hips coming completely off the bed at each pelvic thrust.

Gretchen quickly released her and as soon as she was able she rolled herself into a tight ball and lay perfectly still, so that Elaine was afraid that she was in pain. 'It's all right,' explained Gretchen. 'For her, the feelings are so intense that she has to stay like that for a while in order to calm down and collect herself.'

Sure enough, after a few minutes, Isabel sat up and stretched luxuriously. 'Mmmmmm! Wonderful!' Then she looked down at herself and did a double take. She laughed. 'No blade in the razor!'

'Wouldn't you have minded losing it?' asked Elaine. 'I know I would.'

'Not at all. It felt so good. You should try it some day. I'm glad that it's still there though because I can enjoy the same feeling all over again, sooner.'

Elaine did not understand this thinking at all.

'By the way,' said Isabel. 'In case you thought I was not enjoying myself at times, what Gretchen said about me being unable to stop her doing anything she liked to me was not strictly true. That is a little performance we go through for each other. Whenever one of us is in restraint the other never leaves the room or stops watching what is happening. If we get into difficulties – like cramp or restricted circulation – we say so. Occasionally, we like to wear a gag and then we draw attention to the problem by snapping our fingers and are immediately released.'

'But now it is Gretchen's turn. She has given to me and I know exactly what she likes best.' Gretchen came forward smiling and willingly offered her wrists to be bound. Isabel tied a scarf around each, leaving long ends dangling. She positioned Gretchen beneath a ceiling beam, climbed onto a chair and passed one scarf-end through a large ring in the beam, knotting the ends together and so raising Gretchen's left arm above her head.

'Elaine, would you do the other one?' Seeing a ring about four feet from the first, Elaine climbed onto another chair taking the other scarf-end with her. She passed the scarf through the ring and knotted it as she had seen Isabel do. Then Gretchen was secured with her arms spread wide, almost on tip-toe. Facing the wardrobe's mirror doors she could not avoid seeing her own reflection. 'She likes the blindfold,' Isabel explained, handing it to Elaine, who passed the elastic over Gretchen's head and secured it over her eyes.

'Strip her slowly,' said Isabel. 'Her halter unbuttons at the back of her neck.'

Elaine unbuttoned the garment, then slowly peeled it off Gretchen's large breasts, revealing them little by little. When they were exposed she unbuttoned the strap at the back and threw the halter on the bed. On an impulse, knowing that Gretchen could not see what was going to happen, she stood behind her and reached around her body before grabbing one of her large breasts firmly in each hand, her forefingers

34

scrabbling at the nipple rings. Gretchen's leap of startled delight was exciting to watch. Her head shot back and she thrust out her breasts towards the stimulation, with a succession of, 'Aaaah! Aaaah!' noises, which continued all the time Elaine kept up the treatment.

Feeling pleased at the reaction she had provoked, Elaine slid her hands down over the plump, smooth belly, caressing and stroking her way towards the fastening of the shorts. Gretchen wriggled in ecstasy as she undid them and slowly slid them down and off.

'Now a spreader bar,' said Isabel. Elaine wondered what that was but found that it was rather like a broomstick handle with a ring at each end. Elaine helped to knot a scarf around each of Gretchen's ankles which passed through each of the rings, so spreading her legs wide apart. Isabel took the same cord which had been used to suspend her own nipples, doubled it in two and climbing onto the chair again, put the loop through a ring over Gretchen's head. The ends of the cord were pulled through the loop so that they hung down between Gretchen's breasts. Passing one end through each nipple ring, she adjusted the tension with great care so that there was a small upward pull, which Gretchen could increase or decrease by small movements of her body.

It was obvious to Elaine that this element in her bondage was of great satisfaction to Gretchen, because as soon as the cords were in place, she began to sway her body backwards and forwards, causing her heavy breasts to be lifted by the nipples, then dropped again. Standing in front of the naked, bound girl, Elaine allowed her gaze to travel over the stocky thighs, dwelling for a moment on the pubic area. Then upwards to the bared breasts and captive nipples, the widespread arms, the moistened lips and the blindfold. Maybe it was the blindfold that did it, acting as it did as the ultimate indication of subjugation. A wholly new feeling swept over Elaine, overpowering in its impact. She clasped her lower stomach which was where the shock seemed to be centred. 'Oh, Isabel!' she cried.

'What is it Elaine?'

'I have this strange sensation, right here, and it frightens me.'

'What does it feel like?'

Elaine struggled to explain a feeling for which words were not adequate. 'Power! Excitement! Control! I just want to stare and stare at her and think, "I did that to her". Because I know she can't stop me, I want to touch her and kiss her and be cruel and kind at the same time.'

'Now you understand what I could not explain to you. That is one half of the sensation of bondage. Would you like to explore that feeling a bit more, by being the one who administers her treatment?'

Unreasonably excited Elaine murmured, 'Yes.'

'To be dealt with by someone fresh. Gretchen would like that, wouldn't you?' Gretchen nodded decisively. 'So Elaine, what would you like to do to her? Let's see if it fits into the pattern of her pleasure.'

Elaine knew exactly what she wanted to do to Gretchen. She had felt the strongest of urges ever since she had seen her hanging naked and helpless, but she was too embarrassed to voice her desires.

Isabel sensed her diffidence. 'If you don't tell us, we can't guess. And unless you do tell us it won't happen. I guess you will just have to think about how badly you want what you want and decide whether being coy is the best way to get it. Can you say, now, what you want to do to her?'

Elaine was so stimulated by the pictures which had been going through her mind that she managed to express her burning wish. 'I want to slap her bottom.'

Isabel laughed. 'Is that all. I thought it was something dreadful. Carry on. I think you'll be interested in the reaction you get.'

Elaine went and stood behind Gretchen, a little to one side. She found the soft, white swell of her buttocks absolutely fascinating and the thought of what she was about to do to that bare backside made her wet between the legs. She raised her hand and brought it down in a light slap on one of those plump cheeks. Gretchen exploded into wriggling movement that set her bottom dancing, in spite of her bonds, at the same time cooing with obvious pleasure. Encouraged, Elaine slapped again, harder, provoking an even more violent response. She reached around the front of Gretchen's body and groped her way through her pubic hair until she found her hot, wet vulva, then pushed two fingers in and held them there while she delivered six stinging slaps with the other hand. To her amazement, Gretchen came to orgasm immediately, spilling her fluid all over Elaine's fingers with high-pitched squeals of delight.

'One!' said Isabel. 'She made me have four, remember.'

Elaine was breathing hard with the novel excitement of what she had done to Gretchen's body and the thought of the three orgasms yet to come did nothing to calm her down. Her mind was racing over a variety of ways of driving Gretchen crazy now that she knew her taste for a little bottom punishment. But when Isabel went to the wardrobe and came back with a many-thonged lash, she felt that things were going a little too far.

In horror, she watched as Isabel swung her arm and brought the thongs down across Gretchen's back. The second stroke landed full across her plump bottom and curled around her thighs. Isabel offered the whip to Elaine who recoiled, shocked. 'No, no. I couldn't. That is too much.'

'Gretchen, would you like Elaine to whip you?' Isabel enquired. Gretchen's head nodded emphatically.

'But how can she stand the pain?' asked Elaine.

Isabel laughed. 'Because it doesn't hurt. Look more closely at this lash. It has many strands and they are all made of soft, light leather, over half an inch wide. It makes a very satisfactory swishing noise in the air and an even more satisfactory smack as it lands but is quite incapable of causing pain or injury, however hard it is used.'

Elaine examined the whip. The description Isabel had given was perfectly accurate yet she could not bring herself to believe that being struck with it could be anything but uncomfortable. She said as much to Isabel, who shocked her by suggesting that the only way to find out how it felt was to be hit with it. 'Take off your dress. Now bend forward slightly.' Afraid but inquisitive, Elaine did as she was told and Isabel brought the lash cracking down across her back. To her amazement there was no pain, only a delicious tingling where the tip of each soft strand had landed.

'Again?' Elaine nodded; and received the next blow across the backs of her thighs. Again the delightful tingle. She tried to liken the sensation to one within her previous knowledge. The only one she could come up with was the feel of the needle jets of a powerful shower when she allowed it to play on her nipples. She knew suddenly that she wanted to feel this thing again, and in a sexier place, so she peeled off her brassiere and put her hands on her head, pushing out her breasts in invitation of the next blow, which landed squarely across them and drove every nerve in her into agitated longing.

When no more strokes followed she looked enquiringly at Isabel, who laughed at her and said, 'Gretchen. Remember!' Elaine had forgotten the other woman in the heat of her own pleasure. She took the whip willingly and applied it vigorously to Gretchen's body. She knew that she was sending Gretchen into paroxysms of pleasure with each stroke across breasts, belly, thighs or bottom, even if Gretchen had not made the fact obvious by her noise and behaviour. At the same time it satisfied a primitive urge in Elaine to be able to rain blows on a nude woman.

When she stopped, Gretchen was more than ready for her other orgasms. Elaine knelt in front of her with the little vibrator, applying it to Gretchen's clitoris in the same way she had used it on Isabel, who stood behind Gretchen with her own naked body pressed against hers while she ran her hands over her breasts and stomach. Under this double assault, Gretchen did not hold out very long and came three more times in quick succession.

As soon as Gretchen was released she took Elaine in her arms and kissed her tenderly. 'Thank you,' she said. 'That was so very exciting for me.' Turning to Isabel with a smile she added, 'I think there is now only one person in the room who has not experienced full pleasure today. Do you think we should do something about that?'

Isabel smiled back at her. 'I'm sure we should but that depends upon Elaine's wishes. How do you feel about that, Elaine? Are you curious to find out what it is that we enjoy when we are restrained?'

Elaine was flustered. 'I don't know. I only meant to watch, not to join in – but I *am* curious. I can see that you two enjoy what you do but I can't understand why. I don't know if it would have the same effect on me. Will I enjoy it too?'

'That is impossible to answer,' replied Isabel. 'You may love it or hate it, or be ambivalent about it. One thing is certain; if you want your curiosity satisfied there is only one way to do it.'

Elaine was torn in two by doubt and desire. With her passionate nature there was a strong impulse to sample what might be a new and exciting experience; but on the other hand the notion seemed so strange and bizarre that it was a little frightening. 'If I try it and I don't like it, will you stop and let me go?'

She expected a reassuring answer, but did not get one. 'No,' Isabel said, and seeing Elaine's expression of alarm added, 'Gretchen and I are both experienced in bondage. We know our own, and each other's, feelings, likes and dislikes. Even though we know we could be released at any time, we seldom have to request it, and we can put the thought from our minds. You have no experience and would not be able to exercise the same mind control. To get whatever effect you may feel it is essential, during your first restraint at least, that you should know for certain, that whatever you do and whatever you say, you will remain in bondage until *we*, not you, decide otherwise. Your trust in us must be total. There is no half-way position. It is all or nothing. The choice is yours. To experience, or not to experience what we feel?'

Elaine thought about this for quite a while and the more she thought the more she was filled with a strange sense of adventure and excitement. Her animal instincts and her feminine curiosity were getting the better of her. She knew that she could not walk out of the room without satisfying that curiosity. The thought of doing that was intolerable. She made up her mind.

'Yes.'

'What does that mean?' asked Isabel.

'I mean, yes, I want you to do it to me. I want to find out how it feels.' Her voice was no more than a whisper.

'In spite of the fact that I have told you what the conditions are? You give yourself to us, to do with as we please, for as long as we please?'

Elaine's heart was thudding and her voice was barely audible. 'Yes.'

Isabel smiled. 'Then you have taken the first and most important step. You have surrendered your will to ours. You are already in bondage. The physical restraints are only the visible signs of that bondage.'

Gretchen went over to the wardrobe, slid back a mirror door and brought back a long, wooden pole with various holes and attachments. She set one end of this in a small, brass socket in the floor below a beam then climbed onto a chair and slid two bolts at the top of the pole into sockets in the beam, thus forming a firm and immovable support between floor and ceiling.

Isabel led Elaine, who was wearing only her silk French knickers with the wide legs, to the post and instructed her to put her back against it. She then pulled her wrists behind her around the pole and crossed them. 'Wait there!' she ordered and went to the bed to fetch a silk scarf. Elaine knew that this was the moment when she could stop all this. Could change her mind. Say that it had all been a terrible mistake. Pretend to faint. Run away. She did none of those things, and a few seconds later she felt the silk scarf being knotted securely about her wrists, and knew that it was too late. The thing was done, for better or worse. She tried to raise her arms by bending her elbows, but realised that the scarf must have been passed through a ring on the pole, because she was unable to do so.

Gretchen went out of sight behind her with another scarf, and she felt it pulled tight around her arms, above the elbows, straightening her back and thrusting her breasts forward. At this point she began to experience the first, faint, stirrings of a feeling she had never had before. It was so faint that she could not be sure if it was pleasant or unpleasant. She only knew that it was a little exciting.

The two women stood in front of her. 'Now Gretchen is going to pull your knickers down,' said Isabel. 'You will find that you will usually be told in advance what we are going to do, because anticipation of something is often as exciting as the thing itself. For women, these particular garments are more than just pieces of material. They are the guardians of their secrets and their chastity; the last bastion of defence. Without them, naked, they become vulnerable. I suspect that this is the first time in your life that your knickers have been removed from you without you having any say in the matter. You may try to prevent it from happening if you wish. That may add to your excitement, but it won't make any difference. They will come off.'

The faint stirring in Elaine grew and, as Gretchen knelt in front of her, she found that what Isabel had said was true. She looked down to see Gretchen's hands reaching for her knickers and found that the pre-knowledge that these women were going to strip her naked, and that there was nothing she could do to prevent it, was very stimulating. When Gretchen's thumbs hooked into the waistband against her bare flesh, she almost cried out; then they were dragged down over her hips and tossed aside. She closed her eyes and turned her head away, unwilling to meet the eyes which she knew, were drinking in every detail of her body. She opened them again as she felt scarves passing around her ankles, fastening them to the ends of the spreader bar which was now attached to the pole. She could see herself in the mirror and was embarrassed, yet there was nothing she could do to hide her body from her own stare. If, in the wide-legged pose she was forced to adopt, every detail of her sex was plain to her, it must be plain to her captors and she blushed again.

'Well Elaine, this is restraint. How do you feel? Be truthful now,' said Isabel.

Elaine thought before she answered. 'Strange. A little nervous. I keep wondering what you are going to do to me and that is making me feel very sexy. And yet, there is something else. A feeling of pleasure which has nothing to do with any of those things. Something I haven't felt before, just like when I saw Gretchen in restraint for the first time.'

'I'm glad you feel that,' said Isabel. 'I thought you might. I think I know what causes it, but I wasn't able to describe it to you. You had to feel it for yourself. Did you have a happy childhood?'

Elaine was startled at the suddenness of the question, apparently so out of context, but she replied, 'Yes.'

'Can you say *why* your childhood was happy?'

43

'Not really. I've never thought about it. My parents were kind to me, I suppose.'

'Were you allowed to do as you liked?'

'Within reason. My parents were not what you would call strict, but there were certain standards.'

Isabel smiled. 'You were restrained from bad behaviour then. A child is happy because it has no responsibilities, other than to operate within the limits prescribed by those who are responsible on its behalf, in this case loving parents. The child does not have to worry about a job, food, clothing, money. As the child grows older, it yearns to escape from parental restraint and have adult freedom of action. But then, all those worries that freedom brings have to be taken on and the carefree days of childhood are lost. How does Housman put it? . . . *The happy highways where I went, and cannot come again . . .*

'In the restraint of bondage there is the germ of carefree childhood. You are no longer responsible for anything, because your freedom of action has been taken away. There is nothing you can do about anything. You cannot even give yourself an orgasm. It has to be given to you; maybe, even, begged for. I think that abdication of responsibility is what you feel. And there is a bonus. You are not a child. You have an adult's ability to enjoy sensual pleasure, but in a totally new way. For the first time ever, there is no way you can influence the success, or failure, of a sexual encounter. The power to do that has been taken from you. Bound and helpless as you are, you do not give; you only take. All the time you stay like that, nothing matters, except your own sensations and gratification. I think you will find that this concentration magnifies everything you feel.

'We find that it increases our sense of helpless dependence if we are just a little afraid of what might happen during restraint. Trusting and loving as we do, we know that there is really nothing to fear. But in the same way as a child loves scary stories, there is always that teasing edge of doubt. I love to be kept waiting and wondering. Gretchen likes to get straight to things.

'As this is your first time we shall compromise. You will remain like this for ten minutes. At the end of that time we will do something to you. You have our permission to wonder what that will be. Remember that you have given yourself to us, completely. There are no constraints on what we may do. We may, for instance, decide that your nipples should be pierced for rings, like ours. Mmmmm! I see that gets to you. We may choose to shave you, and this time, I promise you, there *will* be a blade in the razor. You said that you wouldn't like that, didn't you? We may turn you up and spank your bottom. I shall give Gretchen that job. She owes you a good spanking, remember? And I haven't forgotten how you reacted to the whip. Added to all, any, or none of these possibilities there will be the certainty of something else; something which you have never experienced before. When we have dealt with you, we may let you go, or we may leave you in restraint for a further period before starting all over again. Now you are to stand and look at yourself in the mirror and think about what happens in ten minutes time.'

Isabel and Gretchen went to the other end of the room and sat down together talking in low tones. Elaine could do nothing, except what she had been told to do. She was forced to look in the direction of the mirror and could not help seeing her reflection. She found that looking at her own naked, bound body, gave her the same sort of thrill as she had got from looking at Gretchen when she was in restraint. Her mind raced over the options Isabel had described. Her powerful imagination kept returning to concentrate upon the mysterious other 'something' which was soon going to be inflicted upon her. Whether she liked it or not she would be unable to stop it from happening. Dozens of masturbation fantasies presented themselves to her fertile brain, each more exciting than the last. She reached a high level of sexual stimulation and felt herself lubricating furiously, so that dribbles of liquid oozed from her excited vagina and trickled down her leg. For a moment she was ashamed of this, then remembered that she had no responsibility for what was happening. There was nothing she could do, except wait.

3
Penetration

When Isabel and Gretchen got up from the bed and came towards her, Elaine knew that ten minutes had elapsed. Her heart pounded and she could scarcely breathe. Her knees buckled and she would have sunk to the floor had it not been for the binding about her arms which held her fast against the pole. What were they going to do to her? Every sense in her body was at full stretch so that, when Isabel reached out and lightly brushed the palm of her hand across her nipple, it felt like an electric current and she cried out with the shock of it. Gretchen laughed. 'I really think we have excited her.'

Isabel took Elaine's chin in her hand and forced her head up to look into her eyes, reading the deep, lusting want there. 'Now, Elaine. Now it begins. Did you know that it is possible for some women to reach orgasm without being touched below the waist? No? I thought you might not. We intend to find out if you are one of those, or not.'

She held up two long, silver-backed hairbrushes and gave one to Gretchen. The hairs on the brushes were very fine and soft and Isabel drew hers across Elaine's right nipple in one long, slow, light stroke. In her worked-up state, the feeling was devastating, as her long, sighing moan showed. The noise she made became more intense as Gretchen did the same thing to her left nipple. Then both women were working together, brushing first in one direction, then the other, always with slow, light, deliberate strokes, never allowing their brushes to leave the skin.

Elaine struggled desperately to bring her arms forward to protect herself. But a lot of experience had gone into the manner of her restraint and she was forced to remain, with shoulders back, the skin over her breasts stretched tight, unable to shrink away by even half an inch from what they were doing to her. Whatever she had felt at first was as nothing when the treatment continued and her nipples became more and more sensitive with every stroke. It seemed to her that there was a direct wire leading from each breast, down inside her body, plugged directly into her uterus. Every touch produced a powerful contraction until she thought she was going to die from the pleasure of it. 'No more, please! No more! I can't stand it!'

'We do not speak when in restraint,' said Isabel, calmly, 'And anyway, you'll be surprised at what you can stand.' Neither woman interrupted their brushing for a second. Elaine went crazy. She could not move her body, but her head shook uncontrollably, her eyes rolling back in their sockets, so that only the whites showed. Her mouth hung open, slackly dribbling. Every square millimetre of her vulva, vagina and uterus yearned for the touch of a penis, a hand, a finger, anything which would bring the relief of the orgasm she so badly wanted; but no touch came, only the slow, gentle, soft, nipple torture of thousands of tiny brush hairs, constantly, inexorably, moving, moving, moving.

'Touch me! Touch me! Stick your fingers into me!

For God's sake, have mercy! I can't stand any more! Give it to me! Finish me! Please! Please!' Elaine barely recognised her own voice, hoarse and slurred with passion.

And then the orgasm hit her; the kind which only nipple stimulation can produce. The waves of contractions became a continuous ripple all the way up and down the walls of her uterus and vagina. Unbearable pleasure engulfed her whole body. It seemed to go on and on for ever. And when it finally died away, she hung limp, in her bonds, unable to support herself on her legs.

Gretchen and Isabel put their arms around her and lifted the weight of her body, propping her up while she recovered. It took quite a while before she could stand. When she could, Isabel held out her hairbrush and said, 'Again?'

'No! No! Please! No! Mercy! I'll die!' The thought of anything touching her sensitised nipples, let alone those tickly hairs, was enough, almost, to bring on another orgasm.

'Oh, well. Maybe later,' said Isabel, with mock regret. 'You have to have four orgasms and since that one wasn't achieved in the normal way, it doesn't count. We have decided that you shall remain in restraint for another ten minutes, to give you an opportunity to think about what comes next. And to occupy your thoughts I will show you this little toy.'

From a clean, white cloth, she unwrapped a long, flexible, rubber penis and held it up for Elaine to inspect, pointing out the salient features. It was thick enough, without being huge. Where the ridge at the base of the glans should have been, there was a ring of thin, flexible, rubber fingers, about a quarter of an inch in length, all around the circumference, sticking

49

straight out. Near the base, in a position to impinge upon a clitoris at full thrust, there was a cluster of longer, thicker, rubber fingers, pointing towards the tip. When Isabel rotated the base, it buzzed and the whole thing vibrated in her hand. When she squeezed the rubber bulb which was attached to it by a tube, a squirt of liquid spurted from the top.

She put the cloth down on the carpet in front of Elaine and placed the instrument upon it. 'Think about it!' she said, and went off with Gretchen.

Elaine stood erect, as she was forced to do, looking at the penis and at her own reflection in the glass. She was finding that her orgasm, although huge, had not had the slaking quality of others and the thought that this tool was soon going to be used on her was not unattractive. In fact, it was definitely exciting. This time her wait was not so much in dread as in impatience, and when Isabel and Gretchen came back to her, she was ready and lubricating freely again.

Both women knelt in front of her and Gretchen explored her with her fingers, pulling her sex lips apart to make entrance easy and her clitoris available. Elaine found this touch delightful and did her best to spread her legs further. Isabel inserted the tip of the penis into her vagina, but had only penetrated an inch or so when she orgasmed, spontaneously. 'Well! That was easy.' said Gretchen. 'One!'

Next time Elaine was able to absorb three or four inches of the rubber instrument, but found the sensation of the feely fingers so delicious that she was unable to contain herself and came again. 'Two!' said Gretchen.

Elaine badly wanted to feel this thing in her to its fullest extent, so she made great efforts to control herself, and next time, actually managed to hold out until the rubber fingers at the base stimulated her clitoris, when Gretchen was obliged to count, 'Three!'

For the fourth and last time, Isabel inserted the long tool and, sensing Elaine's need, was careful not to overstimulate her with it too soon, pushing it further and further up into her vagina in a series of gentle, pumping strokes. Elaine was ecstatic. The feeling was every bit as marvellous as she had thought it would be. The flexibility of the thing made it very comfortable and the rubber projections gently massaged the right places, all the way up to the neck of her womb. Isabel continued to move it up and down in long, gentle strokes, working her up slowly towards a crescendo. When she judged the moment was right, she rotated the base and it began to vibrate along its whole length. 'Yes! Yes!' Elaine groaned. 'More! More! Faster! Faster! The walls of her vagina were gripping the penis tightly, contracting in waves in an effort to pull it further in.

Her voice became a series of shrill shrieks, getting faster and faster in time with the strokes of the penis and rising up the scale at the same time. 'Now! Now! Oh God! Don't stop! Don't stop . . .' Her stomach undulated with the spasms of her orgasm and at the critical moment, Isabel squeezed the bulb and flooded her with a large amount of warm, slippery liquid, provoking a further orgasm which followed on without pause.

Elaine was so drained that when they released her, they had to half-carry her to the bed, where she lay, curled up and panting, while she recovered. When she was able to sit up after some minutes, Isabel said, 'Well now, Elaine, that is bondage. Now can you understand what we see in it?'

Elaine got up, went to them and embraced them

both at the same time, kissing each tenderly. 'I have never, never, EVER, felt anything like that. Thank you both. I understand now what you meant about loving and giving, and about pain and pleasure and next time, I shall be able to do more for you, because of what I have learned.'

The following morning Elaine, healthy young woman that she was, felt physically almost none the worse for wear; just a little sensitive in the areas which had received so much attention the previous afternoon. Still, she had a lot on her mind which needed thinking about. She worked diligently in the office for most of the morning, then her thoughts became too much for her and she took a break to walk in the garden and sort them out.

There was no doubt that she had formed a strong attachment towards Lady Isabel Hamsett which had something, but not everything, to do with their sexual relationship. She found that she admired her kind and loving qualities; her sense of humour and her philosophical wisdom. She had learned a lot from her about relationships and her own sexuality. Trying to analyse exactly how she regarded her, she finally settled on a cross between a mother and an aunt.

If that were true then she, Elaine, in carrying on a hot affair with Sir James, was committing something close to incest. She had never felt guilty before about their illicit liaison, because Isabel had been a distant and somewhat aloof figure and could be dismissed as 'not understanding her husband' or 'no good in bed'. Now that Elaine knew just how well Isabel understood human nature and, she thought with a wry smile, just how good she was at sex, her feelings in the matter could no longer be set aside with such airy disdain.

But what to do about it? It was not James' fault that this new set of circumstances had arisen which made their love-making seem all wrong. Yet it had been his fault that the thing started in the first place. She had resisted his advances at first, but he had persisted. She could not resolve the quandary herself and she could not talk to the only other person she might have turned to, Lady Isabel. She would have to wait until James came back and try to discuss it with him. It was too hard a puzzle for her alone.

Elaine tried to settle herself into her work, but found it hard to apply her usual concentration. Part of her job was to make notes about any messages which might have arrived out of office hours and been recorded on the answering machine. She performed her task perfunctorily and, when the messages ended, continued to sit on, in a daydream. She was startled back to consciousness when, after a lengthy silence, the machine sprang to life again.

'. . . done enough? I was damned nearly caught last time. Come on. Be reasonable. There must be another way.' Elaine recognised Sir James' voice, although it had a whining, petulant quality which she had never heard before.

'Don't be silly. You know that your present, comfortable life is owed to my forbearance.' The other party to the conversation was a woman who had a familiar voice, although Elaine could not place it.

'You had your fun and now you have to pay for it. Remember that I have all the tapes. One mistake on your part and copies go to all the newspapers and to Lady Isabel, and you know what that means. Disgrace. Ruin. Bankruptcy! Is that really what you want James, because you know I can arrange it. Or would you rather take the trifling risk of bringing in a few kilos of cocaine? Remember that it will be just as well disguised as it was last time, and you didn't get caught then, did you? Don't be such a wimp!'

Sir James' voice was hoarse. 'Damn you! Why was I such a fool as to let you trap me?'

The woman's laugh was chilling. 'That's not what you were saying at the time. When I look at the videos, you appear to be enjoying yourself enormously. You're right. You *are* a fool; but not such a big one as not to know when you have no alternative. Your contact in Cartagena will be Senor Peredos, as before. You will stay at the Marata hotel and wait for an invitation to his home at the Hacienda Rodriguez. Your drop at this end will be as before.'

A click signalled the abrupt end of the conversation, without the courtesy of farewells. Elaine sat on in stunned disbelief, trying to absorb the substance of what she had heard. Sir James had obviously set the machine to its memo function and then failed to erase the whole of the conversation. The full import of what she had heard flooded over her. Sir James was in South America at this very moment. Even now, he might be collecting the deadly cargo which could easily bring him a long prison sentence. She was not as certain as she had been that she loved him, but her thoughts were of Lady Isabel. What would happen to her if James was caught? Her whole way of life would be destroyed.

Elaine did no more work that morning, but stewed over this new problem. She could not go to the police without provoking the very disaster that Sir James was trying to avoid. If only she could find a way to get him off the hook. That, she supposed, would involve tracing the blackmailer and recovering the incriminating video tapes. Who could it be? Certainly, the voice had been a familiar one. She played the tape again and this time, as soon as she heard the voice, she knew who it was. Madam Max! The same Madam Max who had found her attractive and had offered her a job. There *was* a way. She would get inside the organisation at Copley Grange, find the tapes and destroy them. Then she, Sir James and Lady Isabel could all live happily ever after. Or could they? Her mind came back to the problem of her growing affection for Lady Isabel, which inevitably meant that she would have to stop seeing Sir James.

It was with a wildly beating heart that Elaine paid off the taxi at the gates of Copley Grange and reported to the gate-keeper, who was expecting her. The gates swung open, the black limousine appeared and she was transported to the great house. Madam Maximilian came into the hall to greet her. This time she was wearing a black silk kimono. 'Elaine! I can't tell you how pleased I was to get your call. Come into the office.' She conducted Elaine to a room further down the hall than the drawing room she had been in on her previous visit. Seating herself behind a massive desk, she motioned Elaine to sit on an upright chair in front of it.

'So, you have decided that you would like to work for me. Why are you leaving Sir James?'

Elaine had rehearsed her story. 'It was the money you mentioned. Madam Maximilian. I need money now.'

'Here, everyone calls me Madam Max. Why do you suddenly need money?'

'I would rather not say, if you don't mind.'

'But I do mind. If I am to take you on, I need to know a lot about you. Come along now. Don't be coy. Why do you need extra money?'

'It's my brother, Madam Max. He has been gambling and he is in serious trouble. I am desperate to get it for him.' That ought to do it, Elaine thought. She was rather proud of her fictitious brother idea.

'And you wish to be employed as my secretary?'

'Yes. I hoped . . . That is, I thought that if the work was the same and the money was better, I ought to try for it.'

Madam Max stroked her sharp chin and pretended concern. 'I hope I haven't misled you, my dear. When I spoke of more money, I had in mind more than simple secretarial duties. Do you know what we do here?'

'No. I thought . . . I imagined . . . Some sort of conference centre?'

Madam Max smiled. 'You thought wrong. This place is a dream. A world of fantasy. For those with lots of money, it is paradise. For those without it, it is something quite different. People come here and pay to have almost any dream turned into reality. Most of those dreams are about sex. Do I make myself perfectly clear?' Elaine nodded, as though surprised and embarrassed.

'Just how desperate are you for cash?' The question was sharp and Madam Max's laser eyes were even sharper. She seemed to hold her breath as she waited for the answer.

'Very desperate. I must have this job.'

Madam Max released her breath in a long sigh. 'Very well. Let us test your desperation. Would you be prepared to join in the sexual activities here if, for instance, I guaranteed you double what you get now.'

Elaine pretended to hesitate for some time before whispering, 'Yes.'

'Good. Then we can consider that to be a starting

point, should I decide to take you on – and I haven't made up my mind about that yet. If you prove to be conscientious in your duties and please me, it may well be that the rewards would be substantially greater. You are not a virgin?'

The directness of the question startled Elaine, but she replied truthfully.

Madam Max nodded. 'I could tell, but I like to be sure. A simpering little virgin is no use at all in most of my rooms. Understand that you are of no value to me if you recoil from sex. I do not expect you to be a professional all at once, but a certain healthy disregard for convention is helpful. Do you have any marks, scars or deformities?'

'No.' said Elaine, blushing a little.

'A bit of blushing is becoming. Not too much of it though, please. Stand up please.' Elaine did so. 'Show me your breasts.'

'What!' There was no pretence in Elaine's shock.

'Come now, you heard. Show me your breasts.' Elaine made vague gesturing motions towards the front of her body. 'But you can see them.'

Madam Max clicked her tongue in annoyance. 'Are you really so dense? I want you to uncover them.' Then, as Elaine still hesitated, she continued in a more conciliatory tone. 'I will make allowance for your youth and the fact that this is a worrying interview. I am thinking of employing you in a capacity which depends on how you look. Would you not agree that I am entitled to inspect what I am buying?'

Put like that, the order seemed to be almost reasonable. Elaine unbuttoned her blouse and opened it. She was wearing a push-up bra which fastened at the front. She unfastened it and held it open. Madam Max came round the desk and stood in front of her, inspecting her. Then she lifted a breast in each hand, palpating and weighing. She went back to her seat. 'There. That wasn't so bad, was it? You may put them away again now, and button yourself up.' With considerable relief Elaine did so.

'Raise your skirt. I want to see your legs.' Elaine did as she was told. She was wearing stockings and suspender belt and she raised her skirt until her thighs showed. 'Very nice legs, my dear. You are to be congratulated on your good fortune. No. Don't drop your skirt. Raise it higher. That's right. All the way to the waist.' Madam Max took in the view of her flimsy panties thus revealed. She pointed. 'Take those off and give them to me.' Elaine did so, her skirt followed them down as she wriggled them over her hips and stepped across to hand them to Madam Max.

'Step back. Skirt up again. All the way round, front and back.' Madam Max leaned forward and examined Elaine's pubic area with a thoroughness which caused her considerable embarrassment. 'Turn round, let me see the back.' She did so. At least facing that way she could not see those eyes eating into the rounded flesh of her bare bottom, though it seemed to her that she could feel them.

'Very nice. You may drop your skirt and sit down again. Congratulations. You have done very well at this audition, all things considered. You do understand though, that what I shall expect from you is unquestioning obedience at all times.' Elaine nodded. 'Then I shall give you a chance to demonstrate that you understand. You masturbate of course?'

By now, Elaine knew that Madam Max's abrupt questions were meant to shock and she was determined not to allow any surprise she might feel to show. By that small extent anyway, she could feel that she shared control of this situation. If the woman was trying to break her she wouldn't allow it. She had come to get that job; to save James, to save Isabel's marriage. It *was* worth it. She looked Madam Max boldly in the eye. 'Yes, of course I do.'

'Do so.'

Without removing her gaze, Elaine raised her skirt, parted her legs and began to stimulate her clitoris and vagina. Madam Max smiled and nodded grudging approval at her show of spirit and after only a few seconds said, 'Well done indeed. You may stop now, and lower your skirt.' Elaine dropped her skirt but not her wary alertness. When Madam Max came round the desk again and leaned against the front of it, she was ready for anything.

When the tall woman whisked open her robe to reveal that she was naked underneath it, Elaine did not blink. She anticipated the next order and, when Madam Max said, 'Masturbate me.' she reached forward as if it was the most natural thing to do. Madam Max gripped her wrist and stopped Elaine's hand before it touched her. She made no attempt to hide her approval. She could appreciate a contest of wills. She would not bend this girl's spirit today, but she felt that she had to make a point by bending her body.

'The next one is not so easy I'm afraid. Kneel down, knees apart.' Elaine obeyed. 'Put your forehead on the carpet.' She did so. Madam Max came behind her and flipped up her skirt to her shoulders, so that the entire area of her bottom and thighs was displayed. 'You will remain like that until told to move. No matter what is said or done you will remain silent and still.'

Madam Max returned to her seat and appeared to

get on with routine office business. Elaine wondered how long this would last and if she could hold out. She would, she told herself. Cost what it may. This woman would not win. Presently, the door opened and a man came in. Elaine could not see him because of her doubled up position but, by his lack of verbal reaction, it was obvious that he saw nothing strange about seeing a half-naked girl with her bottom in the air on Madam Max's carpet.

'Ah, Hans. This is Elaine. I can't introduce you properly now, but you will be meeting her later.' They conducted a routine conversation and Hans left.

Madam Max came and stood over Elaine. 'I commend your spirit, Elaine. I am sure that I can use you. Always remember this moment, though; you kneeling – me standing. That is now, and always will be, our correct relationship. You may get up now and dress yourself.' When she had done so, Madam Max took her by the arm. Come with me. There is something you must see as part of your education.'

She took Elaine up to the second floor of the great house and to a room which was set up as a VHS recording centre. Above a long desk there were dozens of monitors, only three or four of which flickered with images. Each monitor was equipped with two recorders. At one end of the room there was a bank of recorders wired together. There was only one person in the room; a cheerful-looking young man with a shock of brown, curly hair. Elaine was amused and somehow comforted by the fact that, in spite of the esoteric and amazing sex antics on the screen, he was engrossed in a copy of *The Woodworker*.

He put his magazine down and got up as they came in. Madam Max introduced them. 'Elaine, this is

Stewart Ganton. He is my wizard of the wires. He came to us from a professional studio and he knows just about everything there is to know about closed circuit television. I don't know what we should do without him. Stewart, this is Elaine Dartrey. She is on the staff now and wants to learn. I want you to show her how everything works and help her as much as you can.' She glanced at her watch. 'I see that I have another appointment. I'll leave you two to get acquainted.' Turning to Elaine she added, 'You'll need a couple of days to collect your things. Stewart has tomorrow off. He'll be going into town and he can give you a lift when you've finished here. I shall expect to see you in my office at nine o'clock the day after tomorrow. I expect punctuality from all my staff.'

As she left, Elaine held out her hand to Stewart. 'Hi! I hope we are going to be friends, as well as working together.' She smiled, well aware of the effect that had on most young men, and he responded, as she had hoped he would, with a grin of his own.

'What's the magazine for?' she asked.

He was pleased. 'Oh, that's my hobby. My big passion. Working with wires and electricity all day, it's nice to get your hands on something you can touch and see and smell. I made this.' He picked up a small box from the desk and gave it to her to hold.

She turned it in her hands. The craftsmanship was meticulous, each joint dove-tailed by hand with loving accuracy. Her father had the same hobby and she knew enough about the craft to appreciate the skill which had gone into this. 'May I open it?'

'Surely.'

She did so. The inside was as carefully finished as the outside and when she closed the lid there was a little puff of air which testified to the closeness of the fit. 'Stewart, it's absolutely beautiful. I've never seen better.'

'You want it?'

'Oh, no. I couldn't . . . It's too good.'

'Go on. Take it. I'd like it to go to a good home. Put your jewellery in it, or something like that. I never know what to use them for. I get my fun out of making them, not keeping them.'

She was touched. 'Well, if you're sure. I'd love to have it. Thank you.'

'Now. What can I show you? Let me see. We'll start here.' He indicated the row of monitors. 'Each of them shows what is going on in a different room in the house. There are not always cameras alongside the fantasy rooms, so this little number,' he picked one up, 'in the slot under the monitor, is the number of the room the camera is in, that day. Over here,' he crossed to a large chart on the wall, 'is a plan of the different floors in the house, with each room numbered. OK?'

'That's very clear, thank you.'

He went back to the long desk. 'The cameras are just pre-set, pre-focused jobs. No remote zoom or anything. You'll be familiar with the VCRs. Each monitor has two. The top one is the primary. It either records the whole thing or you can do a live-edit by pressing the pause button. When you need a copy, rewind the primary and edit onto the secondary while it plays.

'If you want lots of copies,' he passed along the desk, to the bank of recorders, 'you put the master tape in this primary and it plays to as many of the secondaries as you have switched on. Are you with me?'

She gave him a dazzling beam. 'That's great. It's all so clear. You really have got the knack of explaining things. Even a numb-brain like me can understand.'

He shuffled his feet. 'Aw! It's nothing. It's just a simple little piss-arsed VHS system. A kid could work it. You'd think that in a place like this, they'd at least have a one inch reel-to-reel. The only thing we have here that you wouldn't have at home is this rapid-erase. Just stick the tape in the slot and high-speed, forward or backwards, and it wipes the whole thing in seconds.'

'And what about the finished tapes? What do you do with them?' He showed her a thick ledger. 'This is the recording log. Every blank tape gets a number before it goes into a machine.' He pointed out a number, written in wax pencil on a piece of perspex under each monitor. I just write down the date, time, room number and name, read off the start and finish readings from the recorder and put those down too.'

'Start and finish numbers? You mean these little sort of mileage things, clicking up, here?'

'That's right. To find anything, you just need a tape number and a start number. I don't correlate the names. I should think Madam Max does though. She has the recording log every morning and I expect she's got a card file, somewhere, if you wanted to find a particular person. Bloody card files. Still in the steam-age, just like this VHS system. Never heard of a computer.'

'And the finished tapes?' Elaine asked.

'Millions of the little buggers all over the place.' Stewart went to the end of the room, where there was a large bank of shallow drawers. 'I made these,' he said, passing his hand lovingly over the wood. Pulling out a drawer he revealed it to be full of numbered

63

cassettes. 'These are the most recent. There are more in the basement. If you like, I can show you that on the way out.'

'Won't you need to be here to stop the recording?' He glanced at the monitors. 'No. Just let them run on. They'll switch themselves off and rewind. I can edit them any time later, so there's only what's wanted. Anyway Joe, my assistant, comes on in an hour and he'll probably do the job.

He conducted her through the house and onto the sub-ground floor, which was as extensive as the ones above it. He opened a door which Elaine noted was not locked, and showed her bank after bank of shelves, containing tapes. 'Plenty to choose from,' Stewart said. 'Looking for anything in particular?'

'Not yet, but I'll get Madam Max to explain her part of the system, then I will be. Thanks, Stewart.'

'You bet!' he said, Arizona-style. 'You ready to go now?' He led her out of the house, to his little red sports car, ushered her in and set off in a flashy squirt of gravel. Elaine contrasted this transport with Sir James' Rolls and stole a glance at the young man beside her, intent on his driving.

'Does what you see on your monitors turn you on?'

'Naw! Oh, don't get me wrong. I'm as keen on sex as anyone. I just don't see it as a spectator sport. I like playing cricket, but watching it bores me to tears.' He grinned, disarmingly. It's just pictures and sound. A horse-race or a couple in bed – they're all the same to me. All I'm concerned about is to make sure that the quality is the best the equipment can provide.'

Elaine found that she liked this young man very much. There was a sort of ordinary decency in him.

4
Love

It was almost lunchtime when Stewart drove her up the winding gravel approach to Sir James' estate. He hopped out and opened her door, so that she could uncurl herself and get out. His smile, she decided, was one she would like to have in a bottle on her mantel-piece.

'Look,' she said, 'it's a nice day and I shall be having lunch in the garden. Would you like to join me? I'm sure I can get cook to cut another couple of sandwiches. If sandwiches would be all right for you?' she added, in sudden doubt.

'A sandwich would be super. Thank you.'

'I'll go and see about it.' Half-way to the house, she turned. 'Beer or tea?'

'Mmmm? Oh, tea please. I haven't had a decent cuppa all day.' She continued on her way, thinking, Elaine! What *are* you doing? Inviting a man she hard-ly knew to lunch! She justified herself immediately. He was hungry and thirsty and she was feeding him. Didn't it say that somewhere in the Bible? It had ab-solutely nothing to do with his crooked smile, or the fact that he was the first young man she had spoken to in days.

When she came out with a big tray, he was looking

out over the garden. He came to her and took the tray from her. 'OK, where are we going?'

'Down here.' She led the way into the lower part of the garden where there was a small, shady lawn with a white, wrought-iron table and chairs among the shubbery. He put the tray down and she noticed that he held a chair for her to sit, before seating himself opposite. She went through the social motions of 'being mother' with the teapot and offering sandwiches. He had a young man's appetite and obviously liked tea, because he was on his second cup before he set it down, half empty and sighed, 'Ah, nectar!'

She was amused. Everything about him was in such direct contrast with the rather effete, sober and elderly businessmen with whom she and Sir James mingled. They would have chosen wine or, if forced to drink tea, would have sipped it with little finger in the air. She preferred his tweed jacket to their pinstripes, even if it did come from Marks and Spencers, instead of Gieves and Hawkes. The change was refreshing and she was glad she had invited him to eat with her.

A short time and two sandwiches later, he said, 'This is really nice of you ... Look, what do I call you. Is it *Miss* Dartrey?'

'Yes.' She had gone through a period of calling herself 'Ms', short for Mistress, but when she actually became one, it didn't seem right to advertise.

She poured more tea and they engaged in idle and desultory conversation. Then they sat for a while in companionable silence, broken by Elaine who, when she saw Stewart looking around the garden in apparent admiration, said, 'It's lovely here, isn't it.'

He turned towards her and looked directly into her eyes. There was not an ounce of banter in his voice as he said, 'Miss Dartrey. Everything I have seen here is incredibly beautiful.'

That earnest gaze, from those blue eyes, did terrible damage to Elaine. Crossing the space between them, it ricocheted off the back of her eyeballs and down her throat, drying it and causing her to gulp. Travelling on with undiminished force, it circled her breasts (twice) passed down over her navel and dived into her knickers, where it caused untold havoc before forking and emerging from each leg to lodge in her knees and make them wobble. 'Come *on*, Elaine!' she thought, 'Pull yourself together! You've heard all these lines before. What makes this one so different?'

It was, she decided, the source of the line. There was something magnetically attractive about the man. She looked at his hands which were strong and brown. Hands that could . . . No! Don't think that! There were no rings, but some men didn't wear them. It was a man's world. 'Miss' was unmarried. 'Mr' might be or might not. He had found out that she was single with one, perfectly legitimate, question. She had to go around the houses.

'If you are living at the Grange,' she said artlessly, 'where does Mrs Ganton stay?'

'Oh, she's in Edinburgh!' This young man meant nothing to her. Why did the day get gloomier at his answer? Then he was grinning impishly. 'She's my mother. I'm not married.' Elaine knew that she had been as transparent as well-water and was being teased for it. She flushed.

He was instantly apologetic. 'I'm sorry. That was mean of me. Let me make it up to you. I'm at a loose end tonight. If you're not seeing anyone at the moment, how about having dinner with me.'

'No, really. I shouldn't . . .'

'Oh please. Just to show I'm forgiven. I shall feel rotten otherwise.'

Elaine smiled. He really was rather cute; a bit like a small boy trying to get his ball back. 'All right.'

'Great. I'll pick you up at seven, Miss Dartrey. OK?'

'I suppose if we have a date tonight, it would be all right for you to call me "Elaine", Stewart.' She enjoyed his boyish grin. They went back to the driveway, where they solemnly shook hands before he hopped over the door of his car and was gone. Elaine went back into the house, feeling unreasonably pleased with herself.

She sought out Lady Isabel and explained that she felt tired and wanted to take some time off as soon as she had sufficiently cleared the outstanding paperwork. Sir James was not due back for a couple of weeks, so she could get away to the coast somewhere. Isabel was so concerned that Elaine felt rather mean about deceiving her in this way, even though it was for her own good. She hoped that a couple of weeks would be long enough for her to do what had to be done.

Fresh from the shower, Elaine selected her wardrobe for the evening with more care than she had employed for ages. Simply, she told her reflection in the mirror, because it would be impolite not to look her best. Stockings or panty-hose? Panty-hose were convenient, but stockings were cooler, and it might be a warm evening. It was a pity that all her stockings except the sheer black ones, had runs in them. That couldn't be helped. She pulled them on and examined the result. The fact that they looked incredibly sexy against her white skin was neither here, nor there, she felt.

Suspender belt? It had to be black, to match the stockings, of course. This solid, silky one, or this filmy little lacy creation? The lacy one, she thought, because it might be a warm evening. Looking at the effect, she saw that stockings and belt made a perfect frame for her fair, pubic hair but that, she told her reflection, was entirely coincidental.

Brassiere? This sensible, satin one with the wide straps, or this transparent number? The transparent number, because it might be a warm evening. Nothing, she told her reflection, to do with the fact that her pink, nipple area was plainly visible through the material.

Knickers? These comfortable cover-alls or these frilly French ones, with legs wide enough to allow the back of a man's hand to be caressed by the silk? The French ones, she thought. I know, said her reflection, it might be a warm evening!

Which little black dress? This all-black one with lots of hooks and eyes and zips? Or this one, with a white collar, buttoning from neck to hem? A touch of white was always nice, she thought. Her outfit complete, there was just the matter of a quick brush through the hair and a touch on the make-up. An hour later she was ready and sitting at her window; watching for his car so that she would know when to start keeping him waiting.

The hotel he took her to for dinner was not as high up the price-range as those she was used to frequenting with Sir James, but the linen was crisp and clean and the food good and plentiful. Stewart proved to be a most amiable dinner companion, as she had suspected he would, with a store of amusing anecdotes, a good general knowledge and a sensible, down-to-earth approach whenever the conversation moved onto more weighty current affairs. Elaine tactfully avoided choosing the most expensive items on the menu, noticing that his knowledge of wine was good enough to enable them to have a very pleasant accompaniment to their food without taking out a second mortgage.

They moved from starter to fish and from fish to main course and Elaine found herself more and more attracted to him. There was a plain, ordinariness about him which was like a breath of fresh air after the sycophantic courtiers she often had to endure when socialising with James. They would try to sidle into her panties by stealth, with sly innuendo, double meanings, nudges, and winks. She was fed up with that approach. She had the feeling that, if this young man fancied her, he would come right out and say so. Just before dessert was served, he did.

He leaned across the table and placed his hand on hers. 'Elaine,' he said. 'I think I'm in trouble.'

She was concerned. 'What is it, Stewart?'

'I find everything that you do completely captivating. The way you move; what you say; how you look. Particularly how you look. Ever since the first time I laid eyes on you I have been wanting to kiss you.'

She was stirred, in a way no man had stirred her before. She felt passion rising within her and she knew that she wanted nothing more than for him to get his wish. 'You didn't kiss me in the garden.'

'Too public. Anyone might have seen and interrupted.'

'And you didn't kiss me in the car.'

'It's an open sports car. Same reason.'

Elaine knew then that she could not allow this flirtation to continue. It was too dangerous; too complicated. She could not see how an amorous dalliance with this man could possibly fit into her present circumstances. He was much too nice to toy with and to tease, as she might have done with anyone else. She could feel her loins beginning to respond to the fantasies which his hand on hers inspired, but however attractive the possibilities were, this thing had to be nipped in the bud. Now! Firmly and without equivocation! In her head she formulated the polite phrases which would end this line of conversation, once and for all. She was still doing that when she heard her own voice saying, 'Maybe we should find somewhere more private.'

His hand remained on hers. It did not squeeze or fondle. It was just there, firm and reassuring. As though changing the subject he said, 'I am staying the night at this hotel. The rooms are very nice. Have you ever seen them?'

'No.'

'Would you like me to show you my room?' This was insanity. She must, *on no account*, do this thing.

'Yes please. I think I would like that.'

He smiled at her, that same, lop-sided, schoolboy grin and she loved him for it, because she could see that he had sensed the inner struggle she had been going through.

'Do you really want dessert?' he asked.

'No.' The wry thought crossed her mind that *she* was now on the menu. It did not bother her. She had made a decision or, rather, her young and healthy sexuality had made it for her, and the rest was in the hands of fate.

His room was clean, tidy and well-appointed. He closed the door behind them and she expected him to hurl himself on her. He did not, and they stood looking at each other; both desiring contact; both awkward and shy. She encouraged him gently. 'You were saying something about a kiss.' She put up her face in invitation. Again she expected an all-out assault, but he took her face gently between his palms and kissed her forehead, very softly. Then he allowed his lips to brush against both her eyelids in turn, before their lips met. My God, thought Elaine, what a kisser! And her arms went around his neck to draw him close to her, as his went around her waist. His were not the harsh, brutal kisses she knew from James in passion. They started with little, fluttering pecks and dabs, as if there was all the time in the world, and built up slowly from there, until their mouths were as one, open and constantly moving against each other, their tongues exchanging flickering compliments. Elaine noticed that her thighs were rubbing against each other without her consent and she was getting very damp between the legs.

They drew apart a little and he reached out to the top button of her dress, paused, and raised his eyebrows in a question. She knew that he wanted to undress her and she knew that was what she wanted too. She helped him with the buttons, until they were all undone, then she slipped out of her dress and dropped it on the floor. He unclipped her bra and she slid it down her arms and let it fall, too. She stood quietly and allowed him to examine her body, pleased with the admiration in his eyes, then his arms went around her again, searching for the fastener of the suspender belt. Her bare breasts against his tweed jacket gave her ripples of excitement. 'It's at the back,' she murmured.

He unfastened it and she stooped to unclip her suspenders, so that he could remove it. She went and sat on the end of the bed, rolled down her stockings and took them off, leaving just her black silk knickers. She knew that she was going to enjoy the moment when he took them from her, to leave her naked, and, half-remembering the lessons she had learned from Isabel, she wanted to delay the moment and savour the anticipation. 'Now you,' she said.

She watched as he removed his clothes. Every aspect of his body pleased her as it was revealed. He was not hugely muscular, nor was he skinny. His shoulders were broad and his hips were narrow. He had no paunch at all. His chest and arms were not great thatches of hair, as she had feared they might be. There was, she thought, just the perfect amount for her taste.

Wearing only his undershorts he came and stood by her. She reached up from her sitting position and took hold of the waistband. In a sly imitation of his own question, she raised her eyebrows. He smiled and nodded, and she drew them down and off. He stood still, his arms at his sides, within touching distance. She looked at his nakedness. His penis was erect, jutting fiercely at an angle from a mat of brown, curly, pubic hair. As she gazed at it, and the maleness of his testicles below, she felt herself lubricating, almost to the point of embarrassment.

He knelt in front of where she was sitting and she knew that the moment she had looked forward to had come. She eased her bottom up off the bed towards him, to make the task easier, and he pulled her knickers down and took them off. She savoured her own nudity and, for a while, they stayed where they were – he kneeling, as though worshipping at the shrine of her womanhood – she sitting, leaning back on straight arms, with legs deliberately spread to display her sex to him.

When he got up, he pressed gently on her shoulders and, divining his purpose, she scooted up the bed and lay back with her head on the pillow, waiting for him to take her. Again she expected the assault to be sudden because this was what she was used to. She was surprised when, instead of coming on top of her, or even alongside her, he sat down at the end of the bed and lifted one of her ankles in his hand. Tenderly, he kissed her instep and his thumbs massaged the ball of her foot. Then he kissed her toes and she felt his tongue flickering on them. It was the most delicious feeling and as it went on, repeated on the other foot, she felt her juices beginning to leak from her. This was not James. Neither was it one of the callow experimenters of her extreme youth, nor any of the clumsy gropers who had tried to gratify themselves with her since. This man knew exactly what he was doing and was prepared to take his time over it. Again her sex sessions with Isabel and Gretchen flickered through her mind and she sighed and relaxed under his ministrations.

When he had finished with her feet, he worked his way up her legs, kissing and fondling all the time. When he reached her knees, he exerted a gentle pressure on their inner surfaces, to indicate to her that she should part them. She did so gladly, as far as they would go, opening herself to his further advance. His hands stroked up her inner thighs and reached her vulva. His fingers spread her open. He drew closer and closer and she suddenly realised that he was going to kiss the parted lips – something no-one had ever done before.

The touch of his lips when it came – there, in that secret place – was like a blinding shock. She started and grabbed handfuls of the bedcovers in an effort to control herself. When his tongue flickered along the inner surface and touched her clitoris, she had a mini orgasm. She was afraid for a moment that she had come too soon, but was relieved to find that it was only the forerunner of greater things to come, like the first uneasy rumblings of an earthquake.

By the time his lips travelled on, across her stomach towards her breasts, she was worked up to a high pitch of sexual expectancy and noticed that not only were her nipples stiff and long, but the whole area of pink aureole was swollen and engorged, something she had never seen before. He saw it too, and taking a breast tenderly in each hand, he began to massage the gland behind and above the areola, squeezing it gently between thumb and forefinger and drawing it down towards the nipple. The sensation was one which Elaine had never felt before and it was wildly stimulating. As she revelled in it, a phrase entered her mind which excited her to further lubrication: *I am naked, and my breasts are being milked*. As she formed the phrase in her mind, she became conscious of another new feeling and looking down, was faintly surprised to see a drop of fluid emerging from each teat. She had no idea that such a thing could happen without a pregnancy. Stewart did not seem surprised. Bending, he took her nipples in his mouth, one at a time, and sucked on them while his massage continued.

She was in a state of arousal quite unlike any previous encounter with a man – though not unlike her experience with Isabel and Gretchen. She felt hungry for sex but at the same time relaxed and cosy; well content to accept the gifts he offered. When he placed his body between her legs, it was like a home-coming; perfect and right, and she welcomed it as the culmination of all the pleasures that had gone before. Reaching under him she grasped the shaft of his penis and guided it to her eager vagina. She gasped as he entered – not with savage thrusting, but with gentle, probing movements, rubbing the ridge of his glans around the extreme entrance, in the areas where it was most sensitive. Then his body probed a little further into her and the hard tip of his penis was massaging that *certain* place inside the pubic bone, which she thought only she knew about. She began to shift her hips in rhythm with his thrusts, which grew longer, until she had his full length inside her and his stiff, pubic hairs were massaging her clitoris.

As he rode her, her arms were wrapped about his upper body holding him close. Now she crossed her ankles in the small of his back and used all the young strength of her vagina to grip and suck at his penis as though to prevent his escape. She could feel her time approaching and she tried to delay the moment to enjoy the ecstasy of what he was doing to her for a few more seconds, but her orgasm would not be denied. It came, not as an explosion, but as a warm flood of loving delight, and as it washed through her entire body, she held him to her, whispering his name over and over again, sobbing with happiness at the emotional impact and relief of that final release.

For a while she clung to him, unable to stop crying. He said nothing but just held her close, waiting for the storm to pass. Suddenly she was aware that his penis was still rock-hard inside her and was overcome with guilt. 'You haven't finished,' she exclaimed.

'It doesn't matter. I'm happy for you.'

'It may not matter to you, but it matters to me,' she said, suddenly womanly and practical. 'Come on. Roll over!' She heaved and shifted under him and, careful to hold his penis all the time in the close and loving embrace of her vagina, she manoeuvred herself until she knelt above him, straddling him. 'Now it's your turn; so just lay back and enjoy it,' she said, and began to raise and lower herself on her knees, so that the whole length of his penis was massaged.

She gazed down at him, loving him for his generosity. She wanted to use all her natural talent for sex, plus anything she had learned, in order to give to him the same amount of pleasure he had given to her. She rode him with every ounce of skill she could muster, teasing, tantalising, making it last for him. She brought him close to orgasm, then raised herself so that only the extreme tip of his penis was in her and made slow, gentle movements until she felt that he could go on. Occasionally she stopped moving altogether and pressed down hard on him with the whole of his length inside her, massaging him with just the contraction of her vaginal walls.

A couple of times she felt herself close to a second orgasm, but held out, putting the thought resolutely from her mind. She wasn't going to spoil it for him by violent movement before the last possible moment. His hands reached up and caressed her jiggling breasts and she rejoiced in his touch. Looking down at herself, she could see the thickness of him distorting her vulva as she worked it up and down his penis; the rhythmic meeting and separation of their pubic hairs, hers golden, his brown.

Then she felt the spasmodic pulsing of his organ inside her and knew that she could not prolong his pleasure any further. Her movements quickened until she was bouncing without restraint, milking him as he had milked her. She knew that she was close to boiling point herself but she wanted her climax to come with his, so she staved it off and waited . . . and waited . . . and there it was! He bucked beneath her in the throes of his ejaculation, as though to throw her off, but she would not be unseated. His hot sperm spurted and squirted into her with his powerful pelvic thrusts just as her own climax came, glorious and fulfilling, bathing his penis in her juices, which mingled with his as she collapsed on top of him and they lay panting in each other's arms.

The early morning sun awoke Elaine and she lay for a moment, trying to understand where she was. Then she remembered and became conscious of the warmth and comfort of Stewart as he lay close behind her, the shape of his body conforming to her own. Playing spoons, he called it. She smiled at the recollection and remembered the lovely sense of safety and security with which she had fallen asleep in his arms. One of them still trailed across her breasts. She wanted to look at him, so with infinite care, she lifted the arm and wriggled gently until she could prop herself on one elbow and see him. He looked so peaceful sleeping there, and she felt a great surge of love for this kind and gentle man.

Isabel's words came back to her. 'One day you will meet a man who has the capacity to love and to give. When you do, I advise you to cling to him and not let him escape. They are rare . . .'

Elaine let her mind wander back over the joys of the previous evening and thought, that's what you are, Stewart, my darling man. You are rare! Would she be able to cling to him and prevent him escaping? She hoped so. She would certainly try her best anyway.

She knew that her 'love affair' with Sir James had

been as dead as a doornail from the time she had met Stewart. She had not known what love could be until then, and realised now, that when she and James had used the word it had been just a matter of form; the expected thing to say. Anyway her previous quandary had just shrivelled up and blown away. There was no way in the world she could allow James to touch her again now. The thought comforted her, as did the pleasurable anticipation of being able to tell Isabel all about Stewart. She would want to hear all the details and would be delighted at her good fortune. Elaine could hardly wait.

She resumed her careful study of Stewart's face and glowed as she re-ran her brain's video of their love-making. She felt a warmth between her legs at each high point and was suddenly and unreasonably cross with him. How could he lie there, so peacefully asleep, when she was here wanting to be loved? Slowly and carefully she lifted the sheet like a tent, then laid it back so that his body was exposed. She was intrigued. She had seldom seen any man unaroused, and the view she now had of his flaccid penis excited her with its novelty. She still thought that it was the most beautiful thing she had ever seen. Then a mischievous thought crossed her mind. She wondered if he had to be awake to get an erection. She reached out her hand and, careful not to wake him, took his penis between her finger and thumb in that most sensitive place just below the glans, and began to masturbate him very softly and gently. Purely in the interests of investigative science, she told herself. To her great satisfaction, after only a few seconds it began to engorge and straighten until it reached its full erection. She admired its length and stiffness and then Stewart's breathing changed and he stirred into wakefulness. She leaned over him, her face close to his. 'Hello sleepy.'

He yawned and stretched. 'Mmmmm! Hello, darling. Sleep all right?'

The 'darling' pleased her enormously and she kissed him. 'Yes thank you, darling. Never better.'

'Call that a kiss? Come back here at once and do it properly.' Elaine did so, telling herself that it was not because she wanted to, but because a woman's duty is to obey her man. Several minutes passed, during which she continued to be obedient and her warm, wanting itch for him grew. She broke away and looked down at his body to see that their kissing had done nothing to dissolve his erection. She felt a sudden urge to give to him, unselfishly. She kissed his mouth again, then allowed her kisses to stray down his neck and onto his chest. She kissed and nibbled his nipples, then passed on down, kissing his stomach until she lay with her cheek on his belly and his penis within inches of her face. She had never taken a man into her mouth, but she knew for certain, that she wanted to do that for him. She wanted to be the one in control; to dictate the pace of his pleasure; to feel him squirm; to give and give until there was nothing left in her. He guessed her intention. 'No, Elaine. You mustn't.'

That decided her. There had been enough obedience for one morning. 'Oh, mustn't I?' she said, and took the glans of his penis in her mouth. He gave a great leap and exclaimed with pleasure. 'Gotcha!' she thought. She held it there for a while getting the feel and the taste of it. It felt strange but not distasteful. Nothing she did with this man, however bizarre, could ever be that, she thought.

Because of her inexperience she had to experiment,

to find out what provided the greatest pleasure for him, judging her actions by his reactions. She took more of his penis inside her mouth and, closing her lips tightly around it, sucked and moved her head up and down, massaging it. She could tell that he liked that! She bit, very, very gently. This produced a moment of tension, but, on balance, seemed to be appreciated. She allowed her tongue to rotate around it. That obviously was also a good thing to do! She took as much in her mouth as she could, until the tip touched the back of her throat and she was in danger of gagging, then closed her finger and thumb around the extreme base and masturbated slowly. When he moaned and writhed, as if in agony, she felt that her short course of self-instruction was over and that she could get on with putting all of these techniques into practice.

She set about her task of driving him crazy, licking, sucking, nibbling, then pausing, as she felt him getting too close to climax, extending the ecstasy for him. His sexual excitement communicated itself to her, and she began to lubricate freely as she guessed at what he was feeling. It was wonderful to be totally in control. However, she had overlooked the fact that her present position, on her side with head down, had placed her shapely bottom within easy reach of Stewart's investigative hand. It was her turn to jump as she felt his fingers part her sex lips and begin to massage her clitoris. This wasn't fair. He was supposed to be the one doing the groaning and suffering. She would clamp her thighs together and frustrate his efforts. She tried hard to do so, but was thwarted by her own animal nature, which kept forcing them further apart against her will.

It was too late. She just had to have the orgasm he

was offering her. Without taking his penis out of her mouth, she scrambled onto her knees and got astride him, her thighs widely parted by the thickness of his body and her genitalia presented to him, completely vulnerable to anything he might care to do. Now his fingers had free access to everything and he made the most of it, driving her wild with lust. She could feel herself close to orgasm and her bottom gyrated wildly with his every stimulation. She knew his was close too, and she used everything she had learned to bring it on. She felt his spasms begin and clamped her hands tightly around the base of his penis to hold back the ejaculation for a few seconds, in order to increase the power of the sensation for him, feeling a little disappointed that she was not quite there.

At that moment however, Stewart inserted the extreme tip of his wet forefinger into her anus and with his thumb inside her vagina, massaged the tissues trapped between the two, while irritating her clitoris with the other hand. She came at once, in copious floods, jerking and wriggling. As she released her grip on his penis, Stewart came too, ejaculating with enormous force. She kept her mouth on him, gulping in order to swallow this salty gift of love. As she did so, she wondered why she was able to do that so easily and so naturally, without any trace of revulsion.

Greater love hath no-one, she thought. That's what it was. Love!

5

The Blue Room

Elaine could hardly wait to tell Isabel all about
Stewart. She exercised as much patience as she could
muster, forcing herself to sit at her typewriter in an
effort to pass the time. There were a great many typing errors that morning but after what seemed an
eternity, she saw from the window that Isabel had
come down into the garden. She shot out of her chair
like a scalded cat and ran outside. 'Oh, Isabel. I have
such wonderful news.'

'You're in love.'

Elaine was stunned. How could she know that?
Was she psychic? 'Yes, but . . . I mean, how . . .?'

Isabel laughed. 'How did I know? Not a great work
of deduction, my dear. For instance, I have only to
look at you to see it written all over your face; but I
have to confess that there was circumstantial evidence
which led me to think that it might be happening.'

'Like what?'

'Like you having lunch in the garden yesterday,
with an attractive young man. Like you sitting at
your window for an hour waiting for him to pick you
up. Like you not coming home last night but being
dropped off early this morning, quite some way from
the gate where you thought no-one would see you,

still wearing your evening outfit.' Elaine was amazed. This woman must have her own personal spy network.

'But never mind how I knew. Just tell me all about him.'

Elaine started to pour out her story, words tumbling over one another in her excitement. 'Woah!' said Isabel. 'You're all of a fluster, my dear. Have you had anything to eat?'

For the first time, Elaine became conscious of the fact that it was almost lunchtime and she was ravenously hungry. She tried to remember when she had last eaten then blushed profusely as she recalled the last thing which had passed her lips.

Isabel refused to listen to a word until she had ordered sandwiches and tea and they had taken them into the garden, to the little white table. There, between bites and sips, Elaine gabbled out her story. Isabel listened, thinking how fond she had grown of this girl. There were times when she regretted not having a daughter and this beautiful child was so appealing right now. Talking with her mouth full, flushed with excitement, she was like a schoolgirl after her first trip to the seaside.

Elaine found that she wanted to tell Isabel every detail of the previous night. As she did so, Isabel listened. Nodding and smiling encouragement every now and then. At last, the spate of words abated, slowing down to, 'Oh, and Isabel. He is just so . . . He's . . . He's . . . Ooooh, Isabel!

'I gather that you like him. Wipe your mouth dear, there is a big tomato pip on your cheek. And how does he feel about you?'

'I think . . . Or rather, I hope . . . That is . . .'

'So he feels the same way about you, I take it.'

Elaine nodded, still dabbing self-consciously at her cheek, then suddenly recollecting an aspect to the matter she had not thought about she said, 'Do you mind, Isabel?'

'My dear, I am delighted for you.' Isabel was touched that in her happiness Elaine should have given any thought to their own relationship.

Elaine was relieved. 'I remembered what you said – about finding a loving and giving man – I so badly want to cling to this one. How am I going to do it?'

Isabel sat, apparently in deep thought for some time, before she answered. 'If a relationship is going to last it has to be built on a firm foundation of love and trust based on total honesty. It's like building a house on sand otherwise. If your house is built on a rock, then later on, quite a few buckets of the sand of deceit can be brought indoors without any serious harm being done. You must not conceal anything important from him now. I know most things that go on here, but I must confess that I'm not quite sure how matters are at the moment. Are you still sleeping with James?'

Elaine froze, all the blood draining from her face, unbelievably stunned. She knew! She had known all along. This was awful. 'No . . . At least, I'm not sure . . . I haven't told him yet. Isabel. I'm so sorry. What can I say? When it started I didn't know you. When I did get to know you, I couldn't go on with it. I had just about decided that, even before I met Stewart.' She put her face in her hands and came close to tears.

Isabel crossed to her and put her arm about her shoulders. 'There, there. Don't worry about it, my dear. You're not the first, and you won't be the last. James is handsome and persuasive and always gets what he wants. You are young and I know your appetite for sex. There are hardly any viable men about here. I thought you held out very well, considering.'

'But don't you mind? Don't you love him?'

'You asked me that about Gretchen, and I gave you the answer then. I don't own James. He is a selfish bully and I love him. It is a mistake to love because of the good points. It is better to love, in spite of the bad ones. He appears to be very strong, but that is a cover. He needs to have his ego boosted constantly, otherwise he wilts. You have been his ego-boost for a while and you did it well. Because I love him, I wish only his happiness and I was glad for him. Anyway, it kept him off my back and left me more time for Gretchen.' A light of mischief danced in her eyes as she added, 'Or perhaps I should say that it kept him off my front. He's really not very good at it. But of course, you know that.'

'I used to think he was,' said Elaine. 'But since you, and Gretchen and Stewart . . .'

'Mmm. For a while, I was afraid that James was going to make a fool of himself with you – running off to Gretna Green and all that – he can do that sometimes, you know. That's why I slowed it down.'

'*You* slowed it down?' Elaine was incredulous. 'I don't understand.'

'By showing you how sex could be with generosity and unselfishness. In your inexperience you didn't know that, and if things had gone too far with James it would have spoiled your life as well as his, before you found out.'

Elaine looked at her in astonishment, but Isabel returned her gaze with perfect calmness. There was no doubt that she was telling the truth. She thought that this was an extraordinary woman. Did anything, ever, disconcert her? 'But, how can you have stayed married all these years; with separate bedrooms, and everything?'

'Good sex is not the basis of a marriage. When it happens – and it happens a lot less frequently than you would expect – it is a wonderful bonus. Ask any man if sex with his wife is absolutely everything he could wish for. Ask any woman the same about her husband. You would be amazed at how many great marriages there are where sex is either unsatisfactory or non-existent. What is much more important is that the couple should be good friends, above all else. James is my best friend and I am his.'

And what a friend, thought Elaine. You don't get many like that to the pound. Suddenly she could see where the strength of their marriage lay – the glue which held it together – and it wasn't on James' side of the relationship.

'So you think I should tell Stewart?'

'Probably best. Although if it's over it is of no great consequence. What I am more concerned about is what you tell James.' Isabel laid her hand on Elaine's arm. 'Be gentle with him, my dear. He won't show it, but he is going to be devastated. Not that he loves you, you understand. It's just that someone is going to take his toy away.'

She got up to go, then paused. 'There's just one thing I would ask of you, as a favour.'

'Anything.'

'Never let James know that I knew about your affair. He needs the assurance which comes from knowing that he is much cleverer than I am. Part of the thrill he gets is in being able to keep them secret from me. I know you'll do that for me, dear. Thank you.' She gave Elaine a little hug and left, leaving Elaine gazing after her in wonderment. This really was a most remarkable woman. She was more determined than ever to succeed in her attempt to remedy James' error of judgement and that, if it lay within her power, nothing should disturb Isabel's tranquillity.

When Stewart picked her up that night, their intention was to drive out to a little pub for a drink. Elaine was unusually silent, running over in her mind the words she had chosen to tell Stewart about her affair with James. It wasn't easy, but she thought she had it just about right now. 'Stewart,' she would say, 'There's something I haven't told you. Something you have to know about me because I want everything to be honest between us.' Then she would tell him and he would listen and he wouldn't mind, and he would kiss her and tell her that he loved her, and everything would be all right. That was the right way to do it, she was sure.

Stewart was quiet too, and after they had been driving for a while he said, 'I'm going to pull over and park for a while. It's all right,' he added, with a smile. 'I'm not going to grapple with you in the open air. I just want to talk.'

She returned his smile and squeezed his arm. 'I wouldn't mind if you did. And I need to talk to you, too.'

He stopped on the grass verge, in the shade of some oak trees and for a time the only sound which broke the silence was the breeze in the trees and the tinking of the exhaust. Elaine braced herself to produce her rehearsed speech, but as she opened her mouth Stewart said, 'Elaine. There's something I haven't told you about me. Something I have to tell you, because I want everything to be right between us.'

She was flummoxed. 'But, that's just what *I* was going to say!'

'Oh, really. Ladies first, then.'

'I've been having an affair with Sir James.' There. It was out!

'Been having? Past tense?'

'Yes. It's over.'

'Anything that happened to you before we met is just something which made you the way you are; and I love you the way you are, so no problem. I'm glad you told me, though.' He leaned over and kissed her. 'I just wish mine was as easy.' He was silent for a while, collecting his thoughts. Then he said, 'The first thing to say is that if I hadn't fallen in love with you, I wouldn't be telling you this. I hope it will help if you bear that in mind. Let me get to the end before you say anything.'

His grip on her hand grew tighter. 'I do not work for Madam Max by choice. When I was younger and sillier, I did something very stupid. Oh, nothing dreadful like murder,' he added, seeing her alarmed look. 'I took some money that wasn't mine. Madam Max has evidence that incriminates me. I wouldn't mind if exposure simply meant prison, but the guys the money belonged to were pretty bad men. If she gave me away to them, then I wouldn't be around for long.'

Elaine squeezed his hand. 'I'm so glad you told me, because now I can tell you that I am with Madam Max only to try to recover the tapes she is using to blackmail Sir James. If we can get your stuff at the same time, then you are both in the clear.'

He smiled ruefully at her enthusiasm. 'Wish it was that easy. I haven't been able to discover where she keeps all this stuff yet, but I might. Even if I do, I'm still in trouble. She would only have to give them my name and they would take her word for it. We're not talking about legal proof.'

Elaine refused to be damped. 'Then we'll have to find a way to shut her up. I'm sure we can, now that we are working together.'

'If ever we manage to do that, I have a proposal in my pocket, all dusted off and ready for you. I can't produce it now because I am not free. I just want to warn you what's coming, if ever I shake her off.'

Elaine relaxed against him and snuggled. 'When you do produce it, the answer will be "yes", but I'm just like you. I can't feel free to marry until I have got those people who are depending on me out of the trouble they're in. We have to keep our love a secret, particularly from Madam Max. I'm sure she fancies me and that could be helpful. It will have to be strictly business while we are at the Grange.'

The following morning, Elaine was in the office at the Grange before nine o'clock, at which time Madam Max came in and said, 'I am pleased to see that you are punctual. There is much for you to learn. Come with me now, and your education can begin.'

She led the way along the rambling corridors and Elaine noticed again, that each door was painted with a different colour scheme. Madam Max paused before a blue door and listened, before entering without knocking.

Elaine hesitated, uncertain as to whether she was meant to follow or not, but the door remained open and Madam Max looked back at her questioningly, so she went inside.

As she followed Madam Max into the room beyond the blue door, Elaine could barely restrain a gasp of astonishment. It was a large room and the walls were uniformly hung with dark blue velvet, matching the soft carpet. There were six large tables arranged in a circle, their tops padded with the same velvet, but what caused Elaine's astonishment was the fact that four of the tables were occupied. On each of them, a naked girl was stretched out on her back, her wrists and ankles stretched widely apart and secured by leather cuffs to the table corners. Above each table, a spotlight illuminated every detail of their white nudity, contrasting with the fabric on which they lay and Elaine could see that each of them wore a gag.

As Madam Max advanced into the room, two silent men dressed entirely in black fell in behind her, as if by long-established ritual. Elaine could see that the girls were conscious, their heads turning as far as they could to follow the entrance; their eyes wide with anticipation above their silenced mouths. Arriving at one of the tables, Madam Max beckoned Elaine forward. 'Come and take a closer look, my dear. This is my own personal discipline room, although I prefer to call it my Play Room. It is here that I administer the punishments which I find necessary from time to time to keep my girls in order.

'In this room bondage and discipline have been raised to the level of an art form. Here, everything is quiet, efficient and orderly. No expense has been spared in the provision of the appropriate equipment. You will find no amateurism, no fumbling, no spur of the moment experiments. Everything that happens here has been planned and thought about well in advance, in order to achieve the maximum effect.

'Observe the leather cuffs and anklets. See how they are padded with the softest silk. Look at the ball gag and notice that it is not solid but perforated. There is no danger of a girl suffocating, however long she wears one. The tongue can move for swallowing saliva, but not enough to make intelligible words. The wearer can make lots of noises – and I like my girls to make lots of noise when they are being punished – but no sense at all. In short, in this room, unlike some of the others you will see, you will find no unintentional discomfort. That is not to say that there is no discomfort; any one of my girls will tell you that.' She smiled icily and ruffled the pubic hair of the helpless girl in front of her. 'Just that all discomfort is completely intentional and carefully planned to exactly suit the recipient.

'Remember that these girls are my stock. Part of my source of income. I haven't the slightest intention of damaging them permanently, so my punishments are subtle, but still effective. For instance, notice that the arrangement of the tables makes it possible for each girl to see what is happening to the others, while she waits for what *she* is going to get. That increases the tension and the apprehension for those who are waiting while, for the one being punished at the time, the knowledge that there are others watching adds to the embarrassment and discomfort. And speaking of audiences . . .'

Madam Max signed to one of the guards to go to the far end of the room. He pulled a cord which drew back the velvet drapes to reveal a large mirror completely occupying one wall. 'And now, my dear, the show has begun. Behind that mirror are several individual cubicles, each occupied by a man or by a woman. They can see through the mirror, although we cannot see them, and they have paid a great deal of money to watch what is going to happen next. Perhaps, in the privacy of their cubicles, they will wish to masturbate. No-one knows if they do or if they don't, but every possible gadget and aid is provided for their convenience.'

She turned her attention to the naked girl again. 'This is Shelley. Say hello to the nice lady, Shelley.' Shelley's head turned from side to side in a fruitless attempt to be rid of the gag, through which came a series of unintelligible grunts. 'Shelley is into weight training. See those well developed shoulders.' The girl's flesh twitched convulsively as Madam Max's fingers lingered briefly on her skin. 'Unfortunately, she met some apeman at the gym and thought that it would be all right to let him fuck her, just for the fun of it. That was a mistake. My girls fuck when I tell them to and only with persons I have approved. 'Shelley knows that now, don't you, dear?' The eyes above the gag widened in entreaty and the blonde head nodded vigorously.

'But you knew it before, didn't you?' Again, the nodding. 'And that makes what you did very naughty. So here you are, in the Play Room, where naughty girls learn not to do it again.' Madam Max turned to Elaine. 'I told you that punishments were devised to fit the individual. Well, we are going to help Shelley with her shoulder development and we are going to use the fact that her nipples are un-usually long.' Her hands went to the helpless bare breasts, squeezing and kneading for a while before pinching and rolling the strong, brown teats between finger and thumb. Shelley wriggled and twisted as much as her restraints would allow, but was power-less to prevent this nipple torture which, although un-wanted, soon had the effect of making them stand out like hard bullets.

Madam Max nodded to her guards. 'Attach the cords!' Shelley's writhing became frantic but, despite that, one guard approaching on each side with slen-der nylon cords had no difficulty in tying one around each nipple, low down against the softer brown of the areola. Madam Max nodded her approval. 'You see the same principle in action, my dear. Tight enough to be secure. Not tight enough to cut off the circulation. Proceed to the next stage!'

From beneath the table, the guards produced uprights which slotted into sockets alongside Shelley's torso. They threaded a horizontal metal bar through holes in the uprights and pinned it into position, selecting a pair of holes which placed the bar about 18 inches above the bare nipples. Moving to the head of the table, they unclipped the wrist cuffs from the rings there and re-attached them to rings in each end of the bar. Like a well-drilled team, they produced a sloping backrest and slipped it underneath the upper part of her body, forcing her breasts up to the bar, then buckled a leather collar about her neck, clipping it to a chain just long enough to reach the head of the table.

'Now the finishing touches.' Madam Max smiled as she knotted each nipple cord firmly to the bar. 'Remove the back rest!' Shelley grimaced as far as the gag would permit as her arms took the weight of her upper body to keep it off her nipples. For a while, her head turned and twisted frantically, the only part of her which she was free to move, as though expecting to find some way out of her predicament. The chain at her neck prevented her from sitting up further and getting her elbows over the bar. The wide spread of her wrist-cuffs made holding the weight difficult, but, as long as she could hold out, there was minimum discomfort at her nipples. She was reduced to indicating her discomfort by writhing as best she could and attempting to beg for a short period of suspension, although all that came out of her gaping mouth was a series of cooing gurgles, which Madam Max completely ignored.

'Replace the backrest in twenty minutes time. It is to be removed for twenty minutes in every subsequent hour.' Elaine followed as Madam Max made her way to the next table, turning as she went to develop her theme of punishment. 'Notice that the number of hours is never known by the victim. That is part of the punishment. Next time the backrest is inserted may be the last, or it may not. There is a delightful uncertainty about it. Each time it is removed, the weight goes onto muscles which are already strained and tired, so each period of suspension is more difficult and so less pleasant to look forward to.

'This is Rose.' Madam Max's hand absent-mindedly caressed the peachy flesh of the dark-haired, well-rounded girl stretched out on the next table, squeezing the soft flesh of her breasts and rubbing the nipples into erectness, then trailing her fingers down to the inner thigh and the secret pinkness concealed in the black curls of her pubic hair which, rather than covering, served to accentuate her stark nakedness and vulnerability. Rose's bright blue eyes sought Elaine's in mute entreaty while she squirmed under the invasive touch and struggled to form intelligible words through the perforated gag. All that came out was a strangled 'Nnnngg!' – all she could manage by way of protest.

'Rose has been a naughty girl, too. I demand certain standards of cleanliness from my girls and twice now, Rose's room has been found to be in a mess. That is the sort of fault you'd expect to find in a little girl, and so her punishment is to be that administered to a little girl – namely a well-spanked bottom.' The probing fingers reached the clitoris and manipulated

95

it gently, causing Rose to wriggle her hips in a vain attempt to close her legs.

'The nice thing about punishing Rose is that she squirms and sings so well. She also has as you can see, very well-developed breasts, though quite small nipples, so I have devised a securing method which allows as much freedom for movement as possible. 'Breast straps, please!' The guards moved in from either side with leather straps which they pulled tight and buckled around each breast, close to the chest wall, so that they were squeezed into bulging mounds above the straps. From the side of each strap the cold steel of a metal clip dangled against the flinching, bare skin.

'Over!' Working together, the two silent men unclipped wrists and ankles and, in spite of her feeble struggles, flipped Rose over onto her bare belly and attached the clips on the breast straps to rings set in the table top underneath her. Short lengths of chain reconnected the cuffs to the head of the table and the anklets to the other end. Madam Max admired the result with her head on one side. 'See how this works? Pinned to the table by her breasts, she can move her arms but not far enough to reach the gag or the clips. She can kick her feet, but not far enough to impede the target area. Her bottom is free to wriggle and squirm – and you will see that it will soon be doing that – but not far enough to be able to interfere with her proper punishment, which will all take place on that beautifully plump little behind.'

Reaching beneath the table Madam Max produced a short, whippy leather quirt which differed from an ordinary riding switch in that the tip, instead of coming to a point, was furnished with a flat paddle, about three inches across. 'Observe the instrument of punishment. I do not permanently mark or bruise any of my girls. With this little toy, the weight of each blow is spread over a wide area. Applied with just the right degree of force, the effect at first, is one of almost pleasurable smarting. After ten strokes, the area is a little reddened and more sensitive. After twenty, the smarting becomes so severe that we may expect squirming and bouncing. At thirty, the noise is quite loud, isn't it, Rose?' The dark head nodded slowly and reluctantly.

'However, Rose received thirty strokes last time, yet that didn't seem to do the trick. So that naughty, bare bottom of yours gets sixty today.' The noises from the gag increased in volume and the dark curls swung vigorously from side to side, things which Elaine knew by now would make not the slightest difference to Madam Max, who raised the quirt and brought it across in a swishing slash which cut the air just above the creamy white bottom. Rose gasped and the muscles of her behind contracted involuntarily. Next moment she had more reason to gasp as the first stroke fell on her left buttock cheek. Thwack! Thwack! Thwack! The strokes marched on remorselessly to a steady rhythm; first left, then right, left then right. Not with the full force of Madam Max's arm but hard enough to produce two bright red patches on each bare, white cheek. By ten strokes, Rose's fists were clenched into tight balls and she had great difficulty in keeping still. Thwack! Thwack! Thwack! At twenty strokes she was crying piteously and kicking her legs as far as the chains would allow. Thwack! Thwack! Thwack! By thirty strokes, her naked bottom was a fiery sea of red and every stroke that fell found a sensitive area. Rose screamed through the gag. Her fists pounded helplessly on the table. Unable to move the upper part of her body because her breasts were immovably strapped to the table top, her bottom leapt and gyrated all the more frantically, her feet kicking helplessly and her knees coming up off the table as she struggled to escape the terrible, insistent, smarting repetition. And still the beating went on – Thwack! Thwack! Thwack! – every stroke finding its target with unfailing accuracy and producing a high-pitched squeal every time.

At sixty the punishment stopped and Rose collapsed in a sobbing heap. Elaine could literally feel the heat coming off her sorely tried bottom. Completely emotionless, Madam Max handed the quirt to a guard and moved on to the next table. With what Elaine guessed was calculated cruelty, she stopped midway and turned to the guard who was still by Rose. 'Twenty more every hour!' Rose shook her head, desperately, and her sobs became, 'Nnngg!' noises as she sought to protest, but Madam Max was already at the next table, oblivious to any pleas for mercy.

'This is Chiquita.' Elaine could only admire the flawless perfection of the olive-skinned beauty who lay helpless before her. Long, silky black hair cascaded around a face which must have been beautiful when not distorted by a gag. Large, firm breasts, topped by knobby brown nipples jutted proudly into the air with no hint of sag. The smooth, flat belly and long tapering legs met at a profuse thatch of black, curly, pubic hair. 'A client has complained that Chiquita has been faking orgasms.' Madam Max turned to Elaine with a smile. 'Nothing wrong with faking an orgasm you understand. All the best professionals have to do it from time to time. No! The offence is that she was not good enough at it and so the client suspected what was going on, and for that she has to be punished. In this case, it seems appropriate that the punishment should be a refresher course in what an orgasm is really like, to help her to fake them better in the future. Chiquita has not undergone this form of punishment before, have you dear?' The dark-skinned girl stirred apprehensively, her eyes widening as though in disbelief as Madam Max produced a rubber dildo and held it up for her to inspect.

'I know that you could hardly be expected to respond to an ordinary dildo, so this one is very special. See these two long wires coming from the bottom, with clips on the end of each. That tells you that it is battery operated, but not in the ordinary way. A closer look will allow you to see this little metal button near the bottom.' She twisted the base and the instrument gave forth a buzzing sound. Madam Max turned to Elaine. 'Hold a clip in one hand then wet your finger and put it on the button.' Elaine did as she was bid and jumped in surprise as she felt the tingling jolt of a tiny electric shock.

'The battery drives a little magneto which outputs a minute current through the metal button, returning to earth through the clips and whatever they may be attached to. The penis itself is not huge. It is a myth that all women like large ones. This is just right for comfort. It's not the size, it's the way it's used which is important.'

Bending over the recumbent girl, Madam Max attached a clip to each nipple, then slipped the rubber penis in between her wide-spread legs and began to rub the tip up and down the lips of her vagina. After a few wriggles, Chiquita began to move her hips rhythmically, in time with the rubbing of the dildo.

Madam Max paused, removed the rubber instrument and substituted her fingers, feeling and massaging the inner lips of the labia before spreading them wide apart. 'Come to this part of the table so that you can have a proper view of what is going to happen. You need to know the signs of arousal in a woman, as well as in a man. See how these lips and the sensitive area just inside are swollen and red. Slip your fingers into her and feel how wet she is.' Elaine obeyed, amazed at her own temerity and more than a little excited at the sight of this woman's body, so openly and lewdly displayed. Chiquita sighed and wriggled in embarrassment.

'Chiquita has a particularly prominent clitoris. See how it protrudes when I spread her open like this, almost like a little penis. Imagine what it is going to feel like when this dildo goes in far enough for the metal button to reach it.' At these words, Chiquita's struggles to escape became more pronounced, but Madam Max displayed her usual icy mercilessness. Switching on the penis, she inserted the extreme tip into the girl's spread slot and agitated it gently, in and out. Chiquita's breathing became heavier and her hips resumed their previous rhythm.

'You see that I am beginning to get to her, despite herself. A lot of men think that all they have to do to please a woman is to ram themselves in as far as they can and bang away. We know better. We know that it is the ridge around the knob, gently massaging just inside which produces the sweetest sensations, don't we?' By this time Chiquita was groaning as well as writhing, in time to the movement of the penis, and her stomach muscles were contracting in an effort to draw the thing further in.

'Now she is ready for the longer, fuller strokes!'

Elaine watched in fascination as the rubber tool disappeared into the gaping slot, suiting the actions to the words. Chiquita's head began to move from side to side, her breath snorting through her nose and her moans became more insistent. Elaine could imagine, with a prickle of wetness between her own legs, what Chiquita must be feeling: the embarrassment of being brought to orgasm by force and in front of an audience; the indignity of the fact that her own passionate nature was getting the better of her, and willing this torture to continue; finally, the anticipation of the hitherto unknown sensation which, so the subdued buzzing of the instrument inside her seemed to say, would begin any time now.

At that moment Madam Max thrust the dildo in far enough for the metal button to press against the erect clitoris and held it there. Every muscle in Chiquita's body clenched and unclenched; violent, uncontrollable waves rippling across her stomach as the tiny current nibbled at her nipples and the most sensitive part of her sex. As the fullest force of orgasm hit her, her head shook, rolled and nodded, her fists and toes closed and opened and the backs of her knees drummed against the table top. From her gagged mouth emerged a series of throaty groans and screams as the circuit remained steadily in contact and the orgasm went on, and on, and on.

Madam Max removed the penis and Chiquita relaxed, breathing heavily. However, her respite did not last long. 'I told you that my punishments were suited to the individual, didn't I? I happen to know that Chiquita is quite capable of multiple orgasms and, now that I have paved the way with the first, you will see that the others are very simple to achieve.' With that, she switched on the dildo again and without ceremony, plunged it to the hilt into Chiquita's still-quivering vagina. She jerked immediately to orgasm again, unable to pull herself away from the unbearable stimulation. With calculated cruelty, Madam Max held it there for what seemed an interminable time before removing it, and beckoning to a guard. 'Three more orgasms, now. And then five every hour on the hour!' She paused a moment to watch Chiquita's dark eyes plead with the guard as he picked up the dildo, then she turned and made for the last occupied table.

This was occupied by a stunning redhead whose eyes, unlike those of the other girls, blazed anger and defiance at the approach of her tormentor. Her soft, pink skin complexion was typical of a redhead and any doubt as to the authenticity of that hair colour was dispelled by the huge thatch of red pubic hair. Elaine had never seen such a quantity. It marched up across the naked stomach almost to the navel, and was thick and curly enough to completely conceal the details of her sex, widely stretched though her thighs were.

'I have saved Mary until the last. She is a very, very special case and deserves the fullest attention. I seldom have to deal with my girls for slackness in their professional duties, but Mary seems to have a lot of difficulty in one particular area. She claims not to enjoy servicing our lady customers and several of them have complained about her lack of enthusiasm. This cannot be tolerated and I think I shall have to deal most severely with this little spitfire. As you have already seen, I select a punishment which blends with the crime and the personal attributes of the girl concerned. I want Mary to remember this lesson for some time, so I have decided to shave off all her body hair.' She reached down and grasped a handful of the red, pubic curls, tugging viciously and eliciting a startled howl of anguish from the gagged mouth.

'With a thick, wiry growth like that, just imagine how uncomfortable the stubble is going to be for at least a couple of weeks, while it grows in again. The only alternative to that discomfort is for her to keep shaving and I know she is very proud of that hair. Well, my dear Mary; say goodbye to it now, because I am going to shave you as bald as a baby!'

Madam Max stooped below the table and produced a set of electric clippers, already plugged in. As she switched on and the clippers began to hum, Mary writhed, every muscle and tendon standing out as she sought to avoid the inevitable, but could do no more than watch helplessly, as Madam Max laid the coldness of the clippers lightly on her bare belly and took the first stroke across the uppermost part of her pubic hair. With calculated cruelty she made the torture last. Most of the time she just nibbled at the edges but, now and again, she made a full scythe which sent red curls scattering to the floor and made Mary gasp. As the clipping went on, more and more bare, white belly was exposed to the view of Elaine and the unseen audience. Tantalisingly, just as she reached the beginning of Mary's vaginal slit, Madam Max stopped, leaving a small tuft there and moved on to the hairy inner part of the strained thighs, working upwards. Finally she started to work on the labial lips, clipping with loving slowness and making sure that the vibrating cutters were pressed well into the flesh in the area around the clitoris as Mary jumped and gasped in response.

Then, all that was left of the glorious red patch was a fine stubble; yet Madam Max had not finished. She produced a foam dispenser of shaving cream and a razor and proceeded to lather the redhead's lower belly, lingering with slippery fingers, rather longer than necessary around the vaginal area. While Mary moaned in misery, the razor removed the last traces of hair from her, leaving the front of her body completely bald; the pink lips of her sex gaping slightly and clearly visible to any onlooker.

And still the torment was not over. At a sign from Madam Max, the black-suited attendants erected uprights and a bar, as they had done for Shelley. Mary put up much more of a fight as they unclipped her ankles, kicking and struggling, but she was overcome and her ankles secured to the ends of the bar so that she was doubled up with her legs widely spread and her naked, pink bottom sticking into the air, completely vulnerable to whatever might be coming next.

Madam Max leaned over Mary and looked into her eyes. 'You thought I had forgotten the hairs down here, didn't you? No such luck, my dear. You are going to remember me for some time, every time you sit down.' She picked up the clippers again and set to work on the newly exposed area, scything away the luxuriant growth between her bottom cheeks, until she met with the bald area already created. Then came the shaving cream, and this time Madam Max inserted a slippery finger into Mary's tight sphincter, which involuntarily tightened and puckered around it; gently easing it in and out to the accompaniment of infuriated howls.

Madam Max leaned over Mary's face again. 'Now, you realise that no part of you is sacred or private. As long as you work for me, I, or anyone else I choose will look at you, touch you and use you in any way they like.' With that, she took up the razor again and soon removed the last vestiges of hair. 'That will do for now. I'll have her depilated with a cream to make sure that nothing has been missed, but that is a pretty perfect shave she has there and the real punishment can begin.'

Elaine gulped. This was not the end of it, then. There was more to come. Apparently so, for at another sign from Madam Max the guards lifted the uprights out of their sockets and moved them further down the table, placed the bar in a higher position and re-secured Mary's ankles so that her buttocks were just clear of the table and her legs, again, widely spread. They passed a wide, leather strap around her body, just above the breasts, then re-positioned her wrists, clipping them level with her hips. Two sections of table were removed on either side of Mary's head, leaving her with just a narrow strip for the back of her head to rest on.

On Madam Max's orders, the gag was removed, releasing a scream of abuse and threats. 'Bitch! Bitch! Let me go! I'll kill you!'

The gag was instantly replaced, muffling further words and Madam Max sighed in mock sorrow. 'Oh dear, Mary. You have such a lot to learn.' As the guards held Mary's head in a vice-like grip, Madam Max spread lather on each eyebrow and in a few strokes shaved them clean off.

'Now the gag is coming off again. Will you have any more to say, I wonder, or will you remember that that beautiful head of red hair you think so much of counts as body hair too? I have the clippers, the razor *and* the will to do it. If you think I won't, you can abuse me again. If you think I will, you will be much better behaved this time.'

The gag was removed once more and Mary remained silent, though obviously seething. 'So much wiser my dear. Now, you are going to service me and make a thorough job of it.' Madam Max stepped to the head of the table, slipped out of her black kimono and stood naked for a second, before mounting a couple of blocks and standing with one thigh on either side of Mary's head, her black pubic hair almost brushing the available mouth.

'No Madam Max. Please don't. I don't like it. I'll do anything else. Please don't make me do that.' The tone was conciliatory and pleading, without any trace of the previous defiance.

Madam Max's eyes glittered and she passed her hands caressingly over her own breasts and down her stomach. The girl's helpless subjugation was obviously a complete turn-on for her. 'I can't tell you how glad I am to hear you say that, Mary. If there is one thing I like better than a good, tongue-induced orgasm, it is one which I have to force my server into. You know what you have to do. The sooner you start, the sooner the pain will ease and, if you please me very much, the pain may stop altogether, although I can't promise that because I get a little carried away and I enjoy inflicting discomfort on you.'

She took the little, padded quirt handed to her by one of her men and flicked it down in front of her body so that it landed squarely on Mary's unprotected left nipple. The next stroke fell on the right breast and then three in succession, right on the bald area of her pubic mound, just above the clitoris. Mary jumped and shouted, struggling to pull away down the table but was restrained by the strap across her upper body, under her armpits. She twisted her head from side to side but was forced to return to staring up at the hairy lips, poised just above her face.

Madam Max grinned wolfishly. 'Take all the time you like, Mary. I am enjoying this. This is to be the pattern though. One on each breast followed by three on that lovely bald spot. When you think you can't stand it any more, you may begin your duties and when I begin to feel pleased I *may* ease off a little.' The ritualistic slapping of the leather pad continued and Elaine could guess, by the bright red colour of the tortured breasts and pubic mound, that the smarting was intense. Mary continued to groan and roll her head, trying to hold out against the pain. Finally, almost without her being aware of it Mary's pink tongue emerged from between her lips. Glancing down without breaking the rhythm of her strokes, Madam Max observed the transition from defiance to compliance and smiled. 'Not good enough Mary. I'm not going to come down to you. You have to come up to me.'

The slapping continued for a few more strokes before Mary's head lifted, slowly and reluctantly and her tongue reached out to tentatively separate and lick at the rounded surface of the outer labia. 'That's not doing a thing for me Mary. I think we ought to put a little more sting into the whip to encourage you to do better.' The quirt rose and fell faster and with more bite. Coming as they did on already tenderised areas, the next few strokes broke Mary completely. She probed deeper with her tongue, inserting it between the inner labia and began to lap eagerly and quickly. A beatific smile spread over Madam Max's face and she began to manipulate her own nipple with one hand while the quirt slowed to become light and easy. Eventually it stopped altogether, leaving Madam Max with both hands free to reach between her own legs and spread herself for the attentions of that active tongue. Her eyes began to roll and her knees trembled. 'Find the place, Mary! Find the place! Oh God! That's right! Go on! Go on! Don't stop! Finish me! Do it to me!'

As orgasm hit her, her back arched and she raised a clenched fist to her mouth, biting furiously. Then she fell forward across the naked body beneath her, pressing her hot, wet sex tightly against Mary's mouth and clawing with both hands at the shaven area between the straining and widely separated thighs.

Presently she stirred and got up, slipping back into her kimono and tying the sash. As she rejoined Elaine she was obviously still struggling for composure; breathing a little heavily. 'Well. As you see my dear Elaine, that concludes this part of the show. The thing I want to impress upon you is that although these girls are temporarily restrained none of them are prisoners. Any of them could walk out tomorrow with no questions asked. They don't because they know when they are onto a good thing. Their accommodation is splendid. They are paid a great deal more than they could earn otherwise. They are well fed and their welfare is a prime consideration. In return for that, they agree to submit to my rules and my domination. It is on those conditions that you will be employed here.

'Before we go I have to tell you that there is always a final turn.' She gestured towards the mirror; 'Our audience would be disappointed to be deprived of their expected treat. Today *you* are that treat. Our friends behind the glass will want to look at you, as a new girl, in order to decide if and how they can make use of you – so just slip off your dress and I'll tell you what to do next.'

Elaine shrank away, blushing scarlet, her hands instinctively protecting her breasts and crotch. 'Oh no! I couldn't do that, Madam Max. I've never undressed in front of lots of people!'

'Then this will be a new experience for you. I promised you lots of new experiences. If you want to keep the job, you'll do it. If you refuse I shall simply get my men to strip you. I certainly don't intend to frustrate my clients because of your maidenly modesty. Make up your mind. Which is it to be? Strip or be stripped?'

With the greatest reluctance Elaine unbuttoned her dress, released the belt and drew it off over her head, to stand in push-up brassiere and flimsy panties. She was very conscious of her choice of suspender belt and stockings instead of panty-hose. Madam Max took her by the arm and pushed her towards the mirror. 'Stand here, on Number One, facing the mirror.'

For the first time Elaine noticed a row of brass numbers set into the carpet along the front of the mirror, about five feet from the glass, and guessed that they corresponded with the cubicles on the other side.

'Brush your hair back from your face, child! That's better. Now – hands on head!' Elaine did as she was told and Madam Max, standing behind her, reached around and folded down the top of her bra so that her breasts stood out even further and her pert nipples were fully exposed. She transferred her attention to the panties and skimpy though they were, made them even more revealing by squeezing the crotch into a single cord and pulling up on the waistband, so that the material disappeared between Elaine's bottom cheeks and into the cleft of her sex, clearly revealing a bush of golden pubic hair.

'Now turn around. Hold it! Move on to Number Two. No. Don't take your hands off your head! Face the mirror. Turn. Hold it. Now to Number Three. That's right – you've got it. All the way down the line like that.' Mortified with embarrassment, Elaine did as she was instructed. Finally arriving at Ten, the last number, with a sigh of relief. But Madam Max had not finished with her. 'Now a full strip. Everything off! Come along, child. I haven't got all day. Get them off!' As Elaine hesitated Madam Max became impatient and crossing to where she stood, ripped her panties down to her knees in one swift jerk and un-clipped her brassiere so that her breasts, unencumbered and unsupported, flopped free. Trembling with shame, Elaine made the necessary movements to un-fasten her suspenders, remove the belt and roll off her stockings. Standing, half crouched, she attempted to shield her body with her hands.

Madam Max picked up her little quirt and ran it menacingly through her fingers. 'I shall begin to think that you are being deliberately awkward. Perhaps you should have tasted this before we started?' Elaine hastily dropped her hands to her sides, very conscious that several pairs of eyes were examining her naked-ness. 'Face the mirror. Flat on your back. Legs wide apart. Wider than that. Wider still. Now reach down with your hands and pull yourself apart so that the audience can judge the condition of your inner surfa-ces. Look, when I say "apart" I mean *wide* apart. That's better. Up on your feet! Turn around! Feet *wide* apart! Touch your toes! Now reach around be-hind you and pull your cheeks apart! Good. Up you get and repeat that at every number back down to One.'

In a daze Elaine obeyed. Could any shame be

greater than this? Being forced to reveal her most private parts in this lewd fashion to unknown eyes. She lay down, got up, bent and showed off her body in a mechanical fashion at each position until at last she was back at Number One and the ordeal was finally over.

'You may dress now. I thought for a moment that I was going to have to have you table-topped, but I would prefer to reserve that pleasure for another time, after I have found out a little more about your likes and dislikes and had the opportunity to plan properly. Now follow me. There is much you have yet to see.'

Madam Max swept out of the room, so that Elaine had almost to run to keep up with her. Elaine's thoughts were racing. Maybe she had bitten off more than she knew. This job was not going to be an easy one and she wondered if she would have the nerve to carry it all the way through. She remembered the naked girls and she wished that she could have spoken to them, there and then, to find out whether she could recruit any allies to her cause. Better keep that for another day. They had other things to think about for the time being. The discomfort yet to come. Elaine shivered at the thought that she too might soon be naked, gagged, strapped down and at the mercy of Madam Max's whim. She tried to put the thought out of her mind and followed Madam Max back to the drawing room.

6
Education

Madam Max patted the place beside her on the large and comfortable sofa, in invitation. Elaine sat down wondering what was coming next.

'Would you like some tea, dear?'

Elaine, who had been expecting some further shock, floundered. The banality of the question had taken her by surprise, and it took a few seconds before she could say, 'Yes please.'

Madam Max rang the bell then returned. 'Such a nice custom, tea,' she said, and from there she led the conversation in her easy way, as if the recent, bizarre events had never happened. 'I'm glad I decided to employ you, Elaine. As I promised, if you please me there is a good chance of greater reward.'

'Thank you, Madam Max.'

'Not at all. I think you have natural talent and you are very, very beautiful.' She reached out and stroked Elaine's hair as she had done at their first meeting. This time, Elaine noticed, she did not ask permission, and there was something proprietorial in her manner, rather as if she were feeling the hocks of a horse.

The same maid came in with the tea and again Elaine was struck by a certain oddness about her. The maid stood by the trolley and waited to be dismissed.

Madam Max, noticing Elaine's scrutiny, did not do so. 'You have noticed my maid?' she said. She beckoned to the maid who, finding herself in such prominence, was shaking with tension. 'Come here, Millicent. This nice young lady wants to examine you more closely. Lift up your dress.' The eyes pleaded but disobedience was out of the question. The dress rose slowly, revealing the tops of her black stockings, then the suspenders of a belt. 'Get it up, girl. Or must I lose my patience!' The skirt rose all the way to the waist, to reveal the genitalia of a man, except that the penis was encased in what looked like a steel sheath, from which a chain passed around his scrotum causing his testicles to bulge forward. Another chain went about his body so tightly that it cut into the flesh and the whole thing was fastened together with padlocks. All the pubic area that Elaine could see, including the testicles, was shaved clean and Madam Max passed her hand across it, as though testing for smoothness, before getting up and going to a cupboard in the wall. The doors of the cupboard were formed from the same panelling as the rest of the room and, when open, revealed a large closet.

At this the man fell to his knees, his hands clasped, as though in prayer. 'Mercy! Please! Not again!'

Madam Max was exasperated. 'Get up, girl. For goodness' sake pull yourself together and stop that whining. When I am ready to cane you, you will know all about it. And pull that skirt up again. Who said you could let it down!' He did so and stood, exposed again, obviously in acute embarrassment and fear.

Madam Max came back with a duplicate of the fearsome gadget he wore and showed it to Elaine. 'This is a penis restraint. They are widely used here,

114

and one of the things you must learn is how to put one on. Not now, of course, that can come later. I just want to show you that it is lined inside with sharp bristles. It is uncomfortable all the time but, when an erection comes to mind, the discomfort quickly puts a stop to those thoughts. I think I can demonstrate that best by asking you to stroke the shaved areas. Make your touch nice and soft and gentle.'

Elaine reached out and stroked him as ordered, running her fingers over the extended testicles as well. After just a few seconds the man's knees buckled. He groaned in misery and screwed up his face, as though with intense concentration, as he fought to turn his mind away from what was being done to him, so as to stop the further swelling of his organ.

'How long has it been on now, Millicent?'

'Two hours, Madam.'

'Very well. I think another two hour period is called for.' Then, as if it was an afterthought, she added, 'At least!' The man groaned again. 'You may drop your skirt and go now.' Thankfully, he did so and hobbled from the room.

Elaine could not restrain her curiosity. 'Is that one of the fantasies you were talking about?'

Madam Max smiled grimly. 'It could easily be but, in this case, it isn't. He was foolish enough, whilst in my employ, to try to steal a great deal of my money. I offered him the choice. A very long period in prison, or a short period of my own particular brand of punishment. I'm not sure now, that he thinks he made a wise choice. He is, or was, a very egotistical, arrogant, macho-man. I needed a servant and it pleases me, for the time being, to humiliate him as much as I can.'

'How long has he been . . .? I mean . . .'

'A few weeks. I am getting bored with the game, so

I shall not keep him much longer, but he does not know that.' Elaine shivered, aware that in trying to match wills with this woman, she was playing with fire.

Madam Max said, 'I allowed you to see that because it will be a part of your education to see other men treated in the same way. Men who pay handsomely for the privilege. Yes, it is incredible, isn't it?' she continued, noticing Elaine's expression. 'But that is their dearest wish, and I am happy to make it come true, at a price. I enjoy domination of men or women. It may be that you will find that you have talent in that direction. It so happens that I have such an appointment this afternoon. You can help me with that and then we shall see. For the time being, we will see if we can give you a flavour of the delights which make my clients come back, time and again.'

She conducted Elaine along the corridors again and they went into a side-room. It was completely curtained along one side. There was a drinks cabinet, a table and some comfortable chairs. What was remarkable was that there were two TV cameras on stands, some distance apart, pointing at the curtain. Madam Max dimmed the lights and going to the curtain pulled part of it aside. The wall behind it was transparent and gave a full view of what appeared to be a small dressing, or changing room, softly carpeted and equipped with a large shower.

'We have just a little while to wait,' Madam Max said. 'Let's have a drink.' She went to the cabinet and poured drinks for both of them, then settled herself in a chair and indicated that Elaine should occupy the other. Seeing that Elaine was very curious, she explained. 'All the fantasy rooms, and a few of the others in the house are equipped like this, with another room alongside. The other side of that glass wall is a mirror. I'm sure you will remember the one you saw earlier.'

She smiled sardonically as she saw that Elaine remembered very well. 'From here, I, or any other privileged person, can watch what goes on in the next room. The TV cameras are operated from a central control room. The wall is soundproof. Concealed microphones on the other side relay sound to these loudspeakers in this room and direct to the cameras. To put that in a less complicated way, we and the TV cameras, can see and hear everything that happens next door. Neither the cameras, nor the occupants of the other room, can hear what we are saying. Clear?'

Elaine nodded and sipped her drink, conscious that a lot of money and effort went into the running of this establishment. Just then a green light glowed and there was an electronic 'ping' as the door of the dressing room opened and two women came in. Madam Max crossed to the nearest camera and pressed a button beneath it, waiting until the red 'on' light appeared before returning to continue her observation of the women. They were both elegantly dressed in evening clothes and both had dark hair. One appeared to be about 25 or 26, the other older – Elaine judged her to be in her late thirties. They kissed one another on the mouth – a lingering, hungry kiss which went on for a long time. Elaine was reminded of Isabel and Gretchen. Their hands groped and fondled at each other's bodies, then they began to undress each other.

It wasn't easy for them to do that without interrupting their long kiss, and they had to do that from time to time, but returned to it immediately. They stripped one another naked and Elaine saw that the younger one had a magnificent body, tanned all over, without marks of clothing; beautifully muscled and perfectly proportioned, reminding Elaine of the sleek qualities of a leopard. Her breasts were large, but taut and firm. The older woman was a little heavier. Her breasts were also large, but swung and joggled just a little, with her movements. In spite of that, or perhaps because of it, she was sexually exciting; the whiteness of her skin and the rounded contours of her haunches exuding the same qualities as the lusty women in a Rembrandt or Rubens painting.

They stopped kissing at last. Laughing, they picked up bathing caps, which were provided along with the towels, and put them on, tucking their hair inside with great care. Elaine thought that they were going to take a shower together and was puzzled when they moved to a door which led to whatever was behind the rest of the curtain. She followed Madam Max as she moved along the glass and drew it back. The red light on the second camera glowed red. The other room, thus revealed, was a little larger than the first but carpeted in the same way. It was completely devoid of furniture. In the centre of it was a thing which resembled a child's portable paddling pool, except that it was much larger, about eight feet square, and had rounded edges padded with matching carpet, so that it looked as though it was built into the floor. Elaine looked to Madam Max for an explanation.

'These women met at one of my parties last week and were mutually attracted. They were able to get together only briefly then, but decided that they would like to return together, for this session. This is one of our more popular fantasies – popular with heterosexual couples as well – very simple in itself, but complicated and expensive if they tried to arrange it themselves. The pool is about six inches deep. It is not filled with water but oil; vegetable oil to which a subtle blend of aromas has been added. It is, believe me, a most pleasant sensation to bathe in it.'

The two women stopped beside the pool. The elder waited while the younger got down on hands and knees and crawled in. 'They have been cautioned against standing up,' said Madam Max. It would be extremely difficult.'

As the tanned girl moved, Elaine watched the swing of her muscular, bare buttocks and was again reminded of a big cat. When she reached the centre she turned over and sat down, obviously enjoying the sensation of the oil on her body and between her legs. She cupped her hands and lifted oil to splash on her face. It ran down over her breasts and stomach in a glistening stream and she rubbed her slippery hands over her shoulders and arms. 'Come on, Peggy. It's lovely. Just slightly warm.'

Peggy got down on her hands and knees and crawled into the pool. She stopped by the younger woman, but remained on her hands and knees, her breasts dangling and swaying. 'I'm not ready, Jane. I might slip. Don't rush me,' she said nervously.

'Fraidy cat!' said Jane. And crawled around her, splashing oil up underneath her, wetting her breasts and belly then, as she turned away defensively, scooping handfuls to splash her thighs and bottom. Peggy let out girlish screams and splashed back as best she could with one hand.

'Come on. Get it on your face, like me,' said Jane and crawled towards her menacingly.

Guessing her intention Peggy backed away. 'No, Jane. You're not to. No, Jane. I'm serious!'

She shrieked as Jane hurled herself on her and tried

to knock away her supporting hands. For a while they remained locked together, like two wrestlers, Jane trying hard for grip but finding it difficult with the oil. Then she was on Peggy's back, holding her tightly with interlocked arms, distorting her ample breasts. Her strong thighs wrapped around her stomach, squeezing tightly, heels digging into her pubic hair. For a second or two as Peggy bucked and jumped to dislodge her, she rode her like a horse, until with a sudden outward, scything movement, Jane knocked her arms away from under her. She fell, face first into the oil, squirming and wriggling as Jane, still on top of her, dunked her head under for a second. She came up gasping and blowing and wiping her face, then the action slowed as they came into one another's arms and lay pressed together, breast to breast, belly to belly, with pubic hair intertwined.

For a long time they just lay there, their lips pressed together in a passionate, open-mouthed kiss. The only movement was a slight undulation of their bodies, as each sought – by rubbing and sliding – to maximise the feel of the naked oiliness of the other. Their hands also moved constantly, feeling the texture of the oil as they slid them up and down, massaging and fondling each other's backs and buttocks.

Elaine had seen bodies massaged with oil before, but only with small quantities, which gave the skin a certain shine. Not with these virtually unlimited amounts. The bare, intertwined bodies of these women glistened and shone with oil. She found that, and their movements, incredibly erotic. She felt herself lubricating and wanted to touch herself and, glancing across at Madam Max, noticed that the display had had the same effect on her. She was leaning forward, staring intently. Her hands were inside her kimono – her left massaging her breasts and her right between her legs. From the subtle movements Elaine could tell that she was masturbating.

Her movements increased as the women parted slightly, so as to permit their hands access to the fronts of their bodies, then massaged each other's breasts and bellies before kissing again, each with a hand between her partner's thighs. They stayed like this for a long time until, apparently by mutual consent, they crawled to the side of the pool and got out, their bodies as sleek as seals, and went back to the dressing room. Peggy turned on the shower and adjusted the temperature and they went in together. The shower was large and the entrance faced the transparent wall. There was no curtain or door, so everything they did could be seen.

They took it in turns to soap one another, seeming to take as much pleasure in soaping as they did in being soaped. Jane stood behind Peggy and reached around her, rubbing suds into her breasts, lifting the weight of them and irritating the nipples with her fingers. Then she transferred her attention to her stomach and worked up a good lather in her pubic hair before plunging her slippery hands between her legs to slide her fingers to and fro along her sex. Peggy moved constantly under this treatment, her whole body twitching with excitement.

Then it was Jane's turn to receive the same treatment from Peggy and she raised her arms and stretched back, placing her hands behind Peggy's head, in order to lift her superb, brown breasts to maximum prominence and stretch the skin tighter around her nipples to increase the stimulation they were receiving.

When they came out of the shower, they removed

their bathing caps, spread fluffy towels on the carpet and, without bothering to dry, got down onto them. Jane lay on her back with her head towards the camera, raised her knees and parted her legs wide. Peggy got astride her in the classic sixty-nine position, kneeling and facing her feet. She bent forward, arching her back down so that her pendulous breasts brushed Jane's naked stomach, then began to kiss and lick between the parted thighs. In this way, her plump, white, bottom cheeks were displayed to Jane and to the camera, her sex stretched apart so as to reveal the excited, swollen entrance to her vagina. Jane put her arms around Peggy's bottom and pulled herself up so that her tongue could work on the area so invitingly exposed, lapping and sucking, then biting gently on the spread labial lips, before searching out the clitoris and concentrating on that.

Peggy came to orgasm first, with a great sigh and a frantic wriggling of her buttocks. She kept up her work and Jane soon followed, showering kisses on the bare, white flesh above her as she did so. Elaine thought that Madam Max came to orgasm with them, but she could not be sure and suspected that the woman was not going to reveal that to her, if she could help it.

Elaine took her lunch in her room, which was luxuriously appointed with every conceivable requirement, and where she had only to lift the telephone to have food or drinks brought to her. The one thing she could not have brought to her was Stewart, and she found that she needed the comfort of his presence very badly. She would have to find a way to see him, at least, even if those meetings had to be formal and business-like.

She found her opportunity after lunch when she

reported again to the drawing room. 'Madam Max. I have been thinking about what you have shown me and it seems to me that I shall become useful more quickly if I learn as much as I can about what goes on here. Visiting different rooms with you is the best way, of course, but you are not always available and it occurred to me that if I spent some of my time in the TV Control Room, then I could monitor what is going on in several rooms at the same time. What do you think?'

Madam Max was gratified at this display of enthusiasm by her pupil. 'An excellent idea, my dear. I will tell Stewart to be as helpful as he can. Now to this afternoon's business. I think this will be interesting for you and you can help me. First I have to change.' She went to the closet in the panelling and, opening it, brought out a large box. She set it on the sofa and removed some clothing from it. Then with complete unconcern, slipped out of her kimono and shoes and stood naked. 'Help me to dress, dear,' she said. Elaine did so.

First there was what could best be described as the bottom half of a black, shiny, leather bikini. The triangle at the front was covered in metal studs. At the back there was merely a thong which submerged itself between her bottom-cheeks and disappeared; leaving her buttocks completely uncovered. Instead of a thin waistband it had a broad, studded belt with a heavy buckle. Next came a pair of shiny, black boots, which reached to just below the knee and had incredibly high heels. Elaine helped her to pull them on and zip them up.

The bodice of the costume was a collection of leather straps held together by rings. When fitted, just about the whole of her upper body was clearly visible, including her bare breasts; the straps against her white skin serving only to emphasise her nudity. A pair of elbow-length gloves completed the outfit and she posed for Elaine. 'Like it?'

Elaine felt a sudden surge inside her which reminded her of the time she had first seen a naked woman, bound and hanging, helpless. She was a little breathless as she answered, 'Yes,' and meant it. This was pure fantasy and it was exciting.

Madam Max looked hard at her for long seconds, then there was a knock on the door which broke the spell. 'Wait!' Madam Max snapped then crossed to the closet. She came back with a whippy cane with a hooked handle. Holding it in both hands across her body, she faced the door and struck a pose – legs apart, pelvis thrust forward. 'Come!' The door opened and a man entered. He was aged between thirty and forty. He hung his head as though in shame. 'Well, Gavin. Have you brought it?'

He replied, 'Yes, Mistress.'

'How dare you address me in a standing position.' He fell to his knees at once. 'Bring it here then. On your knees.' He shuffled across and handed her a sheet of paper. She took it from him, then barked, 'Who said that you had permission to look at me? Get your face down on the floor, where it belongs, while I look at this.' He obeyed meekly, burying his forehead in the carpet in a manner which reminded Elaine of her own interview. Madam Max took her time reading the document, then said, 'You are sure it is all here? Every sin? You are aware of the penalty if I find that you have concealed anything from me?'

'It's all there, Mistress.'

She drew the cane through her hands and seemed to be considering. 'I can see that there are many things which need correction. I was hoping that you had learned better, but you are still having impure thoughts and masturbating. Do you think that deserves punishment?'

'Yes, Mistress.'

'Very well. I shall do that. Now stand up and strip! No! You do *not* look at me. Turn and face this young lady. Now get them off, every stitch, and be quick about it!'

The man undressed hurriedly, dropping his clothes on the floor, then stood facing Elaine, his hands protecting his genitals. Madam Max leapt forward and slashed her cane across his buttocks. He yelped in surprise. 'You do *not* cover yourself with your hands. Put them on your head and listen to your instructions. You will return to your room and shower that filthy, objectionable body, most thoroughly. You will return here in twenty minutes time, with only a pair of clean white shorts. Then your punishment will begin.'

He bent to pick up his clothes, but received another cut with the cane which straightened him up again. 'Did I say you could pick up your clothes? You will leave them here and go naked. You will get back to your room by going out through the west door, into the drive, then back in by the east door. You will not walk on the grass but on the gravel. If you meet anyone, you will say to them, "I am being punished by Madam Max." Is that clear?'

'Yes, Mistress.'

'You will be watched. If you disobey these instructions in any way or if you attempt to cover yourself, even with your hands, your punishment will be increased. Now go!'

He left. Madam Max relaxed and smiled at Elaine

as she sat down next to her on the sofa. 'That is domination. Do you think you could do that?'

Elaine nodded. 'Perhaps. I'm not sure yet. I would like to see more first. May I?'

'Of course you may, dear. Did it excite you?'

'Yes, it did . . . a bit. I think. Your costume . . .'

Madam Max looked pleased. 'You find it sexy?'

In truth Elaine did. At the notion of, perhaps wearing such an outfit herself, she grew moist. She was aware of the fact that the bare breasts, unnaturally white against leather and metal, were very close; the nipples long and brown and erect. She knew that she wanted to touch them, but hesitated. As if reading her thoughts, Madam Max stretched, placing her hands at the back of her neck and thrusting herself out provocatively. Unable to resist longer, Elaine stretched out her hands and brushed the nipples lightly with her palms, in a rotary motion. Madam Max gasped and arched her back like a stroked cat, as if this was something for which she had been waiting impatiently. Elaine saw ripples of pleasure pass across the muscles under the skin of her bare stomach. She remembered the occasion on which she had been brought to orgasm by nipple stimulation alone and resolved that she would not allow herself to be tempted into fondling or stroking. She continued her movements, softly, gently, insistently.

Madam Max's hands came down and stroked across her belly, towards her thighs, but she was thwarted in her desire to touch herself by the leather and metal of the triangle which covered her pubes. She sighed softly in acute pleasure then, as the soft, irritating delight went on, unable to stand the frustration further, she gripped Elaine's wrists and pulled her hands away, grimacing as she did so. 'Perhaps this is a conversation we should contine later.'

Elaine, feeling the dampness between her own thighs, found that she shared that sentiment.

When the timid knock on the door announced Gavin's return Madam Max resumed her former pose and bade him enter. He was wearing only a pair of white shorts. She beckoned and he came forward, falling on his knees in front of her and pressing his face into the carpet. She stung his back with her cane. 'Did I say you could wear the shorts?'

'I thought . . .' His voice was muffled. He got no further, but received three more stinging slashes.

'Arguing?'

'No, Mistress.'

'I should hope not. And you are late.'

'No, Mistress. I was most careful . . .' Three more cuts of the cane.

'Are you calling me a liar?'

'No, Mistress. I wouldn't . . .'

She was impatient. 'Oh, stop your whining. You may apologise for your lateness by licking my boots.' He did so, his tongue slavering all over the shiny surface. 'Enough! Get up! Turn round! Hands behind your back!' She slipped a pair of handcuffs on his wrists and clicked them shut, squeezing the ratchet hard, so as to nip the skin. 'Face me!' Are those shorts clean as I ordered?'

'Yes, Mistress.'

'Let me see. Take them off and give them to me.'

He indicated his cuffed hands. 'Mistress, I can't . . .'

In mock fury she rained blows on his back and thighs. 'Then I shall just keep caning you until you find that you can.'

He managed to pull the back of the shorts down a certain way, then sank to the floor and, by wriggling about and rubbing them against the carpet, induced them to come off.

The caning did not stop. 'The order was that you should give them to me.'

He grovelled about until he could grip them with his teeth, thus exposing his buttocks to the assault, then staggered upright and held them out to her.

She took them without a glance. 'On your belly. On the floor.' He sank to his knees and flopped, face forward, onto the carpet. She tossed the shorts across the room. 'Fetch!' He made to get up on his knees but she thrashed his backside again and he flopped down. 'I did not tell you to get up,' she hissed. 'You will crawl, and as you do so, at no time will your penis be out of contact with the carpet.' Snake-like, he began to wriggle towards the shorts and Elaine could appreciate what the rough carpet must be doing to the sensitive parts of his penis. Madam Max went with him, beating his bottom all the way. When he had almost reached his goal she kicked them a little further away.

She returned to her position and he began to crawl back. Madam Max looked across at Elaine and seeing that her face was flushed and her eyes bright, she held out the cane to her, handle first, with a look of enquiry. As she did so, Elaine remembered how it had felt to whip Gretchen; that part of the feeling which had nothing to do with the pleasure she was causing, but only with her own desire. She wanted to do this thing, so she took the cane and went over to the naked man. He saw her coming and redoubled his efforts. She went back with him, caning his buttocks, back and thighs.

When they got back, she received a nod of approval as she surrendered the cane to Madam Max, who then crossed to the closet and came back with a gag, a blindfold and a little leather device, which looked like two tiny dog-collars, linked together. She slipped one half of this gadget over his penis, buckling it tight. The other half went around the root of his testicles. When buckled it was clear that it could not slip off. The gag was a black, rubber ball with a stick through it. She forced it into his mouth and buckled it harshly behind his head, distorting his face and stretching the sides of his mouth, before adding the blindfold.

'Bend over. *Right* over. Keep your hands up in the small of your back, out of the way. Your bottom is going to be caned.'

Again, she offered the cane to Elaine, who took it with a feeling of fierce pleasure. 'You are going to receive twelve strokes,' said Madam Max. 'If you move your hands, or change your position, I shall begin again.' Elaine slashed at the naked flesh, so conveniently presented. This was something else she had learned about herself. The feeling of whipping Gretchen was slight compared to this. The stimulation was so great that she felt herself close to orgasm when the twelve strokes were given.

Madam Max attached a short chain to the penis restraint and led Gavin to the closet, which resembled a small cell, about four feet square. She hitched the chain to a hook on the wall, pulling it short, so that he was on his toes. Without another word, she closed the door and left him there.

'Will he be all right?' asked Elaine.

'Oh, sure,' replied Madam Max. 'There is a camera in there with him and he is under constant surveillance. The minute anything looks like going wrong an alarm is sounded and I get him out. It is not good business to kill your clients. Tomorrow,' she added, 'I want him back at his job earning money so that he can afford to come again. He is no use to me if he is in hospital for a month. That goes for everything done here. There are no scourges, or metal tipped rods, or cutting whips here. The crazies who want that go to amateurs. I am a professional. I can cause plenty of pain with a strap or cane. The recipient remembers next day, when he or she sits down, but there is no serious damage done.'

Disturbing thoughts were going through Elaine's mind yet she was diffident about expressing them. Certainly she wanted to stay on the right side of Madam Max and what she was considering would achieve that, she was sure – and yet – she was a little panicked to find there was another reason. Her recent experiences had brought forward a latent imp which had been lurking ever since her first experience of bondage and masochism with Isabel and Gretchen.

'Madam Max, I've been thinking about what I have seen here. I have been thinking, in particular, about the canes and whips; about what we have just done and about what you did to the girls in the Blue Room.' She hesitated, unsure how to continue. 'I find that there is something in me which responds to those images. What you do interests me. If I learned from you how to do it, do you think I could have a costume like yours?'

Madam Max was pleased and flattered, as she had hoped she would be. 'Of course you could. I can have anything you like made for you. We have a contract with a saddler who does all our leatherwork. It would be my pleasure to teach you.'

'I wonder if mine could be a red one? Red calf leather?'

Madam Max considered the idea, her head on one side. 'Hmmm! Madam Max and The Red Dragon? That could work very well. Each of us could threaten to turn a client over to the other, with the implication that this would result in even more severe treatment!'

Elaine caught the idea and elaborated. 'And we could work together . . .'

Madam Max was impressed. 'Fantastic! What a turn-on that would be!'

Elaine seized the moment to reinforce her access to the Control Room. 'Are there any videos of you working? I could learn much more quickly by watching those.' Madam Max nodded approvingly, so she went on quickly, 'And I could take the tapes back to my room and watch them in the evening to make the most economical use of my time.'

That night in her room, Elaine had a great deal to think about. She had secured the job she wanted but as far as she could see, she was no nearer to saving Sir James, Isabel and Stewart than she had been before. She had to get further into whatever was going on in this house. The evidence she needed was going to be found, she assumed, in the form of documents and, more particularly, videos. Very well, she would try to get closer to the office administration of the place – that is where documents were likely to be. As for the videos, it seemed to her that she had made a promising start by gaining virtually unrestricted access to the Control Room. If what she wanted was not there now, at least it *had* been there originally, and there might be some sort of trail to be picked up.

But so far, Madam Max had made no mention at

all of her secretarial duties. She would have to work on that. Still puzzling, she showered and put on her nightdress. She was sitting in front of the mirror, brushing her hair when there was a knock at the door. At her invitation it opened and, in the mirror, Elaine saw that it was Madam Max.

She did not come right into the room but closed the door behind her and leaned against it, watching Elaine who, after a pause, continued with her brushing. 'I just came to see that you were settling in all right.'

Elaine brushed, puzzled for a while over just what it was that was different about Madam Max. Then it came to her. She had always seen her dressed in a kimono. Now she had on a flowered housecoat and there was something faintly housewifely and domestic about that very ordinary garment. Also her hair was always drawn back tightly in a bun. Now, although still off her face, it was more loosely bound.

'Thank you,' said Elaine. 'It *has* been a strange day but I'm sure I'll get used to it.'

Madam Max crossed the room and stood close behind her. 'May I do that?'

'Of course.' Elaine handed her the brush and she began to run it through the silky, golden hair, obviously deriving great pleasure from doing so. Elaine watched her in the mirror, seeing the need in her eyes. Any minute, this woman was going to order her to strip so that she could take her pleasure with her. However she did not do so, and after a while she stopped her work and gave the brush back to Elaine who, unable to rely on a reflection, stood and faced her, the better to examine what she thought she saw. She had been right. This woman wanted her. But not as a slave, forced into sex. She wanted love, freely offered. The certainty of this gave Elaine a little thrill of power. Here was the lever she had been looking for. She reached out and took Madam Max's hand, knowing now how satisfactory that would be for her. 'Thank you for being patient with me. I will try to learn as fast as I can. I don't think I could ever be as elegant and sophisticated as you but I'll try.'

Dare she go a step further, she wondered. She must be very careful. This was not a stupid woman. 'Madam Max. Your hair . . . It always looks so beautiful. I wonder if you would let me take it down and brush it.' It worked. Madam Max smiled and sat down at the mirror. Elaine fumbled for a moment with combs and pins, then the coal-black locks cascaded down in abundance. She had not been exaggerating. The hair was truly beautiful. Elaine picked up the brush and began, making long smooth strokes which produced a rich gleam.

'I feel I would progress more quickly if I had a better overall picture of what happens here. In my other jobs I used to be able to get that, quite soon, by dealing with the correspondence and filing.' She smiled. 'After all you did take me on, first and foremost, as a secretary.'

Madam Max smiled back. 'I'm not sure that's quite true but you're probably right. I will introduce you to the office work, tomorrow.'

'Thank you,' Elaine said, and began to gather up the black hair into a loose bundle and replace the pins and combs. When she was finished, she smiled brightly and said, 'There! You're done!'

Madam Max got up and faced her. To forestall what might be coming next Elaine said, 'What are we doing tomorrow morning, apart from the office?'

The mention of business steered the other woman

away from her previous thoughts. 'Dormitory inspection first, then a little bit more of the educational watching we did today.'

'Thank you for coming to check up on me,' said Elaine. 'I feel much better now.' She took both Madam Max's hands and kissed her lightly on the cheek, then went to the door and opened it making sure that the gesture was one of simple politeness and not a dismissal.

Madam Max stared at her for a moment, her laser eyes switched off, then brushed her cheek with her hand murmuring, 'So beautiful.' Then, 'Good night, my dear child. Sleep well.'

Elaine felt that she was a little closer to understanding this woman, and that was helpful. One should always understand the enemy.

7
On the Scent

In the morning Elaine found Madam Max in the office. 'Ah, Elaine. Good morning. You have a good habit of punctuality.' She smiled indulgently. 'This morning we are going to inspect the dormitory. You have seen some of my professional girls. They have their own rooms, are well paid and are here voluntarily. However there are many tasks about the place for which a professional is not necessary or which are, in fact, performed better by amateurs. Then there is the cooking and cleaning to be done. The dormitory girls do these jobs. They are not here voluntarily. They are here because I know things about them which they don't want anyone else to know. Often they are criminals who don't want to go to prison. Sometimes they are runaways, who don't want husbands or lovers to find them. For whatever reason, they find that working here for a month or so is a convenient way of avoiding something worse.

'I demand order and discipline in everything that goes on in this house, and that includes the way the dormitory girls live and behave. You have seen me discipline my professionals. These other girls do not have the constraint of a job to be looked after, so the method of dealing with them has to be slightly different. I have chosen to use the technique employed, at one time, in the armed forces. But you will see.' She glanced at her watch. 'Come with me.'

She led the way through the house and, arriving at a door, threw it open and walked in. Immediately a voice called, 'Ten-shun!' Following her, Elaine saw that it was a large, light and bright room; one end of it the usual mirror-wall. Down each side of it, regularly spaced, were eight army-style beds framed with tubular metal. In each bed-space there were two lockers one short and one tall. The doors stood open, all at the same angle. Each mattress was covered with a single blanket, tightly stretched, on which were laid out various items. At the head of each bed, the bedding was neatly folded in a pile, with front edges exposed and aligned; blanket-sheet, blanket-sheet, blanket, with a fourth blanket tightly wrapped around to secure them, the corners squared.

Elaine could see that the contents of the lockers were similarly displayed, a section of each garment appearing to have been wrapped around folded cardboard so as to present a neat appearance. At the foot of each bed a girl stood rigidly to attention. Elaine judged them all to be in their twenties. They were uniformly dressed in white, polo-neck sweaters, black PT skirts, white ankle socks and white plimsolls. She followed Madam Max as she began her inspection, stalking down the line, her laser eyes everywhere. She began by looking each girl up and down, from head to toe, before passing on to the items laid out on the bed: knife, fork, spoon, mug, toothbrush, hairbrush, and so on; picking up something at random, for a closer look, then throwing it back again. As she finished with each girl and passed on, the girl remained at attention, but a relaxation of tension was apparent.

Arriving at the last girl, her inspection was unusually long and Elaine could see that it was causing considerable disquiet, not only for the recipient, but for the rest of the room. Finally, Madam Max said, 'You again, Lilian. Look at yourself, girl. You are filthy. Your plimsolls are filthy; your socks are filthy; your skirt is wrinkled and . . .' here, she took hold of a handful of hair and pulled the girl towards her, '. . . your hair is filthy. Don't you ever wash it?'

Elaine was not close enough to speak for the hair but, looking at the points Madam Max had made she could see only a small mark on one plimsoll, extending onto the sock, where the wearer had obviously caught her foot against something. There *was* one tiny wrinkle in her, otherwise, immaculately-pressed skirt.

Madam Max picked up a mug from the bed. 'Filthy!' she said, and threw it down. 'Look at the hairs in this brush!' Moving on to a locker, she pulled out the neat contents so that they fell on the floor. They were followed by a cascade of dirty laundry, half-empty sweet packets and crumpled magazines. Lilian went white and began to tremble. Turning to the rest of the girls, Madam Max said, 'I was quite satisfied with this inspection until I reached Lilian. I'm afraid she has let you down again. Double fire-buckets!'

She swept out and Elaine followed. Outside, she could not contain her curiosity. 'Double fire-buckets? Whatever does that mean?'

Madam Max smiled and pointed to a group of four sand-filled fire-buckets in the corridor. They were painted red on the outside and white on the inside. 'They will have to scrape all the paint off those, inside and out, using just their dinner knives, then polish

137

them until I can see my face in them. They show them to me and if I think they are good enough, I pass them. Then they repaint them. They will have to do that, twice; except that they use a different set of buckets second time around. Otherwise the paint would be soft and it would be too easy.'

Seeing Elaine's puzzlement she continued. 'You were expecting some more physical and perhaps, erotic punishment? Believe me; this one is effective. It is dirty and dusty. It spoils their hands and nails. It is totally pointless which removes even the satisfaction of a job well done. They hate it. But we must move quickly now, or we shall miss something.' She drew Elaine into the room next door explaining on the way. 'Mine is not the only discipline exerted in the dormitory. They have their own way of ensuring *esprit de corps*.'

She drew aside the expected curtain and revealed the room they had just left. 'As I thought. You are going to see a "roust".' She held up her hand to stop Elaine's question. 'Just watch and you'll see exactly what that means.'

Lilian was cowering on the floor, by her locker's scattered contents. The other girls were grouped about her, menacingly. One of them said, 'You did it to us again, Lilian. Now you're going to get it.' Lilian scrambled up and made a dash to escape, but she had no chance. She was thrown to the floor and they pounced on her. She fought and struggled like a wild thing, but she was held fast while her sweater was pulled up over her head, muffling her shouts and trapping her arms. Eager hands unclipped her bra and flipped it up so that her well-developed breasts flopped about, uncontrolled, then the sweater was removed completely and she was pinned down on her

138

back, gripped by her wrists and arms. Other hands were busy at the same time removing her plimsolls and socks, before moving on to grope at the waistband of her skirt. Her shrieks grew louder, but it was unfastened and pulled off. The same hands went into the waistband of her white, regulation knickers, dragging them down. For a while, she managed to keep her legs crossed, so that the panties came only halfway down her thighs, revealing her pubic hair and jiggling white bottom, then they were ripped from her and she was stripped. Her legs flailed wildly, regardless of the way this revealed all the details of her body, but were quickly brought under control. Panting, they held her, wriggling and naked. 'Get the mattress off her bed!' The mattress and blankets were dragged off onto the floor and she was lifted by her arms and legs, still struggling, to be flopped unceremoniously, face down onto the springs, her bare breasts and belly shrinking from the contact with the cold metal.

Her ankles were spread and tied to the foot of the bed with stockings; her wrists crossed and tied together to the centre of the tubing which formed the head. Two girls lay under the bed, trying to pull her breasts down through the wide mesh, but, aware of what would happen when they did that, she thwarted them for a while by heaving herself up on her arms. 'We can't do it. Sit on her, will you?' There was no shortage of girls to do that and her dangling breasts were pulled through the gaps in the mesh, tightly bound about with stockings, then tied together so that she could not retract them.

They paused for breath, then four girls took plimsolls in their hands and stood, two on each side. Lilian looking fearfully over her shoulder, began to shout, 'No! No! No,' the shout rising to a scream as the beating began. Each girl started to smack her bare bottom with a plimsoll, with no particular timing or rhythm, just as hard as she could, so that the sound of them was like a heavy shower of rain. The screaming and howling never stopped. Neither did the leaping and jumping of her rapidly reddening buttocks, the cheeks clenching and unclenching spasmodically, never knowing when to expect the next blow.

When their arms were tired they handed over to the next set of four, until all the girls had had a turn. Lilian lay sobbing, but the ordeal was not over. 'Go to the kitchen and get the stuff.'

Two girls went out of the room and Elaine asked. 'Where are they going? What stuff?'

'They are going to black her all over. They use a mixture they make up themselves from soot and margarine. It comes off afterwards, but only with a lot of scrubbing. By the time the day is over, she *will* be really clean – everywhere!'

Their attention returned to the room where the girls were still grouped around the hapless Lilian. 'She is too comfortable, like that. Let's give her something to think about while we wait.' Two girls went under the bed again, taking clothes pegs with them. Lilian's shouts and screams began again, as a peg was clamped firmly onto each nipple.

'Ow! Ow! It hurts!' Her shouts died away to moaning gasps of pain as she waited for the two errand-girls to return.

When they came back they were carrying two plastic buckets filled with a stiff, black sludge, and some rubber gloves. After some discussion as to who should have the honour, two girls put on gloves and gathering a double handful of the stuff, dumped it on

Lilian's bare back and began to smear it all over her and rub it in. When they got up to her neck, others took Lilian by the hair and forced her head over, so that the goo could be rubbed behind and in her ears and across the side of her face. Then it was smeared into her hair and scalp. The visible parts of her arms were treated and her fingers forced apart, so that it would go in between.

The top half completed, they repeated the process from the waist down. Completely covering her reddened bottom, they pulled the cheeks apart so as not to miss a square inch, even her anus and as far as they could reach between her legs. Down the thighs and legs to the feet; they blacked her soles and parted her toes to squeeze the stuff in between.

She screamed as her nipples were unpegged – the pain of this being almost as bad as having the pegs put on – then her breasts were freed and her ankles untied. She was flipped over and her ankles parted and retied, so that they could work on the front. Dollops of the stuff were plopped onto her bare belly, where a rubber-gloved finger made sure that it got well down into her navel. Working upwards they blacked her breasts, lifting each by the nipple to ensure that no creases were missed. Underarms and the parts of the arms missed before were covered, together with the palms of her hands. Then they were at the neck again and Lilian moved her head constantly, to try to avoid what was coming next, but it was firmly held and her face covered, including the creases of her eyelids and the inside of her nostrils.

They worked from the waist down again, and soon she was completely black, except for the triangle of her pubic hair, which they deliberately avoided. Looking down between her black and glistening breasts, Lilian saw this and knew what it meant. She began to beg and plead. 'No! Please! Not that! This is enough, isn't it?' But it wasn't, apparently. A mug was fetched and half filled with water, into which a white powder was poured and stirred in.

'What are they doing?' asked Elaine.

'It's plaster of Paris. It sets very quickly. They will pour a puddle of it into her pubic hair and keep her tied down until it sets really hard. She'll have to get it off herself, and the only way to do that is to pull out the hairs, one by one. Quite painful!'

Sobbing, groaning, and tugging ineffectually at her bonds, Lilian watched the plaster being poured onto her brown, curly, pubic hair. It was already stiffening. The first bit was rubbed well in, to make sure every hair would be trapped. Then the rest was puddled on, building to a flattened point, a bit like a soft ice cream cone. When they had finished they sat about, admiring their handiwork and gossiping, waiting for the plaster to dry. She was a pitiful sight lying there, tied down and helpless, her naked body completely black and shiny, except for the startling white of the cone of plaster.

After testing it a few times by tapping it, they satisfied themselves that the plaster was rock hard and released her. 'Off you go to the shower, Lilian! Get yourself clean, for once. Perhaps you'll think twice before you drop us in it again.' She trailed off dejectedly, walking with an awkward stoop because of the plaster and supporting its weight with her hands; her blackened feet slipping a little as she went.

'That is a "roust",' said Madam Max. 'Now you can see why my punishment was more effective than it might have seemed at first.'

Back in the office, Elaine fell into a pattern of

thought which was familiar to her and for a while forgot that her intent was infiltration. Businesslike, she asked all the questions that a new secretary had to, familiarising herself with an approximation of the filing system and the method of dealing with correspondence. 'You will find,' said Madam Max, 'that there are not many letters to type. To tradesmen and suppliers perhaps, but not to clients. You will understand that they prefer all communication to be by telephone, as it is more discreet. Most of them have pseudonyms or nicknames; sometimes just a number. If they have, they are always referred to in that way. Never by their proper names.'

'I'll need to familiarise myself with those,' Elaine said. 'Do you have a central register of all your clients?' She found that there were two basic card indexes; one for proper names and one for code-names, each cross-referenced. Accounts were dealt with professionally by an outside agency, so there was no book-keeping work to do. Madam Max's appointments diary was in the usual form and was always lying on her desk. The whole thing seemed completely open and above-board and Madam Max exhibited no concern about her having access to anything in the office. It seemed likely that, if there was anything incriminating in the house, the evidence of it was not in the office.

She smiled at Madam Max. 'I think I've got the hang of it. There will be a few more things, I'm sure, but it won't be until I get into the job that I will know the right questions to ask. I hope you will find that I can take a lot of burdens from you. I shall certainly try to do that.'

Madam Max returned her smile. 'I think we are going to get on very well, Elaine. Now I must attend to matters with which you cannot help. You will have to amuse yourself until after lunch, when I will show you some more of my clients.'

'That's all right,' said Elaine. 'I'll potter about here in the office, to get the feel of things, then I can go up to the Control Room.'

Left alone, it did not take her long to get the hang of Madam Max's office system, if it could be called that. Elaine was shocked at the inefficiency of it, having been used to computers at work. Badly kept files, badly kept index cards; she flitted through sufficient material to satisfy herself that her first guess had been right. There was nothing incriminating in that office, let alone anything about Sir James or Stewart.

Her mind turned away from the immediate problem to thoughts of her proposed red leather costume and she thought that she would take another look at Madam Max's outfit, if she wasn't using it; so after knocking, she wandered into the drawing room and fetched it from the cupboard where it was kept. She examined it with greater interest and care than before, noting the details of the workmanship in its construction, then re-wrapped it and put it back.

She looked around the large cupboard, wondering what it had been like for the man she had seen imprisoned there. With the door closed it was probably completely dark; and yet a TV camera had been able to watch him. She wondered how that had been arranged and on a whim she closed the door behind her. Immediately, a dim red lamp came on over her head, solving the puzzle. She was about to open the door again when she heard the drawing room door open and someone entered. A little embarrassed to be caught walking out of a closed cupboard in a room where she was not expected to be, she decided to wait, to see if whoever it was would leave again.

She heard the sound of a telephone in operation, then Madam Max said, 'I wish to speak to Mrs Ortez, wife of the Ambassador.'

There was a long pause, then she said, 'Mrs Ortez? I am the person who sent you the tapes. . . . My name is not important, although you will learn it in due time. All you need to know is that you must report to the address given at eleven in the morning, next Thursday. . . . Oh no! You must believe that I am not a person who makes jokes, Mrs Ortez. . . . Of course you must call the Police, if you think that is the right thing to do. I leave that entirely to your best judgement. But in the meantime I expect you to be here at eleven o'clock next Thursday. I do not tolerate inefficiency or disobedience, so if you are late, that will be too bad. The tapes will be distributed as I stated in the note which accompanied them.'

The receiver went down without ceremony, reminding Elaine of what she had heard on Sir James' answering machine. She held her breath for what seemed like ages, listening to rustling noises she could not identify, then, to her great relief, she heard Madam Max cross to the door and leave.

Elaine emerged from the cupboard and went over to the telephone, in case there was a pad with any helpful note, but there was nothing. She went back into the office. No entry had been made in the appointments diary. She went through the meagre records again, but all she could find was a card which bore the single name 'Ortez' and two numbers. She made a note of them and went off to the Control Room to see Stewart.

His smile, when she entered, made the day brighter and more worthwhile. She told him the results of her efforts in the office and what she had overheard said on the telephone.

'Ortez?' he said, rubbing his chin. 'That name rings a bell, but I can't think why.' About the numbers against the name in the card-file he was more helpful. 'You've forgotten what I told you about the video tapes. You need a tape number and a start position number to find any particular recording, and you've got both of those there. It's a fairly old tape, actually. You'll find it in the basement.'

'What sort of stuff is it which incriminates you, Stewart? I know that I am looking for tapes for Sir James, but is that what she has on you?'

'I don't know myself. Probably papers; receipts, that sort of thing. She doesn't really need anything, though. All she has to do is to talk to the wrong people and I'm dead. Evidence or not.'

With Stewart's help, Elaine collected some tapes which showed Madam Max to advantage in her role as a dominatrix, then went down into the basement. The numbering system seemed straightforward and she walked between the shelves of tapes, counting towards the one she wanted.

The only aberration was a section where, for a few feet, numbers gave way to letters of the alphabet. She smiled and shook her head ruefully. Madam Max's filing system again. The numbers picked up again after that, and she arrived at the tape she wanted. With it in her hand, she stopped and pondered. It couldn't be as easy as that. Surely blackmail material would all be stored together, not jumbled up like this with all the rest. What about that alphabet section? They were different.

She went to that section and chose a tape at random. When she tried to take it off the shelf, it wouldn't come. She tugged at it and the whole section of shelving moved. Looking more closely, she saw hinges at one side and realised that she was looking at a door. She pulled on it and it swung open, to reveal another door in the wall beyond. Hopefully, she turned the knob, but it was locked. Then she noticed the dial of a combination lock and her heart sank. Damn! She was willing to bet that everything she wanted was beyond that door and she couldn't get in. No chance of stealing a key, either. The combination must be in Madam Max's head.

She closed the shelving and went back to her room. Inserting the Ortez tape into her video, she rewound it and set the counter to zero, then went fast-forward to the second number on her pad. When she pressed 'Play', the screen flickered and she sat forward, staring with interest, which quickly turned to disappointment. She was looking at a bed, occupied by a young couple who were copulating enthusiastically, if not very expertly. She judged the girl to be no more than eighteen, dark-haired and olive-skinned. She was on top, bouncing vigorously, her breasts joggling with the movement. Her partner, white-skinned and not much older, was having a great time. Elaine watched them to the inevitable orgasm, when the tape flickered and the sequence ended, to be succeeded by a different couple. There was something here she did not understand. The girl did not look old enough to be Mrs anybody. And what she was doing was not blackmail material. It was perfectly standard sex. Millions of people all over the world were doing just that, right at this moment.

She checked the numbers again. There was no mistake. She had the right part of the tape. This must be a different Ortez. She was not as clever as she thought she had been. She ran quickly through some of the Madam Max tapes so that she could claim knowledge of them, if asked, then took the Ortez tape back to the basement. She would just have to get inside that locked door.

Elaine took her lunch in the canteen. She wanted to sound out some of the other girls to see what the chances were of recruiting one or more of them to her cause. Seeing several of the professional girls at one table she carried her own tray across there. 'Hello. I'm Elaine. Mind if I join you?'

Shelley said, 'Not at all. Draw up a chair. This is Claire, and Jill, and Diana. You've met me; I'm Shelley, and I expect you remember Rose, and Chiquita, and Mary. We've been wondering when we'd get a chance for a natter, ever since we saw you in the Blue Room.' She spoke of that with total unconcern, as though the occasion had been tea and sandwiches at some vicarage. It was to take Elaine some time to grasp that almost nothing could throw these girls off balance. No aberration or human foible surprised them. They had seen it all yet somehow, risen above it and remained untouched by it. In some mysterious way they could detach their personalities from their bodies, as though there was no connection between the two. The body went to work. The mind stayed at home, knitting socks.

'Gossip says you're going to be a fem/dom,' said Rose.

'I think so,' Elaine replied. 'I don't really know much about it, yet.'

'Well, just go easy on *my* bum if she sets you loose on us. It still bloody smarts from last time.'

Elaine was astonished. These girls could talk about the possibility of being disciplined by her without turning a hair – even make a joke of it. 'Why do you put up with that?' she asked.

Chiquita shrugged. 'The money's great. There are drawbacks to everything. It's better than getting punched about by some bloody great, ham-fisted ponce.' They all nodded agreement.

'So you really like Madam Max?' Elaine addressed the question to them all.

'I wouldn't go so far as to say that,' said Shelley. 'She's too weird to really like.'

Mary chipped in, 'Spiteful bitch, if you ask me. My arse is going to itch for days. Like ants in the pants.' There was a general giggle.

Elaine was genuinely curious about something. 'I'm new to all this. How do you manage to go with . . . I mean, deal with . . . I mean, so many different . . ?'

'Oh, you mean, how do we manage to screw lots of different blokes on the same day,' said Mary. 'You just get used to it. After a while, they're all the same.'

There was a chorus of disagreement. 'No, they're not,' said Rose. 'What about the White Rabbit?'

'Oh, well. The White Rabbit. Yes, he is different,' said Mary. She explained to Elaine. 'He's a dear old boy. Wife's an invalid, but he sticks with her and does everything for her. Comes here every now and again for a bit of what she can't give him any more. Won't use the same girl too often, in case he gets attached. Lovely in bed. All soft and gentle – no grabbing and groping. Even makes me come sometimes. Oh, yes. We all volunteer for him.'

'Polite too,' said Shelley. 'Always takes his hat off.' There were more giggles.

'Then there are the weirdos,' said Shelley. 'We get a few of those. What about Mr Smith?'

'Oh Gawd! Mr Smith!' said Rose. 'You strip off and he strips off and you both stand in front of this

149

mirror. Then he reaches round from behind you and feels your nose, while he wanks himself off. Honest! Nothing else. Just a nose groper!' More giggles.

'And Circus Dan!' Mary contributed. 'Just wants you to prance about, in the nuddy, with an ostrich feather up your bum. Weirdos! Another cup of tea, anyone? I'm in the chair.'

All in all, a very educational business lunch, thought Elaine. After that, she made it a habit to eat in the canteen and took the opportunity to talk to everyone she could. The dormitory girls did not take such a philosophical view of Madam Max. They were not free to leave and they hated her for it, and for her disciplinary methods. Still, Elaine could not see any way of using this disaffection to her advantage. The dormitory girls were like slaves and had very little freedom of movement to help her in her quest.

After lunch, Elaine discussed with Madam Max the design of her red leather costume and they jotted down their ideas on several sheets of paper, to be sent off to the saddler. Then Madam Max led the way along the corridors, explaining as she went. 'We try to cater for every type of fantasy. No trouble, or expense is too great to provide exactly what the client wants. Sometimes, I have to admit, it is hard to understand *why* they should want it but that is not my business. I have to know only that they do, and can pay accordingly.'

Opening the door of a side room, she led the way in saying, 'Now, this one is not hard to understand. I think you will agree with that. She comes only once a month, which was why I was glad to catch you.' She drew the curtain. The room beyond was large and contained a large, four-poster bed. The only light was provided by a hearth, from which an open fire projected a cosy glow. A large part of the floor was covered with a thick, plastic sheet, the edges of which were supported, so that it formed a very shallow dish. In the centre of this was a group of naked people and, for a moment, Elaine could not make out details in the gloom. As her eyes grew accustomed to the dark, she saw that a naked woman was lying in the centre of the sheet. She was in her thirties, with auburn hair and a very good figure. She was surrounded by six naked men, three on each side. The men seemed all to be in their early twenties, tanned and muscular. They were lathering the woman all over with soap. Their hands never stopped moving as they rubbed and massaged every part of her: breasts, belly, back, buttocks, thighs, seemingly all at the same time. Twelve hands were in constant contact.

Even from where she stood, Elaine could tell that what was happening was enormously satisfying to the woman. Her eyes were half-closed and she seemed to be almost asleep, responding languorously to the feel of what was being done to her. Occasionally, she would reach out to one of the young men and pull his head down, so that they could exchange a long, open-mouthed kiss. At other times, she would reach out for one of the erect penises which were so conveniently close and soap and massage it, then leave it and find another to play with.

The scene, with the firelight glinting on the bare bodies, was extraordinarily erotic and Elaine found herself becoming most stimulated by it. She caught herself smiling at the thought of the delicious pleasure the woman must be experiencing.

Then the woman seemed to find a penis which particularly pleased her. She rolled onto her back and spread her soapy thighs, guiding the young man by the penis, around between them, until she could introduce it into her vagina. He came down onto her breasts, crushing them beneath his chest, and her slippery hands caressed his broad, muscular back, as he gave her what she wanted. His slow and deliberate thrusts were matched by her pelvic movements as she contracted the muscles in her buttocks, so that her pubes rose up to meet his each time.

All the time, the hands of the other men never stopped stroking, massaging and lathering the parts of her body they could reach. It was not easy to tell the moment when she came to orgasm. It was not a violent one, but from her movements, Elaine could tell that it was deeply satisfying. The young man rolled off and took his place at her side, again. The lathering and kissing continued for a while, then she guided another young man between her legs and took her pleasure again, experiencing another dreamy and leisurely orgasm.

She rested awhile by turning onto her stomach, her soapy breasts flattened against the plastic, while they devoted their attention to her shoulders, back and bottom. When she got up onto hands and knees, the kissing began again, until a third young man mounted her from the rear, plunged his long, erect penis between her soapy thighs and brought her to climax. She sighed deeply, and slid over onto her back again, so that the process could continue.

'We believe her to be capable of an infinite number of orgasms,' said Madam Max. 'The young men are self-disciplined enough to be able to service her many times without ejaculating. Sometimes though, she is too much for them, even though there are six of them, and by taking them so often she induces them to climax, in spite of their best intentions. Usually, the end for her, comes about through sheer physical weariness. I think we are getting near that point now; see how the movement of her hips is slowing down.'

Just then, the naked man who was on top of her increased his motion, his soapy belly sliding easily on her equally slippery skin. He gave way and, with a great cry, pumped sperm into her, his buttocks jerking in hefty pelvic thrusts, his testicles rising and tightening as he did so. That seemed to be the last straw for the woman too, and her orgasm was more apparent than any of the others had been. She lay back panting, making feeble gestures with her hands. 'Enough! Enough! No more . . .' Her voice died away and she seemed on the point of fainting with weariness.

They gathered around and lifted her up onto her feet, where they had to support her to prevent her knees from giving way and allowing her to fall. One brought a hose with a spray attachment and they showered away all the lather with warm water, then wrapped her closely in a big, fluffy towel and patted her dry. One picked her up in his arms and carried her to the bed, which was turned down and ready. With help, he posted her under the crisp, starched, linen sheets and tucked her in. She snuggled into the soft, snow white pillow, murmuring, 'Thank you, boys . . . Thank you . . . so much . . . That was . . . lovely . . .' and she was asleep.

The men busied themselves about the room, like a well-drilled team. In no time, they had drained the sheet through a tube in one corner, collected all the signs of their recent activity and left, closing the door gently behind them. The woman slept on. Her face, in the firelight, a picture of peaceful relaxation.

'She will sleep right through, until tomorrow morning, then be as bright as a button and right on top of her executive job,' Madam Max said.

Elaine was intrigued. 'That was a lovely fantasy. Did you think of it?'

'No. It has been all her own doing. Not arrived at all at once, you understand, but by a process of gradual development, over a period of time.'

Elaine was imagining how it must have felt, to be soaped all over and serviced by six men, then allowed to sleep it off in a huge, comfortable bed by a warm fire. Lovely! 'It must be very popular,' she said.

'To any woman who can have an unlimited number of orgasms and exhaust six strong, young men – yes.' Madam Max's smile was sardonic. 'I can't understand why they aren't queuing round the block.'

She led Elaine back into the corridor. 'What you saw there was an example of some of my professional staff dealing with a client. Sometimes, the fantasies of two clients complement one another and it is convenient to unite them.' She led Elaine into another room. This one overlooked quite a small bedroom. A nude woman was bending over the bed, her back to them. She was substantially overweight; her hips wide and her breasts huge. There was a man on the bed. His hands were strapped behind his back and his ankles and knees were strapped together. He wore a diaper about his loins, fastened with a large safety pin. He had a frilly cap on his head and a large dummy in his mouth which was retained there by a ribbon around the back of his head. The woman climbed onto the bed and lifted his head and shoulders, so that she could sit beneath him, his upper body in her lap. In this position, Elaine could see that her nipples were extraordinarily long and large, set so far down her breasts that they pointed almost directly downwards.

She leaned forward, so that one of her breasts rested on his face and almost completely concealed it, while her right hand reached down and slid into the top of the diaper.

'Oh, good. You don't need changing yet. Feeding time.' She untied the ribbon and removed the dummy then cradling his head in the crook of her left arm, she raised her left breast with her right hand, squeezing it with thumb and finger, so that the nipple stuck out even further. She brushed his lips with her nipple and, after a few moments, he opened his mouth and took it in. The movement of his mouth and jaw showed that he had begun to suckle and the woman threw back her head and gasped with pleasure. Her unoccupied right hand went under his body and between her legs and Elaine could see, between her parted thighs, that she was masturbating. After quite a while, she withdrew her hand and used it to pull the nipple from his mouth, replacing it with the other. Then her hand went back to its masturbatory activity. Quite soon after that, there were definite signs that she was enjoying a massive orgasm.

She replaced and retied the dummy. Again, her right hand dipped into the napkin. 'Time for a change, I think.' She heaved him up and wriggled down until she was under his hips, placing pillows under his upper body to support it. She unfastened the safety pin and laid the napkin open, exclaiming in apparent surprise at the size of his penis, which was erect. He had been shaved, smooth and hairless. 'Better just check your temperature while we're about it.' She heaved again and turned him over, face down, his bottom sticking up and his erect penis clamped between her thighs. Taking a bottle of baby oil, she trickled a generous amount into the cleft of his buttocks and, pulling his bottom cheeks apart with one hand, she rubbed the oil into the area all around his anus. She took a thin vibrator and slavered oil on it, then put the point of it in the centre of his sphincter, which twitched and puckered at the touch.

He writhed, as though to get free, but was held by the penis and restrained by the straps, so there was nothing he could do to prevent the entry of the vibrator. She switched it on and his efforts redoubled when he heard the noise. 'Hold still, baby. This is for your own good,' she said. And parting the cheeks again, she inserted the tip of the buzzing instrument a tiny way and held it until his movements and moans had subsided a little, then advanced it, in gradual steps, until the whole length had disappeared.

Elaine decided that he must be experiencing the most intense sensations because he continued to move and groan the whole time it was in there. Then she withdrew it, slowly and carefully. Judging by his reactions, this was as traumatic a feeling as having it inserted. She held it up and pretended to read it as if it were a thermometer. 'That's normal,' she said, and turned him face-up again. By this time, his penis was purple with engorged blood. The glans hugely swollen and the veins standing out. 'We'll just put some oil on you to make you comfortable,' the woman said, and poured baby oil all over his penis and testicles.

She massaged it in, beginning with the shaved, pubic area, then moving on to his testicles; handling these delicate objects with great care. When she finally gripped his penis with her oily hand, his whole body gave a convulsive leap, his head went back and small, whining noises of desire issued from behind the dummy. She began to massage his penis up and down, slowly and softly, and he moaned and thrust himself up towards the source of pleasure. Without stopping the actions with her right hand, she unfastened his dummy with her left and his mouth immediately sought the nearest available nipple.

Her masturbation of him quickened and became more insistent, finger and thumb gripping tightly around his penis, just below the glans. His thrusting and sucking became more urgent. Then her right hand was just a blur, rubbing, rubbing, rubbing until he gave a great cry as, with massive pelvic thrusts, a fountain of white sperm jetted from the tip of his penis in a long, high arc, which she directed onto her breasts. The woman cradled him even more closely, rubbing his sperm over her nipples and massaging it into his pubic area.

'Time for one more, I think,' said Madam Max and took Elaine to another side room. The room they looked into appeared to be a dungeon, the rough, stone walls realistically shiny with green dampness. From the ceiling, a pair of wires supported each end of a trapeze bar with rings at its extremities. There were two rings in the floor below, the same distance apart. Between the two rings was a short, upright post, on top of which was fastened the thickest and longest rubber penis Elaine had ever seen, pointing upwards at a natural angle. A man she recognised as Hans was waiting in the room. He was naked from the waist up and splendidly muscular, she noted. His lower body was concealed by tight-fitting, black leather trousers.

The door opened and two similarly dressed men came in, pushing a trolley. It was an ordinary, rubber-tyred, commercial trolley, such as is used for taking tea around offices, or carrying domestic cleaning equipment. Perhaps it was the prosaic nature of the vehicle which made it all the more erotic that a naked woman should be strapped to the front of it. Her hips just perched on the front end. Her thighs were parted by leather cuffs about her ankles, which were attached to the front legs of the trolley, so that her sex was displayed; her pubes thrust into prominence by the fact that cuffs on her wrists were secured to the other end of the trolley, bending her backwards. Written in lipstick, in large letters across her bare, white belly, just above the tuft of pubic hair, was the word, 'Masturbator'.

Madam Max explained. 'She has been wheeled about the house in that state for the past half hour. My staff all know that whenever they see her, they are to touch her in intimate places and make comments about the way she looks and what they know is going to happen to her.'

The trolley was turned to face Hans. 'You have been caught in the act of masturbation. That is a wicked, evil practice, and has to be stamped out.' He signed to the two guards and they unclipped her from the trolley and dragged her to the trapeze. Her wrists were clipped to the rings at either end and her ankles to the rings in the floor, spreading her legs wide. One of the guards turned a crank and the trapeze went up until her arms were just above her head, her elbows bent. The tip of the penis was at the level of her crotch, brushing against it.

'Part of your punishment is concluded. You have been exhibited naked. Everyone has seen your tits and your cunt, haven't they?' She hung her head, silent. 'Tell me. What has everyone seen?'

'I . . . I . . . I can't say those words.'

'I think you'll find that you can, after I have thrashed your bare arse for a while. Do you want me to thrash your bare arse?' She shook her head. 'Speak, then!'

'I . . . I can't.'

Her inquisitor took a leather strap from a hook on the wall, stepped up beside her and slashed it across her buttocks. Again and again, the belt fell with a slap, striking indiscriminately on her bottom, thighs and back. She jumped at each stroke and cried out, but Elaine noticed that she was pushing back towards the punishment, not pulling away from it and her shouts were not those of pure pain without pleasure.

She sagged. 'All right! All right! I'll speak!'

'What will you say?'

'I'll say that . . . that everyone . . .' The belt fell again, three times. 'That everyone has seen my tits and my cunt.' Her voice was a shout, then her head hung again, as though in fear and shame.

'She just loves coarse words,' said Madam Max. They are a big turn-on for her, but she couldn't dream of saying them voluntarily.'

'She *wants* this?' said Elaine, incredulously. 'But, the pain . . . the strap?'

'Oh, there's no doubt it stings a bit,' said Madam Max. Look at the red marks. But it is a broad belt and not heavy, so it is not doing any permanent damage. She knows how much she wants and can stand and she is in complete control. Even if she went berserk and volunteered for more than was good for her, my men are all professionals. They would stop before she could cause herself any damage, without destroying the mood of the game.'

'*She* is in control?'

'Sure she is. This is not reality. It is fantasy. *Her* fantasy, designed by her, for her pleasure. There are some sensations she likes to experience, but in real life modesty or upbringing, conscience or social pressures, prevent that. Here, in this game, she is forced to do those things she wanted to do all along. So long as she maintains the continuity of the fantasy, nothing that happens can be her fault. When she wants the beating to stop, she simply says the awful words she has been longing to say, and the game moves on to the next stage.'

Elaine's attention returned to the room, where Hans was saying, 'Next, I want to hear you beg to have your titties sucked and a finger in your pussy.'

'No! No! I couldn't . . .'

The beating began again. This time the strap fell on bare breasts and stomach. 'Enough! Enough! I'll say it!'

'Say what?'

'I want to have my . . . titties sucked and a finger in my . . . pussy.' He signed to the guards. So you shall, my dear. So you shall. They came in front of her and each took one of her nipples in his mouth, while each of them inserted two fingers into her vagina, masturbating her. She leaned towards them groaning softly with pleasure and her hips began a slow, rhythmic undulation. The men stopped and stepped away before she could begin to climax.

Hans came forward and smeared a liberal quantity of lubricating jelly over the rubber penis. This seemed to Elaine, who could see the woman's own, natural juices glistening on her inner thighs, to be superfluous.

'She's built to take one that size,' said Madam Max. 'Not many women could. She likes to feel herself being stretched inside.'

'Now you are going to beg to be allowed to fuck yourself by taking this big prick up your cunt,' said

160

Hans, and the strapping started again. This time, it was not long before the required obscenity was uttered, and it seemed to Elaine that the woman was inspired, not by the pain of the beating, but by the eagerness of her own anticipation.

'Get it up you, then and be sharp about it.' Elaine understood then, why the woman's arms had not been fully extended. As she was, she had enough slack so that by leaning her body just a little forward and bending her knees, she was able to introduce the tip of the penis into her vagina. '*All* of it!' commanded Hans and slashed with the belt at her marked bottom. Slowly, wincing and grimacing, she sank lower, until she had its full length. Elaine could see her lips moving and guessed that she was repeating the forbidden words, over and over again.

'Now I want to see some movement in that fat arse of yours.' He stepped up and began to slap her buttocks sharply. At each slap she flexed her knees, so that the penis went up and down, first pulling, then pushing at the spread lips of her sex. It was obvious, from her movements and the beatific expression on her face, that she was not far from orgasm.

He stopped his slapping and smeared gel on his right ring finger. He held it up for her to see. 'Now, I'm going to finger-fuck your bum and diddle your clitty at the same time.' His left hand parted her bottom cheeks, exposing her anus. Her inserted his slippery finger and held it there, while she wiggled wildly on it.

She was too far gone to pretend modesty and reluctance. 'Yes! Yes! Finger ... Fuck ... Bum ... Prick ... Big ... Pussy.' Her hips gyrated uncontrollably as she extracted the last ounce of sensation from the penis.

He reached across her belly with his left hand and

fumbled through her pubic hair until he found her clitoris. With his mouth close to her ear, he hissed, 'Bitch! Whore! Masturbator! Shit-eater! Pussy-lapper! Piss drinker! Cock sucker!' Her groans became a scream; a constant stream of hoarse, gasping shouts. All the obscenities she had ever heard poured from her lips, slurred with passion. She came in copious floods, then collapsed, supported only by her wrists and the prop of the penis.

'Time for a cup of tea, I think,' said Madam Max. And they went back to the drawing room.

As they sat, sipping tea from delicate china and nibbling on tiny biscuits, Elaine was struck by the incongruity of this scene and those she had recently witnessed. With growing confidence in her rapport with Madam Max, she dared to voice that thought, saying that she found it strange.

'Why should that be?' said Madam Max. 'You would not find it strange that there should be a contrast between the work and leisure environment if it were a different occupation. The boxer who goes home to tend his aviary; the miner who sleeps between clean sheets. This is no different. It is a trade; a business; an occupation.'

'Yes. But it's . . .' Elaine could not put her thoughts into words which would not sound offensive.

Madam Max supplied options for the rest of her sentence. 'Immoral? Rude? Impure? Prostitution? You are accepting labels and values which society has placed upon sexual pleasure. The assumption that, if it feels good, it cannot possibly be right to enjoy it. How very puritan of you. Does not a composer of great music play upon the senses? The poet? The truly great dramatist? The very funny comedian? They can move audiences to tears or laughter and are applauded and rewarded for it. During Cromwell's Protectorship, music, dancing and fun were evil things. Works of the Devil to be set aside by right-minded persons. Now, they are not. It is only the fashion of the moment that makes what I do seem wrong.

'I, too, play upon the senses. The things I create move people deeply; sometimes make them happier. Who is to judge, and say that to pluck one string of the human harp is right, but to pluck another is wrong? Sensuality and the imagination to fantasise are given to all as an essential part of their jigsaw. Many accept the gifts gladly. Some do not and, through some distorted concept of the 'rightness' of denying their own bodies' needs, bury it deep in guilt. Theirs is the true perversion, not mine.

'Yet, perhaps, I should be grateful that society takes the view that it does. All the while it continues to do so, I shall have a successful and profitable business. Let us not forget that is what it is. I am not a social worker. If people want what I can offer them, they pay for it, and that is what matters to me.' She patted Elaine's arm. 'You see, dear. You touched a nerve and got me on my soap box.'

8
Party Time

The following day when Elaine met Stewart in the Control Room, she told him about the secret door in the basement and about what she had seen on the Ortez tape.

'I may be able to shed some light there,' he said, and produced a crumpled newspaper, opened at a page which showed a rather fuzzy photograph and a trivial news item. It looked as if it had come from some small, local newspaper. 'Could that be the girl in the video?'

Elaine stared at it. 'It's not a very good photo, so it's hard to tell; and the girl in the video had her back to the camera most of the time. It certainly looks like her; same skin, same hair.' She read the short paragraph. She was apparently the daughter of a Bolivian diplomat. Her parents were proud to announce her engagement to Ramesh Khan, fantastically wealthy heir to what appeared to be three quarters of India.

'I suddenly remembered reading about her. Luckily I was able to rescue the paper from the basket before it was cleared.'

'What do you think it means?' asked Elaine.

'If it *is* the same girl, then blackmail is quite on the cards. To marry a Khan, she would definitely have to be a virgin. As the appointment is with a *Mrs* Ortez, sounds as if the target is the proud mum, who, presumably, would do anything to prevent a spanner in the marriage works. If only we could get a record of that meeting, it would be a lever to hold over Madam Max. Then we could get her to cough up Sir James' tapes and maybe even stop her from telling on me.'

Elaine said, 'But that isn't a problem, surely? I mean, you're up here in the Control Room and . . .'

'That's just the snag. Whenever there is a blackmail meeting, she gets Joe, my assistant up here. He's in it just for the money and he does exactly what he's told. I shan't be able to get near the place while she is doing her stuff. And by the time I get back the tape will have been edited and anything which incriminates Madam Max will have been erased.'

Elaine pretended an optimism she did not feel. 'I'm sure, if we think about it, we can come up with something.'

Just before eleven thirty, Madam Max called for her and took her to the room alongside the dormitory. It was empty. Elaine was puzzled. 'We were here before. Is there more to see?'

'You will not see the dormitory girls in action, today. This requires professionals. We use this room because it is a convenient location and saves having one specially equipped.' As Madam Max spoke, the door opened and four of the professional girls came in. Shelley and Chiquita were there. Elaine had not seen the other two before. They sat about, talking and laughing, until the room lights blinked on and off. Then they got up and began to undress. Elaine watched them without understanding. Then something odd struck her. They were not stripping casually, but with elaborate care, as if on stage. To roll

166

stockings down, they did not sit on the bed, but put their foot up on a chair, hitching skirts to show generous amounts of thigh and suspenders. In pulling dresses over their heads they remained, for long moments, at full stretch with head and arms muffled, showing off their underwear.

Madam Max supplied the explanation. 'The client is outside the door peeping through the keyhole.' The girls continued with their strip-tease, until some were nude and others close to it, at which point the door was suddenly flung open and six more girls bundled through it, holding between them the struggling form of a man. Elaine recognised Rose and Mary among that group. They threw the man to the floor, face-down, and sat on him. Mary said, 'We caught this object peeping at you through the keyhole. What shall we do with him?'

Chiquita feigned astonishment. 'He *was*? The filthy beast. I think he ought to be stripped naked, don't you, girls?'

With a chorus of yesses they set about it. Under the sheer weight of bodies, the man could do nothing as his shoes and socks were removed.

Chiquita was giving instructions. 'Now turn him over. Hold him! Let's have his trousers off. Rose! Get his belt!' The trousers were heaved down and off, emerging in an arc from the writhing heap. Elaine was reminded of a flock of starlings around a bread crust.

'Have his pants off, too. That's right!' These followed the trousers through the air. 'Now pull his shirt up and let's see what we've got.' Gripped by a multitude of hands, the man lay on his back naked up as far as the navel, his penis erect and straining. Chiquita stooped beside him and took his testicles in

167

her left hand. I'm sure you don't want us doing all this work, do you? Perhaps you'd like to take the rest off, yourself?'

'No! Certainly not! Let me go! I ... Aaargh! Nnnngg!' Chiquita had tightened her grip on his scrotum. 'I didn't quite catch that. What did you say?'

'I said, "No!" Aaargh! Aaargh! I mean, yes, yes.'

'You're quite sure now?' Another squeeze.

'Yes, yes! Aaargh! Look, I'm doing it.' His hands were working on his tie. As quickly as he could, he divested himself of his upper clothing, wriggling out of his jacket and pulling his shirt over his head. Naked, he rested on his elbows, looking down at Chiquita's hand in dread.

'Now, we are going to help you up, and we are going to back over to that bed, there. Slowly and carefully, I suggest, because if my hand slips, these little things . . .' She gave another squeeze in emphasis, eliciting another yelp, '. . . could get torn right off.'

They all got up together, and moved in a group, he backing, making no incautious moves. He felt the edge of the bed behind his legs. 'Sit!' He sat. 'Lie back!' He did. 'Pick your feet up!' Done. They took his arms and spread them above his head, securing his wrists to the frame with soft, white ropes. When they had similarly tied his spread ankles to the bottom of the bed, Chiquita relaxed her hold and stood up. He looked ridiculous and helpless, spread out like a naked, white starfish; his rib-cage thrown into prominence and the stalk of his penis exposed, so stiff that it did not touch his belly at all, in spite of his horizontal pose.

'What are you going to do to me?'

Chiquita pinched his penis delicately between fin-

168

ger and thumb. He craned down to see what was happening. 'First, we are going to give this naughty thing a good spanking, to make it nice and tender. Somebody find a ruler.'

He squirmed and begged, 'No! No! Please!' She loomed over him, flexing the ruler in her hands. 'No! Please! Not that! I'm sorry. Ow! Ouch! Ow!' The middle of his body bounced up off the bed to meet each stroke, as it was applied. Elaine noticed that she was using the flat of the ruler and not really striking hard, just tapping. All the same, the maltreated length of his penis grew quite red and must have smarted. She stopped and he lay still. The only part of him moving was his penis, which twitched convulsively.

'Suppose you were a girl. You wouldn't like to be peeped at, would you?' Then, as if the thought had just occurred to her, 'That's it. You *shall* be a girl. Just a minute though. Too much hair for a girl. Never mind. We can fix that.' Razors and a can of shaving cream were brought and, amid lots of giggles, the cream was squirted onto him and many hands spread it all over his body until he was covered from shoulders to knees. Then they set to and shaved him, four or five of them at a time, working on different parts. They shaved under his arms and across his chest. Down across his belly and down his thighs. They lingered long on his pubic hair and testicles. When they finally wiped away the remnants of lather with a damp cloth, the whole of the front of his body was completely hairless and smooth.

'Now, clothes. Stockings first, I think.' Chiquita trailed a pair of sheer, black stockings across his face. 'Feel how silky they are. You'll love them.' She sat down on the bed beside him and resumed her grip on his testicles. 'When we untie your ankle, you will not struggle. You will raise your leg straight up in the air and point your toe.' He obeyed and a couple of girls slid a silky stocking onto his leg and pulled it up to his thigh. The other leg was similarly dealt with and his ankles temporarily secured again. 'Now, a nice, black, frilly suspender belt for the little girl.' They slid this garment under him, fastened it, then rotated it, so that the clip was at the back and did up the suspenders.

'Nice girls don't go about with no knickers on. How about these nice, silky, black ones?' She gripped him again. 'Same rules. We let your legs go and you co-operate.' They slid the garment up his legs and refastened his ankles, tying them together. Not until he was secured again did she remove her hand from inside the knickers. She rubbed the material against his bald pubes and penis. 'Doesn't that feel nice? Now, a nice bit of make-up.'

They applied foundation and powder, lipstick and eye-liner and, for a finishing touch, put him into a blonde wig. 'His breasts are a bit small. We can't do much about that but we can make his nipples more prominent. Chiquita took a good pinch of skin on either side of his nipples and applied a clothes peg to each. He groaned and writhed in discomfort, trying to shake them loose, but the girls took no notice.

'Now, it's rape time, and it's going to be a gang bang. Pull his knickers down!' When he was exposed, Chiquita sat on the bed by him. 'Listen. You are going to be raped and we all want to have you. If you dare to come before we've all finished, I shall shave all the hair off your head and put clothes pegs all over you. I guess your penis would take about twelve. You've been warned. Don't forget!' With that, she straddled him. Facing his feet and with an ease born of long practice, she slipped his penis into her vagina and began to move up and down on him, stimulating her clitoris with her fingers. The man's face bore a grimace of intense concentration as he fought to hold back his natural instincts and prevent an ejaculation. Chiquita looked over her shoulder. 'There's a perfectly good mouth going to waste, there.' Rose straddled him, behind Chiquita but facing the same way, and thrust her buttocks backwards until her cleft ground into his face. Chiquita said, 'Don't worry. If you can bring her off like that, she won't need to rape this end and your troubles will be over sooner. Rosie. Let me know if he isn't doing his duty and I'll give his balls a reminder.'

Judging by the man's mouth, throat and jaw movements, and Rose's expression, Elaine judged that he was doing a good job. Presently, Chiquita shuddered into orgasm; whether faked or not, Elaine could not tell. She got off and her place was taken by another girl. When Rose had taken her pleasure, she too was replaced. In this way all ten of them satisfied themselves. Elaine noted that when Mary was riding him, it was clear, from his discomfort, that her hair had grown to a prickly stubble.

After that they took it in turns to masturbate him, judging the moment precisely, so that just as he was about to ejaculate, they stopped; leaving him for long minutes, his penis twitching with pelvic thrusts into empty air in a vain attempt to finish as he begged them to go on. When Shelley finally took him in her strong hand and did *not* stop, his ejaculation was massive; sperm flying high in the air in great, white spurts.

* * *

The large room was a glittering, sparkling scene. Lights from the chandeliers overhead glinted off the glasses and bottles, as well as showing to best advantage the expensive jewellery worn by many of the women. Madam Max and Elaine sat side by side on a comfortable couch in the adjoining room, behind the one-way mirror. Small tables held their drinks, obtained from the usual cabinet. Madam Max said, 'There is a lot of competition to be invited to these parties. I don't have too many of them so they have a scarcity value which puts the price up. This is *the* place to be. Here you will see a selection of some of the richest and the most famous people in the land. Lawyers, politicians, pop-stars: they are all grist to my mill.'

Elaine studied the scene with renewed interest. Now that it had been mentioned, there were some familiar faces, as well as some she felt she ought to know, but didn't. Waitresses moved amongst the guests with drinks and snacks. Elaine recognised them as dormitory girls. They were all stark naked, or at least, she thought they were until one came and stood very close to the transparent mirror so she could see that she wore a minute fragment of material, smaller than her patch of pubic hair and held on by a slender thread around the waist and between the legs. Following the direction of her gaze, Madam Max said, 'Somewhere to put their tips.' Indeed, at the very moment she spoke, one of the male guests pushed a note into the top of the garment. Elaine noticed that to do so he used his whole hand, shoving it well down, and taking his time about removing it.

The girl showed no emotion or reaction. Looking around the room, Elaine saw that the other girls were being groped in a similar fashion, as well as having other parts of their bodies molested; and not only by the male guests. It satisfied the feminist in her to note that there were male waiters as well, with equally inadequate covering. They, too, were receiving their share of attention from male and female alike.

Among the female guests Elaine observed the older of the two women she had seen making love to each other in the oil bath. She looked around but could not see the other half of the partnership. Indeed, as far as she could make out, Peggy was with a new companion. Younger, dark and petite, she was never allowed far from Peggy's side. There was some evidence that she did not entirely welcome this attention because a couple of times, when Peggy affectionately placed an arm across her shoulders or around her waist, she shrugged off the embrace.

Elaine drew Madam Max's attention to this. 'Peggy seems to have a new friend tonight. Where's Jane?'

'It is a very interesting story and a juicy piece of gossip. Peggy went out of her way to see that Jane wasn't invited. She is very taken with the little, dark one – Annie – but she hasn't made much progress so far. She plans to make her move tonight and she doesn't want Jane around to get in the way.'

Elaine nodded. The information was interesting, as gossip always is, but not earth-shattering. As the evening went on and the drink flowed, she wondered what would be the 'special performance' Madam Max had mentioned. Apparently it was not the display of intercourse put on by Mary and one of the guards. Apart from one or two couples who gathered around the raised dais at the other end of the room, on which they gave their performance, there was not a great deal of interest shown. A lesbian display by

Chiquita and Shelley was marginally better received, but it was clear that these were only warm-up acts and that everyone was waiting for more interesting things to happen.

The pace began to quicken when it was announced that there would be a draw for a very special prize: the Dish of the Day. On entry, all the guests had been issued with numbered, mother-of-pearl tokens. A number was to be drawn from a barrel and whoever had the corresponding token would be the winner. Amid much genial cat-calling, a ticket was drawn and the announcement made. 'Number forty-two.'

There was the usual pause, then a short, red-haired girl gave an excited shout. 'Hey! It's me!' There was applause and she was invited to go through the door at the far end of the room to receive her prize. As she went out of sight there was a huge shout of laughter and much excited conversation.

There was something here which Elaine did not understand. 'What are they laughing at? What is the Dish of the Day?'

Madam Max smiled. 'They are laughing at her because *she* is the Dish of the Day. The draw was fixed in advance. Everyone, except her, knew that she would win. Right now she is being forcibly stripped by the dormitory girls, ready to become a dish.'

A few moments went by, then there was a loud shout of approval as the far doors opened and four guards entered, carrying between them a large, round, wooden board. The red-haired girl was strapped to it; on her back, stark naked. Her position was like that of a frog at dissecting time; her elbows and knees forming right angles, her upper arms and thighs splayed and pulled as close to the board as they would go. She was forced to maintain this position by straps through holes in appropriate places on the board.

As she was carried forward into the room, she looked ahead of her, down between her bare breasts and across her naked stomach. When she saw the sea of laughing faces she screamed in embarrassment and flushed bright red. Elaine noted with interest, that this blush did not stop at the neck, but extended all the way down her body. The plate was set down on a table in the centre of the room and the guards retired. Waitresses brought bowls of whipped cream and cherries and placed them on the table beside her. The guests crowded around, male and female. Elaine could see that the position she was in stretched the large tendons inside her thighs to their utmost and her vagina gaped pinkly open, the red tuft of her pubic hair hiding nothing, being confined mainly to her pubes, with very little between her legs.

One of the female guests said, 'What lovely, rosy lips. Just a touch more, I think,' and getting out her lipstick, proceeded to colour the outer and inner lips of her vulva. The girl could not move, even by a fraction of an inch, to prevent this. Someone put a spoonful of whipped cream on one breast and topped it with a cherry. In a twinkling, everyone seemed to be joining in; practically covering her with whipped cream and cherries.

Then the licking and sucking began and Elaine could see that, despite her embarrassment, this treatment had an inevitable effect and she came to climax. This provoked a round of betting as to who would be able to induce another, given only three minutes to do so. A small queue of men and a sprinkling of women awaited their turn, and in an endeavour to win, most of them chose a direct assault, using their mouth on the vagina and clitoris. There was special applause for the man who stripped and mounted her in the missionary position. The cheers turned to derisive boos when neither she, nor he, achieved a climax. Two men and one woman won their bets before it was decided that the red-head had had enough and she was allowed to get up and dress.

Elaine thought that the evening's special show was over when suddenly there was a further burst of applause as two guards carried in a piece of wooden apparatus and set it down in the middle of the room. It was a pillory mounted on a stout platform. At the front of the platform a thick wooden post supported a board, with holes for neck and wrists. The top part of the board was designed to hinge, to allow a person to be put in or taken out. Peggy made her way to it and called for silence.

'Ladies and Gentlemen. We have, for your entertainment tonight, a show called, "Punishment through the Ages", and this is the first piece of apparatus to be demonstrated. Would some kind gentleman offer himself so that we can see how this pillory worked?' A young man obliged and stepped onto the platform, placing his neck and wrists in the appropriate places, so that the guard could lower the upper board.

'A souvenir photograph!' Peggy called, and a cameraman, employed for the evening, took one. 'Anyone else for a souvenir photo before the show starts?'

Another man came forward, was photographed and released. 'Me too!' called one of the female guests and quite soon there was a small queue, all waiting their turn.

'This is the other special entertainment,' explained

Madam Max. 'As you have already seen, there is usually a guest involved and also, there is a prank or trick, so that it is a complete surprise to them to become part of the entertainment. The other guests find this so much more amusing than watching professionals. This one has been engineered by Peggy, who has paid me a handsome amount so that she can get her hands on her little Annie. All the other guests know about it; that's why they are co-operating. The idea is that, when it is Annie's turn, the guard will not release her and Peggy can grope her all she likes.'

The queue dwindled and Annie, unsuspecting, drew closer and closer to her fate. Then someone shouted, 'Come on Peggy! What about you?' After only a small show of reluctance, Peggy stepped onto the platform and placed her neck and wrists in the appropriate place. The guard closed the upper half, slipped a padlock through the hasp and snapped it shut.

The photographer took his picture and Peggy waited a few seconds to be released. When nothing happened, she twisted her head as far as she could and said to the guard. 'Come on then. Let me out.' He said nothing, but turned and walked away. Peggy's amazement turned to anger. She pulled and tugged furiously. 'This isn't funny! What's happening?'

The crowd parted and Peggy paled as the lithe and tiger-like figure of Jane stood before her. 'What's happening,' purred Jane, 'is that your nasty little scheme has gone wrong.'

Elaine was mystified. 'How did that happen?'

Madam Max was openly laughing, something she did not often do. 'Peggy forgot that Jane has far more money than she has. She was pleased to double what Peggy was paying me.'

Peggy's voice was pleading and placatory. 'I don't know what you mean, Jane. Look. If this is a joke . . .'

'It's a joke, all right. And it's on you. Tell all these people what you were planning.'

'Nothing. I wasn't planning anything. I was just . . . No. No. Jane! Don't do that!' Peggy's voice rose to a squeal as Jane came around the pillory, took the zip of her strapless gown between finger and thumb and gave a little tug. 'I didn't do . . .' Another tug. A vee of white flesh appeared and Peggy felt the grip of her gown relaxing. 'All right! All right! I was going to play a trick on Annie. It was all a joke. I was going to let . . .' Another shriek as the zip came down all the way and the gown fell forward and downward, leaving her naked to the waist, except for her strapless brassiere.

'OK! OK! No more! I was going to touch her a little bit, that's all.'

Jane was merciless. 'You mean you were going to unfasten her bra – like this.'

Her hands went to the clasp at the back of Peggy's brassiere, provoking a great scream. 'Not here, Jane. Please! For God's sake! Not in front of all these people! Oh God!' This last was a great groan of embarrassment as the clasp was flipped apart and her brassiere fell to the floor, leaving her pendulous, white breasts dangling and swinging free.

'Then, maybe, you planned to grope her tits – like this.' Pressed close against Peggy's hindquarters, Jane reached under her and took a breast in each hand, shaking and mauling and milking them obscenely.

'Jane! Please! I swear I wasn't . . .'

'Lying bitch! You are going to get yours.' From the pocket of her dress Jane produced two little silver

178

bells, attached to nipple clamps. Peggy bucked and squealed, so that Jane was obliged to grip a nipple in each hand and pinch and twist until the pain caused her to stand still and quiet, trembling like a frightened horse. Under that threat, she allowed her nipples to be clamped, the bells hanging down from them.

Jane was triumphant. 'Ring your bells, Peggy. I said *ring* them. Or do you want your dress taken right off?' Peggy shook her upper body so that her heavy breasts jiggled and the bells tinkled. There was a roar of laughter and approval from the audience.

'Please, Jane. Please don't do this to me.' Peggy pleaded.

'This, and much, much more, bitch. I haven't even started, yet.' She pulled Peggy's dress down over her hips and, after a minor struggle, pulled it away from her legs and dropped it, revealing the fact that Peggy was wearing pink silk knickers and a pink suspender belt.

Jane addressed herself to the crowd. 'Not pantyhose, you notice. What more evidence do we need of the intention to grope and be groped?' The crowd roared. 'None!'

'Do we find her guilty?' asked Jane.

'Yes!' chorused the audience.

'Cane or strap?' enquired Jane.

'Cane! Cane! Cane!' yelled the onlookers.

Jane beckoned to a guard and he brought her a thin cane. While she ran it menacingly through her hands, so that Peggy could see it, the guard tied Peggy's ankles to the rear edge of the platform so that her legs were braced apart.

Peggy's bottom was wobbling and trembling in dread; her white cheeks protruding on each side, beyond the edge of the silk knickers. She continued to beg. 'No! Please! Jane. You mustn't ...' Her voice rose to a scream of terror as Jane disappeared from view, behind her. She could not turn her head to see what was happening, but could tell from the faces of the crowd, that her caning was about to start.

Thwwwtt! Right across the tightly stretched, pink silk. The sting was unbelievable. Peggy jumped and wriggled, her bells chiming furiously as her great breasts bounced and joggled. Thwwwtt! Thwwwtt! Thwwwtt! Five more in all. Peggy sobbed, her backside on fire. In the crotch of her knickers a dark stain appeared followed, a few seconds later, by a trickle of urine down her thigh. The crowd cheered. Peggy wanted to die of shame and embarrassment.

'Oh dear,' said Jane in mock concern. 'You've peed in your panties. That can't be very comfortable for you. I should pull them down for you, but then everyone would see your bare bum.' Then, to the crowd, 'You don't want to see her bare bum, do you?'

The audience shouted 'Yes!'

Peggy was too far gone in humiliation to protest as she felt Jane's fingers in the waistband of her knickers. To the accompaniment of a cheer, they were pulled down to mid-thigh, revealing her plump, white bottom cheeks marked with six, crisp red lines.

'Anyone got nail scissors?' asked Jane and, selecting a pair from the many offered, she cut the material on each side of the panties and removed them altogether. Jane went back to where Peggy could see her and stared into her tear-stained face. 'Don't worry. I'm not going to cane you any more.' Then, as Peggy began to gabble out her thanks, she added, 'But, Annie is.' Annie came forward and Jane put her arm possessively around her shoulders. 'Annie and I have been getting it together for some time, now. She

180

didn't appreciate your attentions and I think she is ready to show you that your little scheme was not to her liking either.'

Jane handed the cane to Annie, who passed out of Peggy's sight. Peggy was sufficiently recovered to beg again. 'Please, no!'

Jane grabbed her hair and pushed her face close. 'I want to watch your expression and hear you scream for mercy.'

'Jane! Please don't let her do it! Jane! Jane! I'll give you anything. Please. Ow! Ow! Ow!!' Six times more, the cane fell with all Annie's strength behind it, across the already tenderised, bare buttocks.

But Peggy's debasement was not over yet. Amid her sobs, she looked up to see that Jane was stripping. She was at a loss to understand this for a while, then, when she saw Jane strapping on a long, flexible, plastic dildo, she realised what she had in mind. She jerked and wriggled as much as she could, her bells jingling. 'Oh no! Not that! Not here!' There was nothing she could do, though, to prevent Jane from raping her in full view of hordes of cheering people. As she felt the tip of the dildo at her vulva, she tried to delay the moment by standing on tiptoe, then by gyrating her bottom, but there was nowhere to go and she had to accept its full length. To add to her humiliation, Jane made sure that she came to orgasm by reaching under her and stimulating her clitoris.

When she withdrew, Jane offered an invitation to the watchers. 'Anyone else want the bitch?' By now, they were sated and stimulated enough to be thinking of their own pleasures, with their own, chosen partners and they were merciful in declining the offer.

'Hell hath no fury ... Maybe I've lost one customer, although that is by no means a foregone conclusion,' observed Madam Max philosophically. 'But when word of this gets around, I'll get lots more.'

That evening, showered and in her nightdress, Elaine sat in front of her mirror, brushing her hair. She was aware that she had been profoundly affected by what she had seen at Copley Grange. The most recent episode, the caning of Peggy's bottom, had released an urge in her which she had only half-recognised before, but now knew that she had: a predilection for dominating and inflicting pain. Not severe pain, she hastened to reassure herself, but enough to make the recipient aware of her presence. She did not understand the reasons for it. She only knew that at this moment she was feeling sexually alert and itchy. She wanted satisfaction, an orgasm. If Stewart had been there, it would have been ideal, but he wasn't.

She toyed with the idea of masturbation, but somehow that was not what her body craved. She wanted close contact with another human being. This thought interlocked with her wish to establish more intimate contact with Madam Max, in order to worm her way into secrets which might, otherwise, never be revealed to her. After all, why not? She had found the woman attractive enough to stroke her nipples earlier. The recollection of that incident decided her. She definitely needed an orgasm. Whatever else happened when she visited Madam Max, she was fairly confident of one of those.

She discarded her nightdress in favour of a semi-transparent negligee. As an afterthought, she put on a blue velvet collar with a bright jewel at the front. With her fair skin and hair, when the time came to discard the negligee – leaving only that collar – she felt that she had a good chance of seducing anyone.

Having noted the position of Madam Max's bedroom on the chart in the Control Room earlier, she made her way there and knocked on the door.

Upon invitation, she entered. Madam Max was sitting on the edge of her four-poster bed and looked up in slight surprise. On impulse Elaine shrugged out of the negligee and let it fall on the floor, behind her. 'I think we had an unfinished conversation.'

Madam Max stood up and let her own robe fall so that she too, was naked. 'I remember very well.'

They moved towards each other, and suddenly they were in each other's arms, kissing, open-mouthed, clinging tightly, their pubes rubbing, blonde hairs on black. Elaine felt her vagina liquefy and flow. She knew that she was having the same effect on Madam Max. Still clinging, they shuffled to the bed and fell onto it, bodies intertwined in lust.

At last, Madam Max held Elaine away from her. 'Too fast. Too fast. I have longed for this ever since I first saw you. You are so beautiful. Just lie back and let me look at you.' Elaine complied, her loins burning for satisfaction, but content to let the older woman set the pace.

Madam Max inspected her minutely, picking up her hand to study her nails, twining Elaine's hair in her fingers and massaging her breasts with it. 'I can force any woman in this house to have sex with me. It is so long since anyone made me a gift of love that I find myself moved.' She trailed her hand down the naked stomach and into the blonde, pubic hair. 'Will you allow me to look at you, down there?'

In her turn, Elaine was moved at this humble request from a woman who could order anything. Willingly, she raised her knees and parted her thighs, making the cleft of her vulva available for inspection.

Madam Max wriggled around until her head was close to the object of her interest. In this position, her own pubic hair was close to Elaine's face, and she noticed with interest, that it was not stiff and curly, but long and black and silky, like the hair on her head. As she lay on her side, the elegant white curve of Madam Max's haunch, contrasting with the jet black pubic hair, blending into the flat, white belly was unbelievably erotic. Elaine stretched for a soft hairbrush on the bedside table and began to brush the black hairs.

Madam Max sighed deeply, and placing a thumb on either side of Elaine's vulva, she spread her open so that she could see the vaginal entrance. 'Such soft, pink lips,' she murmured, and bent to kiss them. It was only the second time Elaine had been kissed in that place and the effect was just as dynamic as the first. More so in fact, because this was a woman, dealing with a woman's body and understanding exactly what to do to provide maximum stimulation. The wet, urgent, probing tongue drove Elaine wild. And when Madam Max took her clitoris between her lips and sucked on it – hard – she nearly took off. She tried to contain herself, but her orgasm hit before she was fully prepared for it and she writhed and moaned in ecstasy; both hands pressed against the back of Madam Max's head, lest the sensation should stop too soon.

Elaine lay for a while, breathing hard. 'Wonderful! No-one has brought me off that way, before. Now you must let me do it to you.' Madam Max took Elaine's place and spread herself, as she had spread Elaine. Elaine parted the black-haired lips and positioned herself. 'I've never done this before. You'll have to tell me if I'm getting it wrong.' She extended her long, pink tongue and began to lap gently at the insides of the labial lips.

Madam Max groaned. 'Yes! Yes! Just like that. Now a little deeper. Yes! Oooh yes! Now a little higher. A little . . . higher . . . Can you see my clit? Nibble it, very, very gently. Ooh! Aaaah! Yes! Like that . . . Now your lips . . . take it . . . and . . . Oh God! Yes! Yes! Aaaargh! Do it! Do it! Don't stop! For God's sake, don't stop! Now! Now! I'm coming! Oh Jesus!' Her head thrashed from side to side, her upper body rising completely off the bed and her thighs closed tightly on Elaine's ears, pressing almost painfully as she ground her sex into the willing mouth. Her love juices flowed over Elaine's cheeks until she flopped back, exhausted and relaxed her grip.

They lay in each other's arms for a while, stroking and fondling. 'Mmmm! I needed that,' said Elaine. There was silence for a while, then Elaine, feeling a familiar quickening of interest said, 'Would it be very greedy of me to want another one?'

Madam Max smiled and stroked her hair. 'Very greedy. Almost as greedy as I am, myself. Have you ever used a double dildo?'

'No, I haven't,' said Elaine. 'But I'm always willing to learn.'

Madam Max leaned away from her and took the instrument from her bedside drawer. It consisted of two rubber penises, joined together in the shape of a broad vee. The cleft at the bottom of the vee was filled with small, flexible, rubber fingers. Madam Max, lying on her side, raised and bent her upper knee to stretch herself open and inserted one end of the vee into her vagina with a grimace of pleasure. 'Part your legs,' she said, and rolled between them, to insert the other end of the vee into Elaine.

Elaine found the sensation most pleasant. Her share of the device filled her and massaged her, promising more than a clitoral orgasm. The novelty of Madam Max's bare breasts hanging down onto her own, so that their nipples brushed together, was an added stimulant. The small rubber forest in the cleft was impinging on her clitoris, into the bargain.

As she felt the up and down movement, it occurred to her that Madam Max must be holding it by the contraction of her vaginal muscles so, after a while, she gripped it in a similar way and said, 'Now you.'

The older woman nodded and eagerly worked her body up and down her share of the dildo, her silky pubic hair sending shivers through Elaine as it rubbed against her pubes.

Madam Max felt her orgasm coming and whispered, 'I'm nearly there. I want to wait for you.'

Elaine was breathing hard. 'I'm nearly there, too. Just let go whenever you like.' Their rubbing and grinding movements became more violent, pubes pressing urgently on pubes for maximum excitement, then they both came at the same time, collapsing into one another, breasts crushed, as they rode the wave together.

They rolled onto their sides, still embracing, still joined by the dildo. They left it where it was. There seemed no hurry to remove it. Every now and again, one would stir, making the other gasp with the movement of the tool against sensitised tissue. They spent some time, just holding each other and giggling at the sensations they could generate with such small movements.

Elaine was the first to make the obvious suggestion. 'Maaaax?'

'Mmmm?'

'Are you thinking what I'm thinking?'

Max twitched her end of the dildo. 'I could be. It depends on what you're thinking.'

'I'm thinking how nice it would be to have just one more. Just a teensy, weensy one.' Elaine returned the twitch.

'Then you are not thinking what I am thinking, because I am thinking how nice it would be for you to have another truly enormous one.'

Elaine giggled. 'How will you do it? Let's make it something different. You know so many things I don't. Teach me.'

'Different? Let's see, now. Do you remember the man who had his temperature taken?' Elaine did and felt her juices flowing again.

'And do you remember the woman in the cell and the slippery finger? Have you ever tried that?'

The flow increased. 'No. Does it hurt?'

Max twitched the dildo again. 'Not if I use a specially thin vibrator. I just happen to have one, here.' She reached down and withdrew herself from the dildo, leaving Elaine to extract her half. She squirmed around and took a slender, white instrument from her drawer. She demonstrated it. It was flexible and it buzzed.

Elaine was excited and fascinated. 'How do you want me?'

'You could lie on your back and pull your knees up into your chest; but I think you would be more comfortable if you knelt up for it.' Elaine climbed up onto her knees. 'Knees apart. Now put your head down and stick your bottom out.' As Elaine did so, Max caught her breath. She thought she had never seen anything quite as perfect as those softly rounded, bare, white buttocks, so innocently and freely offered.

187

'Since this is going to be a part of your tuition there are some things which, as a professional, you should know. An anus is an anus and a vagina is a vagina and never the twain shall meet. Never use the same finger, or vibrator or whatever on one as you do on the other. That way, you don't put your client in the hospital when she could be earning money to pay to you. And bottoms do not lubricate naturally. You must always use plenty of gel or cream. In your case, cold cream, I think.'

While getting the jar, she also took out a second, larger vibrator and placed it conveniently to hand. Taking a smear of cold cream, she parted the cheeks of Elaine's bottom and dabbed the chilly stuff onto her sphincter. Elaine jumped.

'Keep still. I haven't started, yet.'

Elaine could feel the cream being worked all around her anus and the thought of what she might feel excited her again, so that her juices began to leak out onto her thighs. When she heard the buzz of the vibrator, she gasped expectantly. When it touched her tight, puckered sphincter, she tensed and clenched and was smacked lightly for it. 'Relax and enjoy!' She did so, and felt the insistent pressure of the thing, trying to force its way into her.

'Oooh, Max! It's so tickly. I don't think I can stand it. It's lovely, but it's . . . it's . . . Ahaaagh! Oooooh! Ooooh!'

She was penetrated, pierced. She felt the buzzing irritation inside herself, in this new and stimulating place. She knew that she wanted an orgasm, and wanted it very badly. Using only the top inch of the instrument, Max worked it slowly in and out, at the same time reaching with her spare hand for the second vibrator. She rotated the base of this one between finger and thumb and, when it was buzzing, reached through the parted thighs to insert it between the wet lips of Elaine's cleft. She eased it forward until it lay flat against the clitoris, then slipped her forefinger past it to search for that elusive little column of gristle. When she found it, she pressed it against the buzzing vibrator, holding it there and massaging it up and down. Elaine thought she would burst. Every nerve and muscle in her stomach, thighs and buttocks, quivered and shook. Her orgasm struck her like a bolt of lightning and she screamed, trying to agitate her clitoris against the vibrator in her vagina and simultaneously thrusting back to engulf the one in her anus.

Max moved with her, keeping up the clitoral stimulation and taking care that she received no more than an inch of the smaller tool. Another orgasm hit her, then another and another, in quick succession. She was no longer a human being, but an animal, completely overwhelmed by lust.

When it was over, she remained as she was; her cheek against the bedcover, her bottom sticking up and her breasts dangling down, making cow-like, lowing noises. Max gently removed the two vibrators and, turning her onto her side, took her in her arms and cradled her, rocking gently. When next she looked down she saw that Elaine had fallen asleep. She continued to hold her, content just to be close to this beautiful, golden child.

9
Incriminating Evidence

A few days later Elaine was called to the drawing room. When she got there, Madam Max was very excited. She had a large cardboard box on the sofa. 'It's your bitch costume, Elaine. Do try it on. I'm dying to see it.'

Elaine opened the box and took out the contents. It was certainly made with great skill and care, the red calf leather a marvel of suppleness. 'Oh, come on! Hurry up and put it on.'

Elaine stripped and Madam Max helped her to pull on the knee-length boots and zip them up. The heels were very high and she tottered for a few seconds until she got used to them. Then the bikini bottom, two red triangles, one front and one rear. The front one hardly concealed her pubic hair. The rear one left large areas of her shapely bottom on view. There were wide gaps at the sides, with criss-cross leather thongs, so that it would be apparent that she wore nothing underneath.

The bodice was hardly worthy of the name. From a broad, studded, leather collar, two straps supported what might be described as a couple of ledges, one under each breast, throwing them into prominence while concealing nothing. They were held against her body by a leather strap across the back, brassiere-fashion. The finishing touch was a red leather headband, shaped like a tiara, with a great paste diamond in the centre.

Elaine posed provocatively. 'Like it?'

'Like it! It's fantastic! You're going to be a great success. I shall have to watch out.' Madam Max surveyed her, head on one side. 'It needs something else. Oh, of course. A cane.' She went to the cupboard and brought one back. 'Now, dear. Stand just so, feet apart.' She demonstrated. 'Now – push your hips forward. Run the cane through your hands. Look fierce. Lovely!' There was a knock at the door. Before Elaine could protest, Madam Max went to it and opened it. Elaine heard *that* voice.

'Madam Max. Sorry to trouble you. Is it convenient to go over next week's schedules?'

Elaine was rooted to the spot. Oh God! Not Stewart! Not now! Not when she was dressed like this! Beam me up, Scottie! Then he was in the room. To his enormous credit, he did not even blink. Madam Max was ruffling through her drawers for papers.

'I'll be with you in a moment, Stewart. Sit down. There. On the sofa with Elaine. I'll order some tea. Elaine, dear. Amuse Stewart for a minute while I find my notes. Oh, of course. You know each other.'

Elaine tried her voice, found it was a high soprano, cleared her throat and tried again. 'Yes. Of course.' She felt an almost irresistible urge to pull down a skirt that wasn't there. She found herself still holding the cane and jerked it behind her, stuffing it down the back of the sofa. Madam Max found her paperwork, handed it to Stewart and settled herself into an armchair opposite them. 'So, is everything going well in your department, Stewart?'

'Pretty well, within the limitations of the equipment. You already know my views on that.'

'Yes. I've been thinking about it. Do you think that upgrading would be cost-effective?'

'I'm not the one to tell you that, because I work here. What you need is an independent consultant. He could run through what you do and advise you about what you need. If he agrees with me that your requirements are not being properly met with the present kit, he'll tell you so and give you a ball-park figure on cost.'

'Thank you, Stewart. That's very fair of you, in the circumstances. Let me see, now. You've never sampled our wares, to see what quality we offer. What would you say to a massage, with extras? On the house.'

Elaine thought that he was bound to refuse. After all, he was a gentleman, and she was there, listening. 'Thanks!' he said. 'That would be great.' The pig! The rotter! The scumbag!

Madam Max continued, 'Elaine dear. Who do you think would be right for Stewart?' Elaine did not hesitate for a second. 'Oh, Mary I think. Definitely Mary.' She gloated at the thought that Mary's stubble would still be at its most prickly; like mating with a hedgehog.

Tea came just then, and Elaine excused herself. 'Mr Ganton, I wonder if you'd mind if I slipped away and changed?' She gathered up her clothes and walked to the door with as much dignity as she could muster on her wobbly high heels. She was very conscious of the amount of bare bottom showing below, and on both sides, at the back of her costume. She wondered if it had creases in it, from the sofa.

There were now at least two reasons for Elaine to

want to talk to Stewart alone, and it was with some impatience that she was obliged to accompany Madam Max on more of her rounds. In the observation room next to a bedroom, Madam Max explained what they were to see that day.

'This is a very sensible approach to marriage. A delightful young couple, but neither has the slightest sexual experience so, rather than put them through one of those disastrous, fumbling, embarrassing honeymoons, their parents have clubbed together and sent them here for a short training course. They are taught separately, so as not to spoil the anticipation and magic of their first sexual exploration of each other's bodies. This is Anna.' She drew aside the curtain and Elaine saw a very attractive, dark-haired girl in her early twenties. She was being undressed by Rose and Shelley, who were already naked.

'Now slip this silk robe on, dear,' said Rose. 'We want to show you how to be attractive without apparently trying. Just lie on the bed. No! No! Not like that, dear. You look about as appealing as a sack of spuds. Come off it and watch Shelley. See. On the side, with the top leg drawn up. See how that creates this wonderful S-shape from chest to thigh and makes her bottom stick out. Now you try it . . . There. Much better! Now adjust the robe so that your bottom and thigh are bare. No! No! Too much! It's all there, on a plate. We want to keep a little bit of mystery, don't we? Make him want to move the robe so as to see more. Same with the leg position. Make sure he can see some hair, but not everything. Now. The door is opening. Here he comes. Big sigh, as though you are just waking up. Keep your bottom half where it is, but turn the top half towards him, making sure that your robe comes partly open. Mmmm! Not bad, but the robe didn't gape enough. Try again, but put in a little stretch and a yawn. Yes! Lovely! Perfect! Push those breasts up! Eyes half-open, sleepy and sultry. Coo! I fancy you myself.'

Shelley took over. 'Give me the robe for a minute. Watch! If we do it up like this – without a big overlap – we find that when we walk, our leg pops in and out, bare to the thigh. Now, you try. Good! Very good! Now practise standing so that your whole leg is exposed and just the tiniest suggestion of hair at the top. Only a hint! That's it! OK. Come in, Hal!'

Anna grabbed at her robe and dragged it closed, but Rose chided her gently. 'Come on, now. Don't be shy. He's an instructor, same as we are. He's seen it all before and it will be very impersonal; just a game. Think of him as a tailor's dummy, or that model they use for practising resuscitation. Look him straight in the eyes. Now, without moving your eyes, let your robe slip down your arms. Stop there! See how, with it at your elbows, you are pretty well naked and your arms are held behind you. He's not going to be able to resist grabbing at you. Let the robe go all the way and sit on the edge of the bed. Right on the edge. Now lift your left leg, bend the knee and set your foot on the bed. As he comes at you, to kiss you, take his head in your hands and guide it down between your legs. Come on now, don't be coy. Get it in there.'

As Hal's lips touched her labia, Anna gave a little scream and her mouth stayed open, in astonishment. Shelley stroked her hair. 'It's wonderful, isn't it? Oh Rose! Do you remember your first time? Makes me feel all sentimental.'

Anna gasped and wriggled, her knees jerking and trembling spontaneously. 'Oooh! Oohooo! It's so good! My God! Is it always like this?'

'Even better, because when it is for real, it will be with a man you really care about and the fact that it is a gift from him will make it all the sweeter. Hal is an expert of course, but your fiance is learning all about it and you'll find that a combination of that training and his instinctive wish to please you, should do the trick.'

Anna's head began to roll, rhythmically and her hands grabbed at her breasts. 'Steady on!' said Shelley. 'We don't want you to have an orgasm right now.'

Hal stopped his ministrations and Anna looked questioningly from Rose to Shelley. 'What's an orgasm like?' she asked. 'I've never had one, I don't think.'

'You don't masturbate?' said Rose, incredulously.

'No.'

Shelley scratched her head. 'I don't think we can explain it in words. But I've a feeling you're going to have one today and, when you do, we'll tell you that it's happening then you'll know what it feels like.'

Anna nodded, absorbing this novel idea. Shelley said, 'Now you get to undress him. Unbutton his shirt. No need for you to do it all. Make a start on the buttons and make some pushing gestures. He'll get the message and take it off himself. Now the trousers. Never dealt with those before? Well, there's the belt, then a sort of hook and eye affair at the top, then the zip. Do the belt first, then the zip, but leave the hook until last because it will help you with the zip.

Anna knelt in front of Hal and, with instruction from Rose, unfastened the belt of his trousers. Then Shelley took her place. 'This is a good way to deal with the zip.' She leaned forward and took the tag of

196

the zip between her strong, white teeth and, with little, teasing jerks, pulled it down. Nuzzling Hal's crotch between each pull.

The girl resumed her kneeling position, unfastened the last hook and lowered Hal's trousers. He stepped out of them. 'Now the shorts,' said Shelley.

Anna hesitated. 'I've never seen a man's ... a man's ... you know. His thing.'

Shelley met Rose's glance and sighed wistfully. 'Come along, dear,' she said, encouragingly. 'That's the idea of this course. So that you get a bit familiar with things and smooth the way for your honeymoon. We can't teach you unless you uncover the exhibit, so get them off him.'

Hesitantly at first, then more confidently, Anna eased the shorts from his hips and dropped them to the floor so that he could shuffle them off and stand naked, before her kneeling figure, his penis at face level. 'Why, it's just like the statues at the museums,' she said, sounding surprised.

'That's because Hal has been selected for his self-control. His penis is not erect,' said Rose matter-of-factly. 'I was so ignorant when I started that it was ages before I found out that a man's penis could be soft and floppy. By the time I got around to feeling them, they were always rock-hard and I imagine that is the way your young man is going to be on your honeymoon. Just in case, though, you have to know what to do to get it hard.'

She knelt beside Anna, the better to point out the salient features. 'First of all, see this loose bag or scrotum, with the balls or testicles in it. You can fondle those, or kiss or lick them, but always very carefully. That is the most vulnerable part of a man's body. If you were to take them in your hands now,

197

and squeeze hard, suddenly, he would pass out with the pain. You might even kill him.'

Rose lifted the limp penis. 'This is the bit that grows and hardens. You can be quite rough with that at times, particularly when it is hard. But when it is soft, like this, you should be gentler. Now, take it in your hand and close your fist around it. Gently! Move your hand backwards and forwards. Good! Now you are masturbating him. If you went on doing that for long enough, he would ejaculate, which means that white sperm would shoot out of this little hole in the tip. That stuff contains millions of little tadpoles, any one of which could alter a couple's tax-code. So be careful what you are doing with it and see that it doesn't get into places where it can do its stuff, unless you have taken other precautions.

'Notice where your thumb is. Holding it, as you are, your thumb naturally comes to rest underneath, just below the head. That is the most responsive place of all. Wiggle your thumb about. See how that makes him gasp? Look up at his face. Notice that little frown, the closed eyes, the lips drawn back? That's how you tell you are getting to him, apart from his hip movements and . . .'

'It's getting bigger!' exclaimed Anna.

'Ah! Now feel it, Anna!' said Rose. 'The power of a woman over a man. The clear and conclusive evidence that you are a mature woman and sexually desirable. The thing that he can't fake. Come on, now. Let's drive him crazy. Lick it like a lollipop. Run your tongue up and down the underside. See how hard it is, now? You did that, all by yourself. Now clamp your breasts together, on either side of it, so that he can work it up and down between them.

'Now take the tip in your mouth and run your

tongue around it. Always clamp at least one hand around his penis when you put it into your mouth, so that you can control the amount you take in. Don't forget that you are driving him wild with excitement, so that he might get carried away and grab you by the hair or the ears and shove too hard.

'Hear that gasping and moaning? Feel the thrusting of his hips? He's getting close to coming. Glance up at his face. You can tell by his expression that something big is going to happen soon. Keep sucking and rubbing! He's very near, now. You'll feel his penis pulse in your hand and you'll see his testicles rise up to the very top of their travel. When that happens, you have a choice. You can carry on, allow him to come in your mouth and swallow it. Don't worry. It doesn't taste bad. Just a little salty. And it is the most loving and close thing a woman can do for a very special man. If you don't feel you want to do that, you must never let him see that you find his ejaculation unpleasant in any way. At the last minute, you stop sucking and put it between your breasts again, or point it at your face or some other part of your body – breasts are favourite . . .'

At this point, Hal's movements became uncontrollable and he gave a hoarse shout. Anna removed his penis from her mouth and pointed it at her bare breasts. 'Keep rubbing! Don't stop!' cried Rose, then copious spurts of white liquid jetted from Hal onto Anna's body. 'Keep going! Keep going! Don't stop until you are absolutely sure that he has finished. Now, stay close to him. Don't pull away. Show that you are pleased about things by rubbing his sperm over your breasts.'

Rose stepped up to Hal and kissed him lightly. 'Thanks!' she said. 'Nice one again. That's all for now, Hal. We'll take it from here.' Hal returned her kiss, picked up his clothes and left.

Shelley handed Anna a towel. 'Here. Wipe yourself off. You did well. What did you think of that?'

Mopping at her breasts and stomach, Anna replied, 'It was OK. Not as frightening as I thought it would be. I loved the idea that I could make a man so excited. I think that when I'm with Nick, it will be lovely.'

Shelley grinned. 'These are just the basics, you understand. We shall show you more in later lessons and you will learn a lot all by yourself, with experience. Now we come on to the serious stuff and Rose is going to play the part of your Nick. That's because he wouldn't be too keen on the idea of you being with another man.'

Rose had put on a tight, black garment, rather like a panty-girdle, with a plastic facsimile of male genitalia attached to the front. Shelley made Anna sit on the edge of the bed again and spread her legs, then knelt in front of her. 'We want to make this as comfortable as it can be,' she said. 'I'll just check a couple of things. She reached out; Anna jumped and tried to close her legs but Shelley was between them. 'It's all right. Don't be scared. I have to make sure you are wet enough and see how much of a virgin you are.' She gently inserted two fingers into Anna's vagina and pushed a little. 'Some girls think they are genuinely virgins when they are not,' she explained. 'Oh, you are, right enough,' she reassured, seeing Anna's surprised look. 'By the feel of things, though, you won't have too much trouble. Just to make absolutely sure, we'll put some lubricating jelly on Rose, first.'

Rose got on the bed and lay on her back, while Shelley smeared cream over the plastic penis. 'Now

Anna,' said Shelley, 'when you're ready, get astride her, face to face. That's it. Hitch forward a bit. Bit more. That's it. Now ease back onto your heels.' With deft hands, Shelley separated Anna's labia and inserted the head of the penis. Anna gasped and wriggled. 'It's OK. Take it easy! You are in complete control. You can take as little or as much of it into yourself as you think you can manage. There's no rush. We've got all afternoon.'

Slowly, slowly, Anna sank back and a little of the penis disappeared inside her.

'Oooh! Ooooh!' she whispered. 'It feels good, but it's up against something. I don't think I can go any further.'

'That's all right. Stop there. Bob, very gently, up and down. Doesn't that feel good?'

'Mmmmm! I wish I could take more.'

'Reach down and touch it. Now bring your fingers up to just above where it goes in. Wiggle them round and round. That is your clitoris and you are masturbating. Like it?'

Anna did not answer, but her expression was eloquent. She bit her lip and frowned in concentration. When Rose's hands came up to fondle her breasts, she gasped and her buttocks began an involuntary twitching. 'Oh! Oh! What's happening to me? I never felt ... I feel ... Oh God!' Her movements grew larger, her white flesh blushed pink and a faint dew of perspiration made her breasts shine.

'Oooh! I want it right in me.' Her whole body shook and quivered like jelly. Her head rolled convulsively, her stomach muscles contracting rhythmically. 'Oh! Oh! Something's happening! Something's happening! Aaah! Gimme! Gimme! It's ... Aaaaaaghaaa!'

With a great shriek, she sank right back so that the whole length of the penis disappeared and she jigged up and down on it frantically, her fingers whirling at her clitoris. Shelley hissed loudly in her ear, *'That's* an orgasm!'

Suddenly she collapsed onto Rose, their breasts pressed together. 'Wonderful! Wonderful!' Then 'Ow! Ouch!'

Shelley and Rose both kissed her tenderly and helped her off, to lie on the bed next to Rose. 'It's OK, Anna,' said Shelley. 'It's done. You're not a virgin any more. Rest a while now. That's enough for today. Tomorrow we will show you some more positions but nothing will be as sore as today was. Believe me, you are going to have a great honeymoon.'

As soon as Elaine could get Stewart to herself, she flew to the attack. 'Warty rat-bag!' she said.

'What do you mean?'

'You know exactly what I mean, you crawly lizard! Massage Stewart? Oh, yes please, Miss! How could you?'

'I had to think quickly, dearest. You don't think I wanted to hump Mary, do you? I had to do it because that is what a young, uncommitted chap *would* do. So that Madam Max wouldn't suspect us of having an affair.'

Elaine was a little mollified. Stewart counterattacked. 'Anyway, what about you and that costume. That's not standard secretary-wear, is it?'

'Just like you, dearest. I had to do it. You don't think I wanted to, do you?' Score, one-all. They could get onto more important matters.

'I've thought of a way of getting a full recording of Madam Max with Mrs Ortez,' said Elaine.

'It's not dangerous, is it?' said Stewart. 'Because, if it is . . .'

'No, I'm sure it will be all right. Just leave it to me.' She outlined her plan, briefly.

He nodded approval. 'I wish I could help, but I don't see how I can.'

'You come in later. There's no way I can get through that locked door by myself. As soon as I've got some evidence we can use, that will be the time for you to try your skill as a burglar.'

On the Thursday of the appointment, Elaine set about putting her plan into action. She dressed with care, in a loose-fitting summer frock with a low neck-line. She wore no stockings or panty-hose. After several tries and rejections, she selected a pair of flimsy panties. They were white and practically transparent in the crotch, cut so skimpily that bunches of her blonde, pubic hair protruded on each side. To satisfy herself of their merit, she sat on the bed, in front of her dressing-table mirror, lifted her skirt, then drew up her knees and parted them. She scrutinised the effect with care. They would do. To finish the job, she applied liberal quantities of her sexiest, muskiest perfume to her inner thighs.

She made sure that she was in the Control Room before the appointed hour and she busied herself at the drawers, selecting a little pile of recent tapes to take away. Joe was checking the picture on the drawing room monitor and Elaine could see Madam Max, sitting on the sofa with a drink in her hand. As far as she could tell from the angle, the camera must be behind a mirror which, she knew, hung over the great fireplace. Glancing along the row of monitors, she checked the picture of the entrance hall and saw that a woman was being conducted towards the drawing room by one of the guards. Keeping an eye on Joe, to make sure that his attention was still on his monitor, she put her hand up her skirt and pinched herself, very hard on the inner thigh, about two inches from her panties. She hung on for long seconds, pinching and twisting, until tears came into her eyes. Then she leapt up and began to flap the loose skirt of her dress.

'Eeeek! Oh! Aaargh! A bee! A bee! Help me Joe. Get it off me!' He turned towards her and she hauled her skirt up to her waist, making searching movements and giving him a good view of the panties.

'I can't. I've got to live edit this one,' he said.

She screamed again and danced about, sounding hysterical. 'Oh, just switch your silly camera on and leave it to run. I'll help you to edit it afterwards. Come and get this thing off me, now!' She played her ace. 'Ouch! Ow! It's stung me.' She slumped into a chair, pulled her skirt right up and parted her legs, as though to inspect herself. She raised her beautiful face, to him, with its frame of golden hair, large tears rolling down her cheeks. 'Oh, Joe. Won't you help me, please?'

There were probably men in the world who could have resisted her appeal. Any blind, homosexual, unfeeling bastard could have done it. Joe was none of those things. He switched on the camera and came over to her, kneeling to inspect the damage. 'Oh, wow! He got you in an awkward place.' The red mark was clear to see. So was her pink sex through the transparent material, and so were the fair hairs between her parted white thighs.

'Ow! It hurts. I can't see. Is the sting still in there? Have a look for me, Joe.' He bent close. The heady musk of her perfume made his head swim. 'Get a magnifying glass, Joe. You must get it out, if it's still there, or it will swell up dreadfully. Please, Joe.'

He had a magnifying glass somewhere, he knew. He ruffled through drawers and papers while she sobbed pitifully; seeing, on the monitor, that Madam Max and Mrs Ortez were now talking together. It took Joe quite a time to find the glass, then he came back, polishing it on his sleeve. To use it, he had to get really close again. The perfume engulfed him and he noticed how warm the room was. 'I can't see any sting. He must have pulled it out himself. They do that, sometimes.'

'It hurts like anything. Is there something you can put on it?'

'I don't know what you put on bee stings. Is it soda? Or is that wasps?' He scratched his head.

'A First Aid book. Have you got a First Aid case?' She knew that there was one and that she had moved it from its usual place into a cupboard. He went off to look for it and she saw, on the monitor, that the Ortez–Max conversation was continuing. Unsurprisingly, it took him a long time to find the case. By the time he came back, leafing through the booklet, she saw that Mrs Ortez was naked and there was a man in the room. She did not understand what was happening, but she could sort that out later. 'What does it say?'

'Ice. Haven't got any of that. Bicarb. There's some in the box. Cold compress. Have you got a hankie? I'll wet it in the washroom.' He went into the little toilet adjoining and she took the opportunity of his absence to pinch up some more redness, as it seemed to be fading fast. Joe wetted her handkerchief and brought it back, dripping. He poured a few bicarbonate crystals into it, screwed it up into a compress and pressed it against the red spot, very conscious of the fact that her pubic hairs were tickling the back of his hand.

She looked over his bent back and saw that the interview must be over. Mrs Ortez was dressed again; was leaving the room; was walking down the hall. Elaine said, 'That is so much better. Joe, you are a gentleman. Come on. I'll hold the handkerchief now. We must edit your tape so that you don't get into trouble for helping me.'

They went over to the desk together and he, seeing that the interview was over, switched off the camera, then rewound the tape in the primary recorder. 'This won't take a minute. I know the signal I'm looking for.' After a few seconds he paused the tape, made a few adjustments, backwards and forwards, then set it to play. Madam Max said '... for the benefit of our hidden camera.' She turned to face the camera and raised her hand. Joe hit the play-record buttons on the secondary recorder and the tape, there, began to turn.

Mrs Ortez and Hans, the chief guard, were the only two people visible on the monitor. Mrs Ortez stripped slowly, while Hans watched. Then she knelt in front of him and smiled up at him. She unzipped his fly and took out his penis. She took it into her mouth and sucked on it. After a few minutes Madam Max appeared from where she had been standing, out of shot, and raised her hand. Joe stopped the secondary recording, back-tracked a couple of seconds, then erased Madam Max and her wave. 'Done,' he said. 'Easy!'

'Oh, good,' Elaine said. 'Joe. Do you think you could wet my hankie for me again. I don't like to go into the Men's Room.' He grinned and took it from her. She knew she did not have much time. She ejected the tape from the primary and scrabbled frantically, with her fingernail, at the sticky plastic label which bore its number. For precious seconds it refused to come, then it did and she grabbed a blank tape from the pile and stuck the number on it, putting the now unmarked master tape on the pile she was going to take away. She made a rush back to the primary recorder but didn't quite make it. Joe came back too soon.

She turned to meet him, the tape in her hands, giving him one of her best smiles. 'I was just being helpful. We want to erase this, don't we, so no-one knows you didn't live-edit.' She took it to the fast-erase machine and posted it in. 'Tell me again how this works.' He showed her and she watched, with satisfaction, while a perfectly blank tape was erased, its spurious number removed and it was replaced on the blank pile.

She took the wet handkerchief from Joe, thanking him profusely for all his kindness then, picking up her trophy with the other tapes, she took it back to her room. Once there, she locked the door, put the tape into her video machine, rewound and pressed 'play'.

When the knock came on the door, Madam Max put her drink down and rose to meet Mrs Ortez, shown in by the guard. She was a plump woman in her mid-forties and Elaine guessed that her daughter got her dark looks from her father, because this woman had very white skin. Madam Max extended her hand graciously. 'Mrs Ortez. How nice of you to come. I am Madam Cecilia Maximilian, but you may call me Madam Max.'

Mrs Ortez did not take the proffered hand. 'What is this all about?'

'But you already know what it is about or you wouldn't be here. You got the tape I sent you?'

'Filth! It has nothing to do with me.'

'Which is why you came all this way. Is it not your daughter on the tape, behaving like a demented rabbit?'

'No! Of course it isn't!' Mrs Ortez was grasping at straws.

'Oh, that's all right. I was mistaken. Then it won't matter if I send a copy to the Kahn's father and copies to the press?' There was a long silence. Madam Max leaned forward and hissed, 'Listen, you fat cow. If you go on like this, I shall think that you are very stupid and of no use to me at all. Pay attention and you can still save your daughter's marriage.'

Mrs Ortez sank onto the sofa and put her face in her hands. 'How much do you want? I don't have much money of my own, but . . .'

'I wouldn't dream of taking your money, Mrs Ortez. When you travel abroad, you do so as part of a diplomatic entourage. Your baggage is not subject to search. All you have to do, from time to time, is to carry certain goods between countries for me. The alternative is disgrace and no rich marriage for your daughter. Do you understand?' Mrs Ortez nodded. 'And you agree?' She nodded, again. Madam Max pressed a bell and Hans came in. Madam Max said, 'I require double security to ensure your good behaviour. There is a camera behind the mirror. When I tell you to, you will strip, slowly, and provocatively. You will kneel in front of this man and suck his penis, with every sign of goodwill and enjoyment. Should you decide later, not to keep your part of your bargain with me, this film will go to your husband and all his friends, as well as to the press. Is all that clear?'

Utterly defeated and with no avenue of escape, Mrs Ortez nodded dumbly. 'Then you may begin. Remember to smile, Mrs Ortez. Begin your strip-tease for the benefit of the camera.' She turned to the camera and raised her hand.

Elaine pressed 'fast-forward' and Mrs Ortez whizzed through her strip and suck routine. She slowed to 'play' as she dressed again. Madam Max was saying, 'You will receive your instructions by telephone. Whatever you are told to do, you will do – immediately and without question. Clear?' Mrs Ortez nodded. 'You may go now. I have ears everywhere, and my arm is long. If I hear even the ghost of a rumour that you have spoken to anyone about this, copies of both tapes go to exactly the people you don't want to see them.'

Elaine stopped the tape. She had got it! She had really got it! She could hardly believe it. Then it occurred to her that the tape was dynamite. Not only valuable evidence, but potentially lethal, if it was found in her possession. She had to hide it – but where? Her mind ranged over the options. Under her clothes in a drawer? The first place anyone would look. Under the mattress? Oh come *on*, Elaine. You're better than that! Think! Of course! The best place to hide it was right out in the open, where everyone could see it. She took it, with other tapes, to the basement vault and walked between the shelves. She took a tape at random, peeled the number off it and stuck it on the Ortez interview. She memorised the number, then took the exchanged tape up to the Control Room and wiped it clean, before putting it on the blank pile.

Now, if anyone wanted to find the Ortez interview, they would have to play every tape in the basement first. It would be only by the most incredible stroke of misfortune that it got played, otherwise.

10
Caught!

Elaine had great difficulty in containing herself until she could speak to Stewart and tell him her news. He looked up as she burst into the Control Room. 'Did you get it?'

She was jubilant. 'Yes, darling. Absolutely everything.'

'You're sure?'

'Of course I am. I checked it.'

'Where is it now?'

'In a safe place, where no-one will find it.'

He was impressed. 'Darling, that's marvellous. Now we can go ahead and open up that room.'

'I've been thinking about that, Stewart. Why do we have to do it? We've taken enough chances, surely?'

He pressed her hand. 'Trust me. I know what I'm doing. All we have, at the moment, is evidence of one squitty little blackmail attempt, when we know that this thing is vast. Ours must be a real threat. One she can believe. Imagine threatening to bring her to trial in a court where the judge, the prosecuting counsel and half the jury are in her pocket, under threat of exposure and disgrace if things don't go her way. We just have to know who she has got to, and who she hasn't, if we are to have any chance at all of stopping her.'

Elaine nodded slowly. 'Yes. I suppose I can see that. But this will be the last thing, won't it, darling? Then, if there turns out to be more to do, you'll let the Police take over.'

'Once we are in that room and know what needs to be known, our troubles will be over. Now, you'd better show me where this door is.'

She went with him into the basement. She swung the shelved door aside and showed him the combination lock. He knelt and examined it. 'It's an excellent lock. Just about uncrackable.' She was downcast, then he continued, 'But it's crappy woodwork. Watch!' He took out a penknife and inserted it between the architrave and the jamb of the door-frame. A few wiggles, and the door sprang open. He folded up his knife. 'Easy.'

They passed into the room beyond, then stopped, in disappointment and disbelief. It was a wine cellar. Racks and racks of dusty bottles lined the walls. Elaine almost cried. 'Oh, Stewart. And we were hoping that all the evidence of blackmail would be in here. I'm so sorry, darling.'

'Shit!' said Stewart, and stood with hands on hips, looking around, wondering where else to look. Then a thought struck him. 'Just a minute. This doesn't make any sense at all. Why go to all that trouble to hide the entrance to a wine cellar? And why is it next to the tape store?' He prowled around the room, examining the racks closely, then homed in on a set at the far end of the room. He took a tiny pen-light from his pocket and, on hands and knees, peered between the bottles then reached into a space and gave a tug. The rack swung out, as the tape shelves had swung out. They both craned forward expectantly. What they saw was a massive, steel door. Worthy of a bank vault; with a time-lock and elaborate combination.

Stewart squatted on his heels and examined it closely, then he stood up and dusted his trousers. 'That's it, then. There is no way on earth anyone is going to get through there. It is the latest and the best. Even explosives or carbon-arc wouldn't shift that door.' He swung the rack closed again and it clicked into place. He couldn't hide his disappointment. Elaine could see it in his face and her heart went out to him. She kissed him, in consolation. He put his hands on her waist and kissed her back. The feel of her lissom hips was putting thoughts into his mind. 'Darling,' he whispered, 'this is the first time we've been alone, in private, for ages.'

The same thought was in her mind. At the first touch of his lips, her vagina had begun to tingle and moisten. She remembered the naughty panties she was wearing and a picture flashed through her mind of herself, with legs spread, while Stewart's finger hooked into the transparent crotch and brushed her sex as he pulled them down. She kissed him again, passionately, her tongue thrusting and probing between his teeth, her hand reaching down to tug at his zip.

She felt a cool draught of air on her thighs and bottom as he hauled up her skirt at the back, then his hands were inside her panties, squeezing and massaging her bottom cheeks. As she felt the flesh of his penis in her hand, growing and hardening, his hands moved to and fro, easing the panties down off her hips, leaving her buttocks bare. With them down to mid-thigh, she bent her knees and pulled him down on top of her, onto the floor. He pulled the panties right down and she kicked out with her feet, to free herself of them. Then she spread her legs as wide as they would go, parting her thighs and opening her sex to him. He flipped up her skirt, so that she was naked from the navel downwards, while she wrestled with his belt and pulled his trousers and pants down. Then he was between her legs and she groped for his penis, to guide it into her wet cleft. As he penetrated her, she arched her back and tore at the buttons of her dress, unclipping the front fastener of her brassiere, to provide access to her breasts. He kissed and sucked her erect nipples and she began to grind her hips, dreamily and rhythmically, in time with his thrusts.

From her position, on her back, she could see over his shoulder. With eyes blurred with passion, she tried to make out what it was that shone red. Suddenly, she clenched and screamed, pushing him away from her. 'Stewart! Oh, my God! Stewart! It's a camera!' The remorseless electronic eye had been watching them, and the electronic ear had been listening to them, ever since they entered the wine cellar.

'That's right!' said Madam Max. 'It's a camera.' They rolled over and sat up, trying to adjust their clothes. She stood in the doorway. Beside her was Hans, and he had an automatic pistol in his hand, covering them.

Madam Max said, 'Get up and face the wall. No, don't bother to pick up your panties. You won't be needing them. Put your hands behind you.' They did so and she came up behind them, careful not to impede Hans' line of fire. Elaine felt cords encircle her wrists and saw Stewart dealt with in the same way.

'Turn round!'

Hans returned the pistol to its shoulder holster and Madam Max came close to them, peering into their faces. 'So, Mr Ganton. You thought you could slip out of my clutches. And you,' she gripped Elaine's chin, squeezing the sides of her face and forcing her head back, 'you have betrayed me. I loved you and trusted you and you rewarded me with treachery.'

Hans pushed them out of the cellar in front of him and ordered them along the corridor to another basement room. This one had a steel door with a barred aperture. He unlocked it and they went in, assisted by pushes. It was lit only by a small, barred window. The only furnishings were two upright, wooden chairs. Set into the walls and floor, at intervals, were rings and chains. Elaine shivered.

Hans produced his gun again and pointed it at Stewart. Madam Max said, 'Hans doesn't say much, but he wants you to sit down.' Stewart sat on one of the chairs. She came behind him and untied one wrist. She pulled his hands around the back of the chair, passed the rope under one of the back rails and retied it.

'Strip the girl, Hans. Everything off. Shoes as well.' With hands still tied behind her, Elaine could do nothing to prevent him. He grasped two handfuls of the front of her dress and ripped it apart in a spray of buttons. Her brassiere was still unfastened and her bare breasts sprang free. She had no covering on her lower half, having left her panties in the cellar. He pulled the dress and bra down her arms, to her wrists. He gripped the wrist cords through the material and lifted her arms, forcing her to bend forward. She was like a toy in his powerful grip. He raised them further and she fell on her knees. He pushed, and she sprawled face down on the floor, her bare breasts and belly against the cold stone.

Hans rested his weight across her thighs and removed the shoes from her kicking feet. He felt through the dress material and unfastened the knots, so that he could remove the dress completely. When she was naked, he hauled her up by the rope on one wrist, dangling her like a doll. Pushing her back against the wall, he raised that wrist above her head, passed the cord through a large ring then pulled the other wrist up to be secured again.

Madam Max came close to her and stroked both forefingers around her nipples in a circular motion, then grasped a breast in each hand and squeezed, making her wince. 'I have such plans for these, dear Elaine.'

She beckoned to Hans and he came forward and pressed his pistol into Elaine's navel. She winced at the coldness and the cruel pressure.

'Now for you, Mr Ganton. I shall release you and you will strip, too. If you have any tricks in mind, remember where Hans' gun is pointing. Her death would be slow and painful. I'm sure you don't want to be responsible for it.' She unfastened Stewart's hands and stood back. He hesitated. 'Get on with it, Mr Ganton. A full strip, please. Every stitch.' She watched, with gloating satisfaction as Stewart removed his clothes. She took each item from him as he took it off and threw it into the corner of the room. When he was naked, she made him sit down again and refastened his hands, as before. With more ropes, she fixed his ankles to the front legs of the chair, then stood back and looked at him.

'We'll soon see how clever you are, Mr Ganton. You and that trollop of yours. I don't like to do things in a hurry and I want to think about what I am going to do with you both, so you can wait here, while I do. It will give you a chance to guess what is going to happen to you.' She signed to Hans and they left the room, locking the door behind them.

Long minutes went by, then Elaine's head drooped

and she began to sob quietly. Stewart pulled at his restraints but couldn't budge them. 'Come on, darling. Buck up. We aren't dead yet.'

'No, but I'm so afraid, Stewart. What is going to become of us?' She raised her head and his heart went out to her.

'You mustn't be frightened, Elaine. That is what she wants. If she scares you, she's won. You mustn't let her break you. Try to think of something else.'

There was another long pause, then Elaine gave him a watery smile and, in a wobbly voice, said, 'I am thinking of something nice, now.'

'That's better. What are you thinking of?'

'I'm thinking of you and what we nearly managed to do in the cellar. I'm thinking of your hotel room and the first time we did it. I'm trying to remember the feel of you inside me, darling.'

'Jolly good, old thing. That's the style.'

There was a gruffness to his voice which she did not understand, then she saw his flaccid penis twitch and light dawned. 'Why, Stewart. I do believe I can do things to you, even at this distance.' Womanlike, she was intrigued with this notion of power.

'Yes,' he said. 'Probably. Time to be thinking of something else, now.'

'Why, Stewart? Don't you like looking at me and thinking about sex?' She was filled with curiosity to see how she could affect him. 'Just think, dearest. If I was all trussed up like this and you were free, you could do anything you liked to me, and I wouldn't be able to stop you. You could rub your hands over my breasts.' She looked down at them and thrust them out, provocatively. 'With my hands bound up here, I could only watch.' She looked across at him and was elated to see that his penis had, most definitely, stirred.

217

She pretended contrition. 'I'm sorry, darling. I didn't mean to make your penis grow. That was naughty of me. I deserve a good spanking.' She wriggled round, ducking under her own arms until she faced the wall, then parted her legs and thrust her body backwards, giving him a good view of the full, white, roundness of her haunches. 'I think I ought to have my bottom smacked, don't you? It would be a good chance, while I am tied up like this. Good, hard, stinging smacks – not love pats – that would make me jump, like this. Ouch! Ouch!' She matched the noises with contractions of her muscles, which made the delectable mass of her backside twitch and wobble. 'Wouldn't you like to spank me, Stewart? I'd love you to smack my naughty, white bottom until it's all red and sore. It would make me want you so much that I would get all hot and wet inside, so that I would just *have* to turn round . . .' She suited the action to the words, '. . . and open my legs, like this, so that you could see me just twitching to feel your penis up me.'

She spread her legs wide and came up onto tiptoe, with knees slightly bent, pushing her pubes forward. By rhythmically contracting her vaginal muscles, she made her vulva pulsate, knowing that he could see it quite clearly. She thrilled as she saw that his once-flaccid organ was now in a state of full erection, showing the power she had over him.

She smiled and relaxed. 'Trouble is, my lover, that by doing that I have made myself *really* want you, and there's nothing either of us can do about it. We'll just have to hang around and try to come off the boil.' They waited on, but now the waiting was easier to bear. The little game had relieved the tension and reduced the anxiety.

When Madam Max returned with Hans she

brought a leather strap and a small cloth bag. Hans was carrying what seemed to be a wooden plank. Elaine saw that it was not the light strap used in fantasies, but a real one – hard and heavy. Madam Max said, 'I have decided how to deal with you both. My punishment will last several days, allowing you time to rest in between sessions, so that you will be fully aware of the discomfort of each. By the time I have finished you will wish that you had never been born, let alone meddled in my affairs. For Mr Ganton, that period of reflection will be short, as I cannot allow him to live. For you, treacherous bitch that you are, the period will be longer because I am going to have you drugged and crated and sent to a brothel in South America, where you will wish that I had killed you, too.

'Hans. I will start by thrashing the girl. Mr Ganton may watch. Turn her to face the wall.' Not wanting to be touched by him, Elaine turned herself, spread her legs and braced herself for what was coming. She hoped that she could endure without screaming, although her whole body trembled in anticipation of that strap. She closed her eyes and prayed. Stewart, watching, saw Madam Max position herself, strap in hand, and raise her arm. For long moments she stayed like that and he thought that she was simply being cruel, delaying the first stroke for maximum terror. Then he saw the play of emotions on her face as she looked at Elaine's naked helplessness and knew, intuitively, that she was having trouble. Elaine had got to her as no-one else had done for a long time and she could not bring herself to do this thing, in spite of what had happened. Madam Max's arm dropped. With fresh resolve, she raised it again, but Stewart knew that she was not going to be able to carry it through. He heaved a mental sigh of relief as her arm fell to her side and, in a voice hoarse with emotion, said, 'I will work up to the thrashing, later. Hans, turn her to face front and tie her legs apart.' Shuddering with relief at her reprieve and unable to understand how it had come about, Elaine allowed herself to be turned. Her legs were widely parted and roped to rings in the wall.

Hans brought the plank and fastened it, upright, to the wall between her legs. From the cloth bag Madam Max produced the rubber penis she had used on Chiquita; the one with the magneto and the metal stud. Kneeling between Elaine's spread legs, she introduced the penis into her vagina and thrust it upwards. She switched it on and it made a whirring sound. Elaine knew that the metal button was live and, to keep it away from herself, she rose on her toes. Madam Max followed the movement and Elaine hitched herself higher. A couple more such moves and Elaine was on the extreme tips of her toes, quite unable to get any higher. At that point, Madam Max clamped the penis to the plank and picked up the dangling leads. With elaborate care, she pinched Elaine's nipples into erection, then clipped a lead onto each.

Satisfied, she stepped back. 'Now we just wait,' she said. The whirring vibration of the penis inside her was causing Elaine to lubricate copiously, so that her juices leaked past the penis. She felt her first orgasm coming, but still managed to hold her position through the throes of it, knowing that to move her body lower – even by half an inch – would bring the metal button onto her clitoris. Her face was twisted with concentration and she stared wildly at her tied wrists and her clipped breasts, as though, by looking at them, she could release them. Then her second orgasm began and, at the same time, she felt the tortured muscles of her thighs and calves beginning to tremble with the strain. Still she hung on, gasping and panting, through the contractions. Then, her tired muscles were leaping and jumping and, in spite of every effort of will, they would no longer support her weight. She sank a quarter of an inch, then jerked herself up. Then, the full half inch. The button made contact and she had never felt anything like it. The intense, tickling irritation of the tiny current linked nipples and clitoris and she saw stars as a huge orgasm overwhelmed her. She jerked herself up in the midst of it, but there was no strength left in her and she fell back onto the source of the stimulation, so that another orgasm followed immediately on the first. She heard herself screaming. She wanted to beg for mercy; to ask to be released; to have the thing taken from her, but she was too far gone to be articulate. She screamed herself hoarse as a never-ending tide of orgasms flowed through her. Only when she began to lose consciousness did Madam Max switch off the tool and remove it. She hung, half-fainting, supported only by her tied wrists. It was the pain of the cords digging into her flesh which aroused her and she took her weight on her feet again, slowly coming back to awareness.

Madam Max had been waiting for her to recover. 'That is just a taste of what is to come. Now it is your turn to watch, while I deal with Mr Ganton.' She crossed over to where he sat, tied hand and foot to his chair, and turning to face Elaine she slipped out of her kimono. She wore nothing underneath, as usual. 'Mr Ganton seems to be a sturdy young man and well built. I thought it would be amusing if, to start with, I took my pleasure of him while you watch.' She stooped and took his limp penis in her hand, massaging gently. 'First, we must get him into the right frame of mind.' She continued the treatment, but the penis remained flaccid. She frowned. 'I hope you are not going to prove uncooperative, Mr Ganton,' she said.

She straddled his half-recumbent body. Holding his head, she pulled his face towards her and rubbed her pubic hair across it. After a while, she stepped off and gave a gesture of annoyance as she saw that her actions had had no effect on his lack of tumescence. 'Hans. Bring the girl here.' Hans unfastened Elaine's ankles, untied her and dragged her across the room by the arm. He forced her to her knees in front of Stewart. 'Let's see what you can do with him, my dear. I want him erect.'

Elaine shook her head, 'No!'

'Very well, Elaine. There are other ways of warming him up. Hans, your cigarette lighter.' She bent over Stewart's helpless body and took the tip of his penis between finger and thumb, extending it. With the lighter in the other hand she said, 'Is this really what you want me to do?'

Elaine shook her head dumbly and crawled forward. 'Forgive me, Stewart,' she said. And taking his limp penis in her hand she began to massage it. She felt an immediate stirring under her fingers and he groaned.

'Nice and stiff, Elaine. I think a little mouth-work is necessary, don't you?' Reluctantly, she bent forward and took his organ into her mouth, tonguing and sucking until it was ramrod straight.

'Thank you. You may sit down and watch. I can manage the rest.' Hans pulled the second chair across so that it faced Stewart's and thrust Elaine into it. She watched in fascinated horror as Madam Max stepped across Stewart's knees and pressed her pubes against his stomach. Slowly, she bent her knees until his erect penis brushed her pubic hair, then reached between her legs to guide it into her vagina. As she sank down onto it, Stewart tugged furiously at his cords but he was quite powerless to prevent her from doing anything she had a mind to. She rode rhythmically up and down his length, pulling his head in between her breasts. 'Mmmm! What a lovely man!' she said, over her shoulder, 'I can see what you see in him.'

She went on like that for a while, then raised herself from him and got off. Her juices gleamed on his straining penis. She turned round to face Elaine, then backed into Stewart's lap, reaching behind her to guide him to the lips of her sex. Again, she sank until his full length was in her. She spread her legs to show Elaine. Stewart's scrotum was raised and tight. The trunk of his erection was only just visible, disappearing as it did between the bright pink labial lips among the soft, silky, black pubic hair. She pulled the top part of her sex apart, exposing her clitoris, and massaged it gently with her wet forefinger. Slowly, very slowly, she straightened her knees a little and rose up the length of his penis, her lips dragging on it with a slurping noise. When she was sure Elaine could see nearly all of it, she sank down again and sat for a while, her stomach muscles contracting, so that Elaine could tell that she was using her powerful vaginal muscles to feel up and down him.

'This is very nice, but what would make it perfect is if you were to crawl over here and give my clitoris some attention. I know you know how to do that, dear.' Blushing, Elaine crawled forward as bid, and

223

spread her open. She applied her tongue to the button of her clitoris and she jumped and began to move, more rapidly, up and down. Elaine had difficulty in keeping pace with her and, indeed, could not do so as her climax approached and her bouncing grew frantic. Faster and faster she moved, her fingers groping for her clitoris. When she found it, she rubbed it, hard and fast. Then she came, shuddering and gasping, her legs trembling with the cessation of effort.

Madam Max sat where she was for a little while, her stomach muscles twitching occasionally, with the sensation of the still-erect organ in her vagina. Then she recovered herself and got off Stewart. 'That will do for now.' She looked at Stewart's hard penis. 'It seems a shame that should go to waste. Perhaps it will keep Elaine occupied while we are away. Bring her here.'

Hans pulled Elaine forward. 'You straddle him, like I did.' Elaine obeyed. Facing Stewart, she stepped over his legs.

'Down you go. Get it into you.' Elaine bent her knees and her vagina engulfed Stewart. Madam Max pulled her arms forward, so that her breasts were crushed against his face, then tied them to a low rung of the chair, to keep them there. More ropes went about her ankles to fasten them to the back legs of the chair, then they were bound together in a permanent embrace. Elaine wriggled in embarrassment. 'You'd better keep still, child, or he might have the ejaculation he has been fighting,' said Madam Max. 'You can stay like that until I come again for the next session.' She and Hans went out and left them alone.

There was a long silence, each of them trying to think of something to say which wouldn't sound ridiculous. Eventually Stewart said, 'I hope you're not thinking of taking advantage of this situation.'

That cleared the awkwardness. Elaine giggled. 'It's where I wanted you, earlier on, but not quite like this. Are you all right?'

'Yes, OK. It's a bit hard to see and breathe down here.'

'Sorry. I don't think I can do much about it, but I'll try.' She hitched herself up, trying to get her breasts out of his face, but her arms were stretched too tightly and she could not get enough leverage in her legs.

After a few tries he said, 'I don't think you should do that any more.'

'Why not?'

'Because every time you wiggle up and down it does amazing things to me and something may happen. I've had a tough job, not letting her get it and I'm about ready to burst.'

She was sympathetic. 'I know how that feels. Well, no need to hold back any longer. You can let me have it and get it off your mind.'

'No. Better not. Keep still, Elaine. Elaine! Don't do that!'

She was using what slack she had to bounce in his lap. 'There's not a lot you can do about it,' she said. 'Why don't you give up and let go.'

She continued her bouncing, feeling him pulse inside her. Soon, he gave a great sigh and ejaculated. She felt the heat of his sperm bathing her and it was comfortingly normal. She rested on him, contracting her vaginal walls to suck the last drops from him as she felt his erection subsiding. He relaxed and she said, 'There. Isn't that better?'

Man-like, once the deed was done, it was done and he could move on to other things. 'Now we've got to get out of here.'

'Out of here? Are you kidding? What about the little details, like these ropes and a locked door, or are you Harry Houdini in disguise?'

'Actually, darling, you are not far off hitting the nail on the head. Houdini's escapes were made possible by the fact that he could conceal things to help him.'

'Oh? And I suppose you just happen to have a sharp knife . . . My God! You *do* have a knife! Where is it?'

Stewart nodded with his head, as best he could, towards the crumpled pile of his clothes in the corner of the room. 'In my trouser pocket. All we have to do is to get over there.'

They set about learning how to make the chair move and, after a few false starts, developed a rhythm which enabled them to work their feet together to lift it and move it, a few inches at a time, in the direction they wanted to go.

They got near the pile of clothes and Elaine said, 'How are we going to pick your trousers up? I can't reach the ground and neither can you.'

'I thought of that. We'll have to tip the chair over, but we'd better get it right, because I don't think we'll be able to move far once we're on the ground.' They guessed at the right place to make their move, then threw the weight of their bodies sideways. The chair went over onto its side with a crash, taking them with it, unable to break their fall.

Stewart said, 'Are you all right?'

'Yes. I'm OK. I've got the trousers. Which pocket?'

'Right hand. You can see your hands and I can't, so you'll have to cut yourself loose, first. Watch yourself. It's very sharp.' It was not difficult and she managed it, first time. Overwhelming relief flooded through her as her hands came free and she could sit back from his face. She rubbed some feeling back into her wrists. Leaning into his face again, she freed his hands, then her own ankles.

She was about to cut the cords on his ankles, when they heard footsteps in the corridor. Her stomach turned to water. Free his ankles? No time! Already, a key was rattling in the lock. She searched frantically for some sort of weapon. The only thing in the room was the other chair. She grabbed it and scooted silently to a position by the door, where she would be hidden when it opened.

The door swung open and Hans came in carrying a tray. He grunted in surprise when he saw Stewart in the corner and took a couple of paces towards him. Holding the chair by the back, Elaine shut her eyes and swung right round in a complete circle, like a hammer thrower, before aiming at where she thought Hans ought to be. She felt the chair connect and opened her eyes in time to see him pitch forward onto his face like a felled tree. There were fragments of smashed chair all over the floor and she held only a small part of the back in her hands. She dropped it and ran to Stewart, fumbling for the knife to free his ankles. 'Oh, Stewart. Have I knocked him out?'

'Knocked him out! Jesus, lady! You've probably killed the poor sod. Remind me not to pick a fight with you!' He crossed over to the prone figure and checked his pulse.

Elaine wanted to vomit. 'I didn't mean to kill him.'

'Don't worry. You didn't. Must have a steel skull. He'll have a lump in the morning. Help me to tie him.' Together, they secured him with their discarded ropes. Stewart put his clothes on and Elaine did the best she could with her torn dress. Stewart took

Hans' pistol from its holster and a spare clip of ammunition from his pocket.

They saw no-one as they made their way to Elaine's room. She changed into respectable clothes, then they went together, in search of Madam Max. They found her in the drawing room, sitting in her usual place, on the sofa. She jumped up as they entered. 'How . . .?'

Stewart drew her attention to the pistol in his hand. 'Don't ask questions, and keep your hands where I can see them. Tie her up with something, Elaine.'

'I can do better than that!' said Elaine. She went to the cupboard in the panelling and came back with a pair of handcuffs. She pulled Madam Max's hands behind her and cuffed them together.

Stewart relaxed and put the gun in his pocket. 'You can sit down again now, Max.' She did so, and Elaine had to admire the way she had, so quickly, recovered from what must have been a nasty shock.

'Well. And what now, Mr Ganton?' Madam Max showed no sign of emotion.

'The game's up, Max. We have the whole of your meeting with Mrs Ortez on tape. The police are on their way. You're going to prison.'

Madam Max did not turn a hair. 'Do you really think I believe you, Mr Ganton? I know you wouldn't dare call the police. You'd only get yourself into trouble, not me. You know that I wouldn't even come to trial and that, even if I did, I would be acquitted. I know too much about too many people.'

'Oh, you'll come to trial, Max. Now you will give me the combination for your secret room.'

She laughed, scornfully. 'Oh, really! Give me a little credit, Mr Ganton. As long as what is in there remains known only to me, I can't be touched, and you know it.'

'Then I'll get an expert in to break into it.'

She laughed again. 'Carry on, if you want him killed. There is a device fitted to the door which cannot be defused from outside. If an attempt is made to open it without the combination, the penalty is death. Which expert is going to volunteer, do you think?'

For an answer, Stewart rose and motioned her to get up. 'Come with me,' he said. And with Elaine following, he took her by the arm and led her to the room where they had been confined.

Hans had recovered and was sitting up. Stewart said, 'Remember how we escaped. Make sure she doesn't have a key on her.' Elaine was startled for a moment, then dived her hands into the pockets in Madam Max's kimono. 'That's not good enough,' Stewart said. 'We'd better take her clothes with us.' He took out his pistol. 'Uncuff her.' Elaine did so and Stewart said, 'Guess it's your turn, Max. Get it off.' Calmly and contemptuously, Madam Max slipped out of her kimono and stood naked. 'Now check everywhere for a key.' Elaine didn't understand. Stewart explained patiently. 'Take the pins out of her hair and comb through it with your fingers. Now look in her ears. And her mouth.'

'There's nothing there, Stewart!'

He sighed. 'You still don't get it, do you. She could have one anywhere.' He waved the gun at Madam Max. 'Turn round. Part your legs. Bend over and hold your ankles.' Seething, Madam Max did so. At last Elaine understood, and undertook the necessary, intimate body search, making Madam Max draw in her breath sharply as her anus and vagina were explored by Elaine's fingers. 'OK,' said Stewart. 'Now you can cuff her to the wall. Separate her hands and use two sets.' Elaine selected a pair of rings about four feet apart, at waist level, and secured Madam Max between them, one wrist cuffed to each ring.

Stewart turned his attention to Hans. Squatting beside him he said, 'The jig's up, Hans. The game is blown and the police will be here soon.' He counted on his fingers, 'Aggravated assault; indecent assault; conspiring to extort; living on immoral earnings; illegal possession of a firearm. Your arse is grass, my old mate, and there is a big, big, lawn-mower on the way. You've got, maybe, half an hour. Perhaps less. Why don't you go and spread the word among the other guards? Do you catch my drift?'

Hans nodded and Stewart released him. He got up, rubbing his wrists. Stewart said, 'I'll follow him, just to make sure he got the message. Why don't you go and tell the girls what's happening? Don't forget to lock the door when you go.'

Elaine and Madam Max were left alone, together. Elaine was burning to ask the question which was on her mind. 'Max. Why didn't you beat me when you had the chance?'

Madam Max stared resolutely at the wall, refusing to meet her eyes. 'I had my reasons.'

'I think I know what they were. Thank you.'

Madam Max was silent for a while, then she said, 'You never felt anything for me, did you? It was all just a pretence?'

Elaine said gently, 'No. I didn't, Max. I'm sorry about that. And I'm sorry for you now . . .'

'You're sorry for me?' Madam Max's eyes flashed. 'I don't need your pity. Soon, I shall be free and you will find that my power and reach are infinite. You are going to regret crossing me.' There was a venom in her voice which scared Elaine and she was glad to leave, being careful to lock the door behind her.

11
Revenge is Sweet

When Elaine and Stewart met again, in the drawing room, he was able to report that the guards had all packed up and left. 'So much for loyalty!' he said. Elaine reported that she had spread the word through the house. The dormitory girls had cheered. The professional girls had been philosophical and she thought they would leave. The kitchen and domestic staff were staying on for a while, in the hope that someone would take over the house and they would keep their jobs. The captive 'maid' had been ecstatic. Elaine had taken the trouble to go to the Control Room to give Joe an opportunity to leave. She felt she owed him that.

Stewart said, 'So, what we have is one tape; one blackmail proposition and no corroborating witnesses? It doesn't look good. We've got to get that combination or we might just as well let her go, now.'

'But couldn't we have her arrested? The police can break her down, can't they?' asked Elaine. Stewart smiled indulgently at her naivete.

'She'd be entitled to the full protection of the law. Not obliged to say anything, and all that.'

Elaine was incredulous. 'But that's not fair. *She* breaks the law as much as she likes and then, when she's caught, it helps her to get away with it.'

'I won't comment on that. The fact remains that, if she is arrested on what we have now, the blackmail won't stop. We've got to get into that room. That's the only way we can be sure she'll lose her grip on the people who are afraid of her now.

'I don't understand,' Elaine said. 'Surely, with the whole lot of evidence . . .?'

'Think about it. If what I think is in that room *is* in there, then the most powerful and influential people in the world are involved. If there was a trial she would make sure that plenty of dirty laundry got washed. The government would collapse – and not just ours. Confidence in banks would be shattered. No-one would have any more faith in law and justice. It would be anarchy.'

'But if all that rotten stuff is there, under the surface, shouldn't it be stopped?'

'And replaced with what? How do you find totally incorruptible people to rebuild what's been lost? And if they're incorruptible when you find them, who is to say they will stay that way? No. The system isn't perfect, but it works. You may eat an apple with a worm in it, but if you never actually see it, it doesn't matter.' Stewart paused reflectively. 'No. The only possible way for everyone to be free, me included, is if Madam Max is put out of business, all her records destroyed and we can be sure she won't start again. There's nothing else for it. If we can't get into that room, we have been wasting our time and taking risks for nothing.'

There was a knock at the door. It was Lilian, the dormitory girl Elaine had seen 'rousted'. 'Has Madam Max been taken away, yet?'

Stewart said, 'No. Not yet. Why do you ask?'

'Me and the other girls got together and they sent

232

me to ask. Before she goes, do you think we could have her to ourselves for a bit?'

'You mean, for a bit of your own back?'

'Yes. Why not? She's a spiteful bitch.'

A plan was forming in Stewart's mind. 'If I allowed that, you'd have to promise not to really hurt her. I don't want a broken, bleeding corpse on my hands.'

Lilian was offended. 'We're not as bad as she is. Nothing worse than what she's done to us and the other girls.'

'All right, Lilian. But if I do that for you, you've got to do something for me. She knows the number of a combination I need. And it's got to be the right one, not a lie, or the safe blows up. Do you think you can get it?'

Lilian rubbed her hands. 'You just watch us.'

'Elaine,' said Stewart. 'Perhaps you'd better do just that. Watch them – I mean. Just to see they don't get too carried away. Are you sure you can handle her, Lilian? She's a fighter.'

'There's sixteen of us, all hoping she does put up a fight.'

Stewart grinned. 'OK then. You go and get your friends and bring them back with you.'

She left and Elaine said, 'Oh, Stewart. This doesn't seem right.'

'Of course it's not right, but we're desperate. The alternative is to let her get away with it and spoil the lives of hundreds of people, like Mrs Ortez. Anyway, although I'm not a vindictive man, I must say I'm looking forward to my next interview with the lady.'

When Stewart went into the cell, Madam Max greeted him with scorn. 'Well, Mr Clever. I guess the great brain hasn't come up with anything. Why don't you let me go, now, and have done with it?'

Stewart was rueful. 'Guess you're right, Max. I'll just have to let you go.' He unlocked her cuffs and she stood still, rubbing her wrists.

She looked at him suspiciously. 'I don't trust you. What's the game?'

'Oh, I don't have a game, Max – but Lilian does. Come in Lilian. And she's brought her friends to see you.' A horde of dormitory girls crowded into the small room. 'They want you to come out to play.'

Madam Max went white. 'You can't do this. I know my rights. I demand to be arrested, at once.'

Stewart smiled. 'You mean, you are ready to confess and give me that combination?'

She chewed her lip furiously. 'Go to hell!' she spat.

Stewart stepped back. 'I was afraid you'd say that. She's all yours, girls. Take her away.'

They cheered as they closed in on her, each of them anxious to grab a piece. They couldn't all get a grip on her, but there were plenty of them to carry her, naked, squirming and kicking, out of the room. Elaine followed them as they bore her triumphantly to the Blue Room and dumped her unceremoniously onto a blue velvet table top.

They didn't bother to strap her down, but seemed to enjoy holding her. 'Damn you! What are you going to do?' Then the crowd parted and she saw Mary, razor and tin of foam in her hands.

'I stayed behind, especially to give you this going away present,' said Mary. 'I hope you enjoy it as much as I did. Spread her legs, girls.'

Max set up a tremendous struggle but there was no way she could prevent her legs being pulled wide apart. Mary applied the foam and shaved, with loving care, until her pubes was smooth and bald. Then they up-ended her, with knees against her chest, so that

Mary could reach the area around her bottom cleft and vulva.

When that was smooth too, Mary paused. 'Oh, I nearly forgot. Remember sticking your finger up my bum? I wouldn't want you to miss anything.' She squirted lather onto the tight, brown sphincter and inserted the whole of her index finger, wiggling it until Max squirmed and shook.

Next, the girls attached leather cuffs to Max's wrists and ankles and dragged her into a kneeling position on the end of the table. Her ankles were clipped to the edges of the table and straps behind her knees parted her legs widely, and secured her in place. A bar was set up just level with her buttocks and Elaine could see that it was studded with many small pins. It was obviously a form of restraint with which she was familiar, because she fought like a wild thing, to avoid the next stage. But there were too many of them and her arms were pulled back and clipped to the table edges near her ankles, so that she was arched backwards, like a bow, straining to avoid resting her bottom against the pins on the bar.

They paused then, and just stood, looking at her, drinking in the abject helplessness of her predicament; her bald pubes were thrust forward obscenely and every detail of her sex was revealed to gloating eyes. When she saw one of the girls approaching with a jug of water and a glass, she moaned.

'Yes. That's right,' said Mary. 'You know what's coming, don't you. How many times have you used this one? Now you can find out how it feels.' She held up the little, padded whip which Max had used on her and flexed it in her hands. 'Oh, I *do* hope you are going to be disobedient.' She held the glass of water to the upturned lips. 'Drink!'

With only a moment's hesitation, but glaring daggers, Madam Max drank and Mary continued to tilt the glass until it was empty. It was refilled and Mary positioned it. 'Again!' This time, it took a little longer for the glass to be emptied, when it was relentlessly refilled and pressed to her lips. 'Another!'

'No! No! Please! I can't!'

Mary climbed onto the table and stood behind her, looking down at the naked body arched back towards her. 'Then you remember what you get for disobedience. One on each nipple and three on your new bald spot, until you decide that there is nothing you would like better than to drink another glass of water.'

She began a slow and rhythmic tattoo and Madam Max gasped and squirmed as much as she could. Her breasts and pubic area slowly reddened under the persistent slaps of the pad and presently she gasped, 'Stop! Stop! I'll drink!'

Mary did not pause for a second. 'You don't sound convinced, Max. I need to hear you beg for a drink as if you were really thirsty.'

'Ow! Ow! Please! Please! Let me drink!'

'All right, if you insist.' Mary held the glass again and watched a third half-pint disappear. When she tried to force down a fourth glassful, Madam Max retched halfway through and water ran out of her mouth and down over her bare breasts and stomach.

'I think she's full up, now,' said Mary. To Elaine, she added. 'Now we just have to wait. We chose this one because it is one of the most ingenious of Madam Max's torments. You have to hand it to her. She really knew how to make a person suffer without inflicting real injury. It is the anticipation which is almost as bad as anything else. She knows that it is only a matter of time before she will need to pee really badly. She'll do what we had to do; hold it and hold it until she is bursting, while we trickle water into a bowl to make things worse. You'd think she would just be able to let it go and not care, but none of us ever could. There's something about going while everyone's watching, not to mention the inhibition of having nothing to go into. So we waited and hoped and, every now and again, she would bring a chamber pot close. Just as you thought you were going to be able to let go, she would take it away again. It's a dreadful, teasing torment. Of course, she knows that she will, eventually, be able to relieve herself. But mixed with that pleasure will be the knowledge that she will then have to drink a glass of her own urine. If she refuses, we simply start all over again with water and waiting. No-one ever refuses.'

Elaine approached the nude, fettered body on the table and noted the tension in the muscles; the short, gasping breaths brought on by the strain of holding her bare bottom away from the pins; the upthrust breasts and eyes staring at the ceiling in wild despair as the sensation of a full bladder began to make itself apparent.

'Madam Max. Why don't you tell me the combination? You could spare yourself all this.'

The eyes did not look away from the ceiling and the voice was a hiss. 'Go to hell! I can take anything they can dish out and still win.'

'Quite the little spitfire, isn't she?' said Mary, and climbed onto the table again. Straddling Max's upturned face, she said, 'You remember what comes next, don't you?'

'Yes.'

'Tell Elaine,' Mary prompted.

'I shall have to service her by licking her to orgasm.'

'Oh, not just me, but all the girls, Maxie. And what did you do to us when we were near to bursting?' Getting no response, Mary tapped her padded whip against Max's bare stomach. 'Come on, Maxie. What did you do to us?'

'Damn you!' Max spat; then, resignedly, to Elaine, 'A full bladder increases sensation in that area. They will masturbate me to bring on a quick orgasm and increase the need to go. Don't worry, though,' she added. 'I can deal with it.'

Elaine realised that there was little more she could do there and, satisfied that Madam Max was not being seriously injured, she went off to report progress to Stewart.

She found him in the canteen and got a cup of tea for herself, before she joined him. 'She's a tough nut, Stewart. I don't think she's going to crack, no matter what they do to her. Her will is far too strong.'

'Damn! I was hoping . . . It almost tempts one to consider the boiling oil and the red hot pokers. I was only joking!' he added, seeing Elaine's horrified expression. 'Anyway, I've a nasty feeling that wouldn't work, either. We seem to be stuck.' They sat on in gloomy silence, for quite a time, each busy with their own thoughts.

They were back in the drawing room a couple of hours later, when they were interrupted by Lilian, who came and sat down on the sofa without invitation. She looked from one to the other, obviously bursting with her own importance then, unable to contain herself any longer, she beamed and said, 'Eighty-two – forty-one – forty-three – zero-six!' They stared at her without comprehension. She repeated, 'Eighty-two – forty-one – forty-three – zero-six! Don't you get it? It's the combination you wanted.'

'You got it from her? She told you?' Lilian nodded happily. Elaine was baffled. 'But she was so defiant – so strong. How on earth did you do it?'

Lilian giggled. She produced two wooden meat skewers, each about eight-inches long and laid them on the table. 'With these!'

Elaine felt sick. 'My God, woman. What have you been doing to her?'

Lilian went all mysterious and laid her finger along the side of her nose. 'Why don't you come and see.'

They went back with her to the Blue Room. Stewart had to admit that he was concerned about what might have happened and Elaine was almost vomiting with apprehension. When they got into the room, their eyes went immediately to the only occupied table and both were relieved to see that Madam Max was at least alive and, apparently, not covered in blood and gore. She was no longer in her kneeling position, but half-sitting on the table. Her ankles were cuffed to the front of it, but her upper half was not restrained, except by a leather collar padlocked about her neck, and a short length of chain which prevented her from rising any further than to rest on her elbows, which she was doing as they came in. When she saw Lilian, she went into a panic. 'Nononononononono!' she screamed, 'Don't let her touch me! Please, don't let her touch me!'

As Lilian stood beside her, she shrank away, in obvious dread. It was clear that she was completely broken. 'Hi, Max!' said Lilian. 'These folk want you to tell them the combination.'

'I told you! I told you!'

'Yes, but they want to be sure it's true, and not something you made up.'

'It's true! It's true! I swear to God, it's true!'

239

'I think they need convincing. Hold her legs, girls!'
A group of girls gathered on either side of her and
held her from knee to ankle, at the same time gripping her toes and pulling them back towards her
knees. That seemed to Elaine to be rather excessive,
but she soon saw that it was not. Elaine went to the
bottom of the table and, with a skewer in each hand,
she gently scraped the pointed end in a figure of eight
on the sole of each foot.

The effect was so sudden and electrifying that it
made Elaine jump. Max went into total hysterics. Her
upper body leapt up from the table to the full length
of her chain, stopping with a jerk which might have
broken her neck. She flung herself about wildly, her
fist beating a tattoo on the table, and screamed,
'Woahoho! No! No! Nononononono! Mercy! No more!
Woahohoho!' Afraid that she would hurt herself,
Elaine stretched out her hand and stopped Lilian's
torture. Max collapsed into a sobbing bundle, 'It's
true! It's true! I swear! It's true!' she wept.

'Is that all you did?' asked Elaine. Lilian nodded.

In some admiration, Stewart asked, 'What made
you think of that?'

'Dunno! She was sitting there, all stuck up and it
just came to me. My sister used to do it to me when
I was little and I couldn't stand it. Some people can't
abide having their feet scratched, and it turns out
she's one of 'em.'

'Well done. If you've finished with her, for the time
being, we'll take her,' said Stewart.

'Yes,' said Lilian. 'We've had a bit of our own back
and that'll do for now. Any time she misbehaves, you
can bring her back and I'll do me stuff again. I enjoyed it!

It was a totally different Madam Max who walked

back to the drawing room with them. She was completely subdued and her whole posture showed it. They gave her back her kimono and made her take them to the basement. They watched while she fed in the combination and opened the door, then they took her back to the cell and left her there. They did not bother to handcuff her. There seemed no need.

They went back to the secret room and went in. There were filing cabinets and drawers containing tapes. They flicked through some of the files. 'My God!' said Stewart. 'Look at some of these names! There is no way she could have been touched while she held something over them.' They looked for a bit longer, now and again exclaiming to each other, 'Not *him!* Not *her!* Well ... Who would have thought of *them!*'

They put the papers back and went to the drawing room. 'What we've got to do,' said Stewart, 'is to establish the same kind of grip on her as she has had on other people.' He thought for a bit then said, 'Got it! She has to be filmed, squealing on her colleagues here and abroad. As many of them as we can make her admit to. A lot of straightforward drug smuggling and pushing is going to stop, now. If they knew she was the cause of it, her life wouldn't be worth a candle, and she knows it. We can hold that over her. We threaten to send them tapes of her confession if we ever hear that she is in business again.'

'I must say, that sounds fair. After all, it's only what she was doing to other people,' said Elaine.

They decided to make the tapes in the drawing room. Elaine went up to the Control Room and switched on the drawing room camera. Checking that there was a blank, long-play tape in the primary recorder she set it to record. Stewart fetched Max from her cell and they sat her down in an armchair facing the camera. She seemed perfectly docile and agreeable and the confession began. Stewart asked questions, prompted by information from the files, and she answered.

She began to recite details of drug-smuggling operations and all seemed to be going well, then something struck Elaine as a false note. Max had been asked about Cartegena and claimed that she did not know Sir James' contact there. Elaine, remembering what she had heard on James' answering machine, held up her hand quietly. 'Stewart. She has begun to lie.'

She explained what she had noticed and he agreed. 'Damn! That means the whole thing is useless.'

'I'd like to handle this. Can you leave us alone together while we have a woman to woman chat?'

'Are you sure you'll be all right?' he asked.

'I'm absolutely positive!' she replied, and there was something in her voice which made him believe her. He did not protest any more but left the room. She sat in silence looking at Max, who squirmed uneasily under her gaze. In truth, Elaine *did* feel capable of dealing with this. She was fed up to the teeth with Max. Just when it seemed that the whole thing was going to be over at last, she had gone and ruined it.

At last Elaine spoke. 'You lied!'

'No! No! Elaine. I made a mistake.'

'You did *not* make a mistake. You lied deliberately. You will have to learn not to do that. You must go back to Lilian.' She crossed to the telephone and picked it up.

Max flung herself on the floor in front of her, clasping her knees. 'Please, no! Elaine, please! Don't give me back to her. I won't do it again, I swear!'

'Once is too often. You have to be punished for it.' She started to dial.

'Yes! Yes! It was wrong of me. I have to be punished, I know. But *you* do it, Elaine. Don't give me to Lilian.' She threw off her kimono. 'Look, you can beat me. Do anything you like.' She grovelled, pleading.

Looking down at her, Elaine felt an urge grow within her which had nothing to do with wanting the truth. She wanted the satisfaction of domination. The recognition of that desire made her heart pump and her vagina tingle.

'I might consider that,' she said, as though in doubt. Although she already knew what she was going to do.

'Thank you, Elaine. Thank you!'

'From now on, you call me "Mistress".'

'Yes, Mistress. Of course.'

'Fetch my costume from the cupboard.' Max almost ran to get it. 'Help me into it.' With the red leather outfit on, she felt a surge of delight at what was coming. She flexed a cane in her hands, then appeared to change her mind. 'No. No. It has to be Lilian. Only that would be severe enough.' She went to the phone again.

Max was in tears, wringing her hands and Elaine gloried in her power over her. 'Please, Mistress. No! You can cane me! You can punish me enough!'

'Later, certainly. But for now you have to learn a lesson in humility. I have received certain requests about you and I have refused them until now. Your lies have made me change my mind.' Into the telephone she said, 'Madam Max will be waiting for you in the Blue Room in a quarter of an hour.'

'Not Lilian! Please, not Lilian!' Madam Max begged, still on her knees.

'No. Not Lilian – *if* you behave yourself and do

exactly what you're told, when you're told to do it. Now we'll go to the Blue Room, where your audience is waiting. No! Don't get up. You'll go all the way on your hands and knees.' Elaine followed the naked, crawling figure along the corridor, exulting in the vulnerability of that swaying bottom to the sting of her cane, any time she cared to apply it.

As they entered the room, a great cheer went up and Madam Max halted, only to be driven on by flicks of Elaine's cane.

'All the girls are here, Max,' said Elaine. 'I wonder if you remember this gentleman? Recently your maid, Millicent.'

Max looked up at the man, now dressed in his own clothes and her head sank to the carpet, in forlorn defeat.

'He has made a most reasonable request, in the circumstances. He wants to take you, from behind, with an audience. You'd like that, wouldn't you?'

The reply was almost inaudible. A mumbled, 'Yes, Mistress.'

'Louder. I don't think we all heard.'

'Yes, Mistress.'

'Now, sir. How would you like her? Any special clothing? A bit in her mouth, with reins for you to pull on? Frilly underwear or fully stripped, as she is?'

The man began to remove his clothes. 'A full strip is fine, thank you.'

'You heard that, Max? He is letting you off easy. Up you get then. Feet apart. Now, bend over. Touch your toes. Remember what you had me do in this room? Reach back and open yourself up, like that.'

Elaine watched, as Madam Max reached around and placed her fingers on either side of her bald and exposed, vaginal slit, to pull the lips apart.

'Oh dear! You don't seem to have understood. It's not that hole he wants to use, dear Max. It's the other one.'

Max shot upright, at once. 'No! No! You can't . . . I can't . . .!'

'Down! Down, I say! Grab those ankles!' Elaine administered two stinging slashes to the unprotected buttocks. 'Remember that Lilian is listening. Did I hear you say No!'

'No, Mistress.'

'Louder!'

'No, Mistress.'

'So, it's all right for this gentleman to use you any way he wants, is it?'

'Yes, Mistress.'

Elaine's smile was icy. She was rejoicing in her power over this woman. 'Mary will help you. You don't deserve it but she will save you some discomfort. Mary!'

Mary came forward with a large plastic tube of cold cream with a long nozzle. Max gasped and grimaced as Mary inserted the nozzle into the puckered ring of her anus and squeezed in a generous amount. Elaine stepped in front of the stooped figure, gathered a handful of hair and pulled her head up to look into her face. 'You know that I can have your wrists tied to your ankles, don't you?'

'Yes, Mistress.'

'Any nonsense from you, and that is what I will do. You will not let go of your ankles until I give you permission to do so. Understood?'

'Yes, Mistress.'

'Then we can begin.'

The man was, by this time, naked and in full erection. He stepped behind Madam Max, who squirmed as she felt the head of his penis against her rectum. He paused for a moment, in anticipation, holding her firmly by the hips. Then with a brutal thrust, he rammed his penis into her. She screamed, her bottom jerking up and down as her knees flexed involuntarily with the discomfort she was feeling, yet she continued to hold her ankles, as ordered. Her breasts jiggled back and forth, wildly uncontrolled, with the vibration of his rapid thrusts.

Mercifully for Max, he did not attempt to spin things out, but pumped faster and faster until he came, with a great cry of triumph, slamming his pubes against her backside as he spent high inside her. His withdrawal was not gentle either, eliciting another cry of pain from her drooling mouth. She continued to hold her ankles, sobbing quietly, while his sperm dribbled from her enlarged and abused hole.

'You can get up now – if you can,' said Elaine. Max came upright, very slowly and stood, crouched over the centre of her discomfort.

'Now to the drawing room. Come on. March!' The cane got Max going again and, with bowed head and parted legs, she shuffled out of the room.

Back in the drawing room, there was no respite. Elaine sensed that she had to complete her crushing domination and finish this haughty woman once and for all. She dragged a heavy chair into the centre of the room. 'This is just between you and me, in private, Max. You are going to get the thrashing you begged for. Get yourself over the back of the chair. Or do you prefer to go back to Lilian?'

'Oh, no! You beat me please, Mistress.' Max hurriedly draped herself over the high back of the chair, resting her hands on the seat in a position she had ordered herself, countless times. Elaine bound her wrists to the front legs, then her ankles to the back legs. Delighting in the picture thus presented, Elaine ran her hands lightly over the upturned and vulnerable bottom; fondled the defenceless, hanging breasts, then slipped her fingers up and down the sex lips which protruded between the parted thighs.

'Why Max, you're quite wet. I really believe this turns you on.' She picked up her cane and swished it through the air. Max cringed. 'Remember this moment, Max. You bent in submission. Me upright in domination. That is how it is always going to be from now on. Which of us is the boss, Max?'

'You are, Mistress.'

'What am I going to do to you?'

'You are going to cane me.'

'I am going to cane your bare bottom because you deserve it. Say it!'

'You're going to cane my bare bottom . . .'

'Why am I going to do that?'

'Because I deserve it, Mistress.'

'Is that true?'

'Oh, yes Mistress. Hurt me! Hurt me!'

'Very well. Kiss the cane.' Max's lips travelled up and down the length of the whippy bamboo.

Elaine raised her cane. 'You're sure about this?'

'Oh, yes Mistress. Cane me! Cane me hard!' With a fierce joy, Elaine slashed with the cane across her buttocks. She let all her anger flow out of her. This *bloody* woman – Slash! – who screwed Stewart – Slash! – and let Hans put his filthy paws on her – Slash! – and destroyed lives – Slash! 'That's right. Let me see your backside squirm; and let me hear you scream!' – Slash! – and now told lies – Slash! – which prevented the business being over – Slash!

In a white-hot frenzy of temper, she struck again

and again at the unprotected buttocks and thighs. In her berserk state, she was conscious of nothing except the quivering, juddering flesh, reddening beneath her cane, and the gasping shrieks which each slash elicited. Suddenly a spontaneous orgasm which struck without warning, like a thunderbolt, checked her in mid stroke and made her fall on her knees, clutching at her pubes through the leather costume.

Jesus God! What had she done! Who was she! The demon within her, hitherto only vaguely felt and regarded as a source of harmless fun, had burst forth and consumed her, revealing a depth of evil which frightened her. Sick, trembling and drained, she looked up at the bound and punished figure of Max, sobbing in pain. She staggered to her feet and stripped off the costume as if by doing so, she could strip off the memory of what had taken place. As she replaced her ordinary clothes, she rationalised. It had had to be done; for all the people who would suffer otherwise. For Sir James and Isabel. And Stewart.

There remained one task, to make sure of her permanent dominance. She picked up the phone. 'Lilian. Can you come and get Max. She needs one more session to convince her to co-operate.'

In the back seat of her taxi, Madam Max sat white and strained, looking neither left, nor right. 'Oh, Stewart,' said Elaine. Are you sure we are right to let her go?'

'There's nothing else we could do. Her power is broken. If she ever tries to cause us any trouble, she is as good as dead, because we hold the video tapes in which she involves some very nasty, unforgiving people.'

They watched as the taxi drove out of sight. Madam Max never turned her head to look back.

'So, that's that!' Elaine signed, contentedly. 'What's next, Stewart?'

'Well, there's a wedding, for a start.'

'Oh? Is there going to be a wedding?'

'Definitely. Most definitely. But first, the cleansing operation.' He picked up a remote control from the front seat of his red sports car, pointed it at the Grange and pressed the button. There was a brilliant burst of orange flame from the ground floor, followed immediately by successive explosions on all the other floors. Within seconds, the whole house was a raging inferno.

'Oh, Stewart. I suppose that was necessary? It seems a shame.'

'It's like woodworm or dry rot, darling. You can't pick at it. It has to be destroyed all at once. We couldn't search the whole place thoroughly enough to make sure we hadn't missed anything. Anyway, there'll be a lot of relieved people in the world, tonight.'

'No-one, not even you, will ever know what I did for them,' Elaine said.

'No, darling.' It did not seem tactful to mention that he had watched the whole of the drawing room tape and had it safely stored away, unedited.

As they drove away, together, into their future, a fragment of red leather poked from the lid of a cardboard box on his minuscule back seat, flapping in the breeze of their passage. After all, he thought, a turn-on is a turn-on. Waste not, want not.

NEW BOOKS

Coming up from Nexus and Black Lace

250

(*Nexus*)

Witch Queen of Vixania by Morgana Baron
March 1994   Price: £4.99   ISBN: 0 352 32900 9
In the mythical land of Vixania, the evil and salacious Queen Vixia has captured and imprisoned the rightful heir to the Throne of Earth. But before she can reduce him to an abject sex slave, she must overcome his powerful sexual magic and a formidable army of Amazon allies.

Elaine by Stephen Ferris
March 1994   Price: £4.99   ISBN: 0 352 32905 X
Elaine, taken on as a wealthy aristocrat's secretary, finds that the job entails taking down more than just notes. As well as becoming his wife's lover, she gets mixed up in a secret sex club where every sexual proclivity is catered for – and someone is monitoring their activities very closely . . .

Wanton by Andrea Arven
April 1994   Price: £4.99   ISBN: 0 352 32916 5
First she was *Wicked*, then she was *Wild*; now she's *Wanton*. This is the third in the series of the salacious adventures of Fee Cambridge, the stunning green-eyed socialite of the twenty-first century.

Jennifer's Instruction by Cyrian Amberlake
April 1994   Price: £4.99   ISBN: 0 352 32915 7
This is Jennifer's personal account of her initiation into the delights of discipline in the experienced hands of the Professor and his wife. An exhaustive education in punishment from the author of the highly successful *Domino* series.

Virtuoso by Katrina Vincenzi
March 1994   Price: £4.99   ISBN: 0 352 32907 6
The sophisticated world of classical orchestra is the setting for this highly sensual story. Mika was once a great solo violinist, but tragedy halted his rise to fame; the beautiful and equally talented Serena, however, is determined to reawaken his passion by any means necessary.

Gemini Heat by Portia da Costa
March 1994   Price: £4.99   ISBN: 0 352 32912 2
Deana and Delia want the same man. In their desperation to win his affections, they are forced to try increasingly daring sexual feats. Jackson's choice is made all the more complex by the fact that the girls are identical twins!

Fiona's Fate by Fredrica Alleyn
April 1994   Price: £4.99   ISBN: 0 352 32913 0
The writer of the immensely popular *Cassandra's Conflict* brings us a tale of two pretty young hostages – a wife and a mistress – awaiting the ransom from their mutual lover. Their captors, a group of ruthless Italian kidnappers, come up with some very original ideas to pass the time.

Moon of Desire by Sophie Danson
April 1994   Price: £4.99   ISBN: 0 352 32911 4
Soraya is in Eastern Europe investigating her family history when she is overcome by wild sexual impulses. As her behaviour grows more and more lubricious, it becomes clear that the answer may lie in her ancestors' dark past ...

Nexus

252

THE BEST IN EROTIC READING – BY POST

The Nexus Library of Erotica – almost one hundred and fifty volumes – is available from many booksellers and newsagents. If you have any difficulty obtaining the books you require, you can order them by post. Photocopy the list below, or tear the list out of the book; then tick the titles you want and fill in the form at the end of the list. Titles with a month in the box will not be available until that month in 1994.

CONTEMPORARY EROTICA

AMAZONS	Erin Caine	£3.99	
COCKTAILS	Stanley Carten	£3.99	
CITY OF ONE-NIGHT STANDS	Stanley Carten	£4.50	
CONTOURS OF DARKNESS	Marco Vassi	£4.99	
THE GENTLE DEGENERATES	Marco Vassi	£4.99	
MIND BLOWER	Marco Vassi	£4.99	
THE SALINE SOLUTION	Marco Vassi	£4.99	
DARK FANTASIES	Nigel Anthony	£4.99	
THE DAYS AND NIGHTS OF MIGUMI	P.M.	£4.50	
THE LATIN LOVER	P.M.	£3.99	
THE DEVIL'S ADVOCATE	Anonymous	£4.50	
DIPLOMATIC SECRETS	Antoine Lelouche	£3.50	
DIPLOMATIC PLEASURES	Antoine Lelouche	£3.50	
DIPLOMATIC DIVERSIONS	Antoine Lelouche	£4.50	
ELAINE	Stephen Ferris	£4.99	Mar
EMMA ENSLAVED	Hilary James	£4.99	May
EMMA'S SECRET WORLD	Hilary James	£4.99	
ENGINE OF DESIRE	Alexis Arven	£3.99	
DIRTY WORK	Alexis Arven	£3.99	
THE FANTASIES OF JOSEPHINE SCOTT	Josephine Scott	£4.99	

FALLEN ANGELS	Kendall Grahame	£4.99	Jul
THE FANTASY HUNTERS	Celeste Arden	£3.99	
HEART OF DESIRE	Maria del Rey	£4.99	
HELEN – A MODERN ODALISQUE	James Stern	£4.99	
HOT HOLLYWOOD NIGHTS	Nigel Anthony	£4.50	
THE INSTITUTE	Maria del Rey	£4.99	
JENNIFER'S INSTRUCTION	Cyrian Amberlake	£4.99	Apr
LAURE-ANNE TOUJOURS	Laure-Anne	£4.99	
MELINDA AND ESMERALDA	Susanna Hughes	£4.99	Jun
MELINDA AND THE MASTER	Susanna Hughes	£4.99	
Ms DEEDES AT HOME	Carole Andrews	£4.50	
Ms DEEDES ON A MISSION	Carole Andrews	£4.99	
Ms DEEDES ON PARADISE ISLAND	Carole Andrews	£4.99	
OBSESSION	Maria del Rey	£4.99	
THE PALACE OF EROS	Delver Maddingley	£4.99	May
THE PALACE OF FANTASIES	Delver Maddingley	£4.99	
THE PALACE OF SWEETHEARTS	Delver Maddingley	£4.99	
THE PALACE OF HONEYMOONS	Delver Maddingley	£4.99	
THE PASSIVE VOICE	G. C. Scott	£4.99	.
QUEENIE AND CO	Francesca Jones	£4.99	
QUEENIE AND CO IN JAPAN	Francesca Jones	£4.99	
QUEENIE AND CO IN ARGENTINA	Francesca Jones	£4.99	.
SECRETS LIE ON PILLOWS	James Arbroath	£4.50	
STEPHANIE	Susanna Hughes	£4.50	
STEPHANIE'S CASTLE	Susanna Hughes	£4.50	
STEPHANIE'S DOMAIN	Susanna Hughes	£4.99	
STEPHANIE'S REVENGE	Susanna Hughes	£4.99	
STEPHANIE'S TRIAL	Susanna Hughes	£4.99	Feb
THE TEACHING OF FAITH	Elizabeth Bruce	£4.99	Jul
THE DOMINO TATTOO	Cyrian Amberlake	£4.50	
THE DOMINO QUEEN	Cyrian Amberlake	£4.99	

EROTIC SCIENCE FICTION

ADVENTURES IN THE PLEASUREZONE	Delaney Silver	£4.99	.

Please send me the books I have ticked above.

Name   ....

Address   ....

            ....

            .... Post code   ....

Send to: **Cash Sales, Nexus Books, 332 Ladbroke Grove, London W10 5AH**

Please enclose a cheque or postal order, made payable to **Nexus Books**, to the value of the books you have ordered plus postage and packing costs as follows:

UK and BFPO – £1.00 for the first book, 50p for the second book, and 30p for each subsequent book to a maximum of £3.00;

Overseas (including Republic of Ireland) – £2.00 for the first book, £1.00 for the second book, and 50p for each subsequent book.

If you would prefer to pay by VISA or ACCESS/MASTERCARD, please write your card number here:

Please allow up to 28 days for delivery

Signature: _____